Praise for

THE SELBY BIGGE MYSTERIES

"I was hooked from the first page..."

Alex Pavesi, bestselling author of *The Eighth Detective*

"This sparkling Golden Age murder mystery, set in the glamorous but repressed world of 1930s London, brings us the further adventures of Selby Bigge, ably assisted by his partner in crime-solving Theo/dora. With murders to solve and secrets to reveal, *A Morbid Passion* is simply irresistible!"

Sean Lusk, author of *The Second Sight of Zachary Cloudesley*

"Selby's second case, a Golden Age mystery set at the decadent Servants' Ball, sparkles with wit and banter. When murder strikes, Selby and Theo are faced with the challenge of unmasking a killer at a masked ball."

Jo Cunningham, author of *Death by Numbers*

"It's a joy to be back in Holtom's vividly realised world: a brilliantly twisty mystery that delivers both laugh out loud wit and real emotional depth."

Eleanor Wasserberg, author of *Foxlowe*

"Crime fans can expect a refreshing treat with all the style and class of a Golden Age whodunit... Lively, exciting and delightfully written. Five stars."

Janice Hallett, bestselling author of *The Appeal* and *The Twyford Code* on *A Queer Case*

"The sharp wit of classic whodunits infused with the pulse of LGBTQ perspectives, all wrapped in a world of wealth, scandal and secrets."

Jeffrey Marsh, author of *How to be You* on *A Queer Case*

"Clever, atmospheric and intriguing."

Greg Mosse, bestselling author of the Maisie Cooper Mysteries on *A Queer Case*

Also by Robert Holtom
and available from Titan Books

The Selby Bigge Mysteries
A Queer Case

A MORBID PASSION

ROBERT HOLTOM

TITAN BOOKS

A Morbid Passion
Print edition ISBN: 9781835413197
E-book edition ISBN: 9781835413203

Published by Titan Books
A division of Titan Publishing Group Ltd
144 Southwark Street, London SE1 0UP
www.titanbooks.com

First edition: June 2026
10 9 8 7 6 5 4 3 2 1

This is a work of fiction. All of the characters, organizations, and events portrayed in this novel are either products of the author's imagination or are used fictitiously. Any resemblance to actual persons, living or dead (except for satirical purposes), is entirely coincidental.

A CIP catalogue record for this title is available from the British Library.

EU RP (for authorities only)
eucomply OÜ, Pärnu mnt. 139b-14, 11317 Tallinn, Estonia
hello@eucompliancepartner.com, +3375690241

Designed and typeset in Minister Std by Richard Mason.

Printed and bound by CPI Group (UK) Ltd, Croydon CR0 4YY.

A MORBID PASSION

A Selby Bigge mystery

BY ROBERT HOLTOM

CHAPTER I

On a chilly November eve in a tall Victorian townhouse not far from the Royal Albert Hall I was seated at a table laid for seven. I was accompanying one Theodora Smythe, third child of the seventh Baronet Smythe of Etherley, to dinner with the Fortescue family. The reasons for our presence were as convoluted as the sentences preceding this one but, for now, my task was to eat without dribbling, drink without spillage and offer comment without irony. So far I'd been doing rather well but we were still on the first course – a salty oxtail broth.

"There needn't be shame in being a heterosexual."

Our hostess had spoken. Helena Fortescue was a proud member of the National Vigilance Association and terribly concerned with the morality of the Empire. She headed one end of the table and I was seated to her left. Her grey-black hair was neatly coiffed and her back incredibly straight. Here was a woman who took herself very seriously.

"This is Hector's great contention," she continued, speaking of her husband, currently absent from the room as he remonstrated with one of the servants. "He's the one who introduced me to the work of Sigmund Freud."

"That's the Austrian chap simply obsessed with his mother."

This quip came from the man seated opposite me, Percival "Percy" Fortescue, the younger son of the family. He was handsome in a prop-in-a-scrum sort of fashion with his hair neatly pomaded and his square frame dressed in a smart dinner jacket.

"I think I've heard of him," I replied politely, hiding the irony from my voice lest Theodora, sitting next to Percy, skewer me with one of her piercing glares.

"Mother doesn't approve of his spectacles."

"They're a sign of weakness," said Helena.

"And he's rather keen on patricide."

"My son is being flippant," she said. "While Freud's work into the subconscious has proven revolutionary in the study of the mind, it is his work into sexuality that most interests Hector."

"Perhaps we could save discussions on sexuality for after dessert," said Percy.

"Why?" replied his mother. "Are we not adults? This concerns us all."

"I'm with Percy on this one, Mother, let's discuss the weather."

This time it was the man to my left who spoke, Lancelot "Lance" Fortescue, the elder son. There were no daughters, and judging by their Christian names, great things were expected of the Arthurian heroes. Lance's appearance was more to my liking, in the back row rather than the scrum, and the Fortescue family staple of strong chin and high forehead better suited his slightly larger skull. The significance of cranial size had been discussed over the aperitif.

"My sons are teaming up against me," protested Helena in good humour. "What say you, Theodora? Surely these discussions are of great import?"

"I agree," said Theodora, sounding ever the polite guest. My friend had opted for a demure maroon dress that, unlike so many of her other clothes, refused to sparkle in the candlelight. "Freud's work has proven essential in the pathologisation of human sexual practices."

"And having a fondness for one's mother," said Percy.

"And struggling with one's father," added Lance.

I couldn't help but laugh. The brothers made quite the double act.

"You are a pair of bullies!" exclaimed Helena, smiling. "I may be a God-fearing woman but even I can see the need for science in moral advancement."

"Freud's work on the libido is proving most revolutionary," said Theodora.

"It's so wonderful to have another intelligent woman at the table."

This occasioned a polite cough two seats to my left.

"Don't worry, Jackie. I was including you in that comment."

"Thank you, Helena," replied Jacqueline "Jackie" Bosanquet, the third and final woman at dinner. One might have described her as self-effacing, given the other occupants of the table and her height, but I knew better than to judge books by their covers. She was dressed elegantly in the current fashion with a glinting diamond on the ring finger of her left hand. Luckily for her, she was engaged to Lance. "Although I'm afraid I haven't read much of Freud's work."

"Your life is the better for it," said Lance good-humouredly, giving her hand a brief pat.

"Perhaps we can take his books on our honeymoon."

"Better not," said Lance, "or we'll have no time for birding."

"Those works are crucial for a happy union," said Helena. "As are the *Married Love* manuals of Marie Stopes. I have spare copies in my parlour. Her insights are freeing the bedrooms of heterosexuals up and down the country."

"Please let us not talk of heterosexual bedrooms," said Lance.

"We must," continued his mother, unyielding. "You should be proud of your father. It's thanks to the tireless work of men like him that the world will know heterosexuality is not an illness."

On that note, the door to the dining room burst open and in strode the head of the family, Doctor Hector Fortescue. An aged version of his sons dressed in a style highly reminiscent of the aforementioned Austrian doctor – three-piece suit, spotted tie, golden watch chain and neatly trimmed beard (but no spectacles). Doubtless there was a cigar case concealed somewhere on his person.

"Hear, hear," he boomed. "My wife, right again."

Helena allowed herself an imperious smirk as her husband took his seat at the opposite head of the table. He whipped a napkin from the table with a conjuror's flourish, tucked it into his collar and began to drink his soup with a silver spoon. Or did one eat soup? The table was laid splendidly with a pristine, white tablecloth; two silver candleholders casting an intimate light and a banquet's worth of sparkling glassware. The room itself was appropriately grand with deep crimson wallpaper, curious artwork and a narrow marble fireplace. The autumn of 1930 was proving decidedly chill and I was grateful for every blazing fire and functioning radiator I could find.

"I wish to offer a challenge to our Victorian forebears," proclaimed the doctor. "Those fusty old men who decreed sex was only for procreative purposes and anything else a sin. But I am a doctor, not a priest. The sins of the soul are not my profession. I'm interested in illnesses of the mind."

I had the distinct impression he'd given this speech a number of times before.

"There are those who would have us believe heterosexuality is one of these illnesses," he continued. "A perversion no better than bestiality or homosexuality."

A frisson of discomfort rippled around the room as everyone looked to their soup bowls. The flickering candlelight danced queer shadows across our faces. Lance, the handsome brother seated to my left, stiffened. It might have been the final word that did it.

"But I believe, like Freud, that the expression of certain erotic desires can be healthy. After all, not all our passions are motivated by a desire to procreate, and I don't think that makes them morbid."

"Hector, surely you're not advocating that men and women be free to have sex whenever they wish?" asked Theodora with an air of shock I saw straight through.

"Good heavens no," he replied. "These passions are to be shared between a man and his wife. Anything else is simply perverse. I will not be associated with the wanton lust-seeking of the working classes and foreigners. My darling wife campaigns vigorously for the abolition of prostitution."

"I do," she beamed.

"I want the liberation of our kind. I want a respectable heterosexuality to be defined not as morbid but as normal."

The room fell silent but I imagined Doctor Fortescue heard the rapturous applause in his mind – his respectable, disease-free mind, that was. I shifted a piece of ox gristle from one side of my bowl to the other.

"How is young Reginald?" asked Helena, finally freeing us from the interminable convolutions of the doctor's mind.

"I'm thoroughly disappointed in him," replied Hector, dabbing soup from his lips. "I expressly told him to purchase only two tickets, but the naughty chap has bought four."

"Four! It's simply impossible to find the staff these days," opined Helena.

She said these words with little regard for the one member of her staff who was still in the room. This was a maid, a young-looking woman dressed in the typical garb of a female servant, which included one of those silly white hats. I hadn't quite caught her name earlier, possibly Grace. She'd served us our soup and would soon be called upon to clear our bowls. It always surprised me how openly people talked of their servants even when they were mere feet away. But it was hardly as if she could complain – she'd be out of a job forthwith.

"Wouldn't you agree, Theodora?" continued Helena.

"Quite so," my chum replied vaguely. "Although I'm afraid I'm a little lost as to Reginald's transgression. Something about tickets?"

"To the ball," said the doctor.

"Which one?" I asked, thinking it a good idea to remind people of my presence.

"The Servants' Ball," said Percy.

My heart gave a jolt, the spoon quivering treacherously in my hand. Theodora and I had tickets to the very event.

"It's tonight," he said.

"Really?" I replied. "I wasn't aware of the date."

I offered Theodora a sideways glance but she was busy trawling the bottom of her bowl, hoping to alight upon a piece of carrot or onion. Perhaps soup was both eaten and drunk, dependent on its ingredients.

"It's a good old jolly for the staff," continued Percy. "Gives them something to look forward to."

"Poor Grace," said Helena, finally acknowledging the woman's presence. "To think of all the balls and parties she's helped prepare me for."

"So, now it's her turn," I said.

Helena nodded. "I'm acquainted with Lady Malcolm. She spoke at one of our meetings, most rousing."

Lady Jeanne Malcolm née Langtry – daughter of the famous actress Lillie and wife to Sir Ian Malcolm, the Conservative politician – had taken it upon herself to organise the Servants' Ball. From parlourmaids to valets, footmen to cooks, servants the city over were able to enjoy a night of dancing. It was said even staff from the royal household attended. The balls had gained a reputation for themselves.

"Some of your staff are to attend?"

"Three was the original number," said Hector, "but our

chauffeur, Max, rather misbehaved the other day."

"Father, we don't need to go into all that," said Lance quickly. "We'll bore our guests."

"But he was rude to you and that shall not do."

"Rude?" I asked, sensing Lance's discomfort.

"He insulted my darling," said Jackie. "Called him a *brute*."

"A brute," said Theodora, piping up. "I can hardly believe it of you, Lance."

"It was an accident," he replied. "I wasn't looking where I was going and knocked the poor chap over."

"Were you running through the house?" Theodora said with a light tone, but I could tell she was up to something.

Lance laughed politely, clearly hoping the conversation would move on.

"I punished him," said Hector, "and forbade him a trip to the ball."

"Quite right," chimed Helena.

"And having previously told Reginald to purchase three tickets – for himself, Grace and Max – I expressly told him to purchase only two. You can imagine how irate I was when I discovered four!"

"I'm sure it was a mistake, Father," said Lance, oddly defensive. "He most likely got muddled."

"How does one get muddled between two and four?" asked Jackie.

"It's sixes and sevens I always confuse," said Theodora, with just a hint of mischief.

"Apparently, he'd been tasked with buying four candles," said Hector, "but got the numbers the wrong way around."

I glanced at Grace, given she worked alongside Max. But if she knew anything further about the curious case of the four tickets her face wasn't revealing any of it. She stood perfectly still, almost part of the furnishings.

"What shall it be then?" said Percy. "Off to bed with no supper?"

"No, no, a stern remonstration was all that was necessary," said Hector.

"You'll let him go to the ball?"

"I will. I'm not a brute but I shall dock the cost of the third and fourth tickets from his wages."

A harsh punishment given each ticket cost five shillings.

"What will you do with the spares?" I asked.

"Perhaps you could give one to Cook," suggested Lance.

"Burn them," said Percy.

"I haven't decided yet," replied Hector. "I'm of the mind to attend the thing myself and keep an eye on my lot."

"Personally," said Helena, "I wish the ball was no longer running."

"Now who's the brute?" said Lance.

"It's a question of morality."

"It is?" I asked.

"I'm all for butlers and cooks getting a night off to dance the foxtrot, but over the years the ball has attracted an unsavoury crowd."

I knew exactly the crowd – I was part of it.

"What my wife means to say, is that the ball is now a site of moral decadence."

Count me in!

"It's simply awful," said Jackie, her spoon clinking loudly against the side of her bowl.

"Thieves, is it?" I asked, and this time the look Theodora gave me was verging on the hostile.

"Oh no," said Hector solemnly, "much worse than that."

"Perverts," said Percy.

"Degenerates," said Helena.

"Men in dresses," said Jackie, aghast.

"And make-up." More from Percy.

"Homosexualists." Hector again.

"Female homosexualists," added Helena.

"Lesbians, I believe," said Theodora.

"Oh my." Jackie once more.

A strange sort of silence filled the room as three of the Fortescue family heads turned to look at the one of their number who was yet to speak. In turn, Jacqueline Bosanquet placed her hand on top of her fiancé's. Lance coughed awkwardly into the expectant silence. I saw his Adam's apple rise and fall as he searched for the words required of him. A glimmer of silver caught my attention and I looked down to his right hand – it was at his side, hidden from the others under the table. In it he held his bread knife. I winced as he pushed his thumb against the blade. Eventually, he spoke.

"Criminals, the lot of them."

"Grace, if you would clear," ordered Helena.

The maid appeared from the shadows and began carefully collecting the empty bowls. I wondered if she was desperate to get away to the ball and put as much distance between herself and this highly opinionated family as possible. The main was meat, potato and cabbage, but spiced in a manner I presumed to be Austrian – yet another ode to dear Sigmund. For the serving of the next course, Grace was aided by a male servant – a good-looking man with pale skin and dark hair slicked very neatly across his scalp.

"Don't look so glum, chum," said Percy, in a jovial manner I was beginning to find grating. "You're off to the ball after all."

"Yes, sir," replied the servant – who must have been the aforementioned Reginald.

"Whatever possessed you to buy four tickets?" asked the younger brother.

The question coincided with Reginald serving a dollop of mashed potatoes to Lance, whose look of disquiet persisted.

"Confusion, sir."

"You weren't buying one for your secret sweetheart, eh?"

"No, sir," replied Reginald, without the least hint of an emotion save obedience.

"More mash," commanded Lance rudely and this time the serving spoon banged against the plate. Helena, to my right, muttered a protest. Something was afoot at 42 Pendragon Rise, and for a fleeting moment, I wondered if Lance found Reginald as attractive as I did. Perhaps this Arthurian hero was another fruit in the bowl.

CHAPTER 2

The spiced cabbage concoction proved rather tasty, even if the potatoes were a little too mashed for my liking, and the meat-to-gristle ratio of the pork chops was in the pig's favour. Part way through the main course, I excused myself and left the room for the water closet. A long corridor ran from the front door through to the back of the house and I had already been told the WC was further down the hall. However, as this was the first time I'd ever visited the house I could still employ the ruse of being a forgetful guest so as to excuse my ending up in places I shouldn't be. Like the proverbial cat, curiosity and I were well acquainted.

Sometimes, in houses such as this one, the servants were confined to the attic along with the children's old toys. In others, they lived in the cellar with the wine. My trip downstairs revealed the latter to be the case. The plush carpet became sparse, the rich walls became drab yellow and even the wattage of the light bulbs lowered. I didn't want to venture too far, but as above, so below, there was a long corridor with numerous doors leading off it. I heard the clatter of pots and pans being cleaned and smelt the distinct odour of silver polish. Apparently two of these servants were off to a ball soon but not before their tasks had been finished.

Personally, I was delighted to be attending the ball. Theodora had kindly purchased our tickets, paying extra for seats in a box, and informed me that all the brightest and youngest of the things would be in attendance. She'd regaled me with an anecdote from last year's ball, held at one of the big hotels – some of her chums had sneaked into a suite to enjoy its bed only for the rightful occupants to appear. One hid in the wardrobe, the other on the balcony, and both had been entirely without clothing!

A door down the corridor opened and I stepped back into the shadows. I saw the profile of a young man, a serious-looking face of light brown skin. He paused to take a long inhalation of breath and his shoulders slumped on the exhale. Fortunately, he didn't look my way and quickly disappeared down the corridor. I wondered if he might be the disgraced Max whom Lance had accidentally pushed to the floor. Suddenly, one of the nearby doors opened and out rushed Reginald. We almost collided.

"I'm awfully sorry," I managed.

"My mistake, sir."

Up close I could make out the chestnut sheen to his dark hair and the delightful dimples in his cheeks. He looked a little younger than my twenty-six years, and for a moment, our eyes lingered.

"It's Reginald, is it?"

"Yes, sir."

"I wasn't looking where I was going."

"Nor I, sir."

"I'm Selby Bigge and rather lost I'm afraid."

"The water closet, is it?"

I nodded, still holding his gaze, as he held mine.

"I'm heading up. I'll show you."

"That's terribly kind."

He passed me in the corridor and I caught a whiff of soap and body odour. In an alternative setting, a meeting such as this might conclude somewhat differently. On the Heath perhaps or over in Hyde Park, the distance of class could briefly be crossed by the mutual nature of our desires. I might kiss his lips and hold his person in my hand as he did the same. It had taken me but a moment to ascertain that here was a man of similar persuasions.

"It would appear you're in a spot of trouble," I said, referencing the purchasing of tickets.

"That's all cleared up, sir."

"Good-o, and you are to go to the ball?" I asked as we reached the top of the stairs.

"I am indeed."

He led me down the corridor, our footsteps silenced by the thick carpet. The walls were wood-panelled and adorned with pastorals and portraits, including one of Freud. I spied a gap where a picture had been. It rested on the floor beneath, its back facing outwards – like a naughty schoolboy sent to face the wall.

"What happened here?" I asked.

"It fell."

I wondered how this could be true, given the hook on the

wall and the string on the back of the frame were both intact. But I noticed a tear of a few inches in the fabric of the painting, about two-thirds up. A strange sort of accident.

"Here it is," said Reginald, pausing outside one of the doors.

"Thank you," I replied, slowly approaching him. "I hope your night proves bona."

A little risk, but one I thought worth taking – *bona* being the Polari for good and Polari being a slang often spoken by the likes of us.

A small smirk raised the corners of his lips. "The khazi is just here," he said – *khazi* the Polari for toilet – and this time it was my turn to smirk. There was mischief in his bright blue eyes. He gave me a brief nod before vanishing into the depths of the house. Well, well, well, this chap was proving more curious by the minute. Not only was he purchasing more tickets than he should have been, he was a definitive orange to my apple. If luck would have it, I might catch him at the ball.

My toilet attended to, I returned to the corridor, readying myself for another course with Theodora and the fearsome family Fortescue. But before that, I stopped by the painting on the floor. The lighting was dim and atmosphere oppressive. Chatter leaked between the gaps of the dining room door, Hector's baritone holding sway. Bending a little, I quietly pulled it back from the wall to discover a portrait of Lancelot. His chestnut hair was neatly parted, chin slightly raised and lips unsmiling – the painter had captured the mythical quality his name heralded. However, a more recent addition had been made to the piece. From the middle of his forehead to the base of his chin there was a thin, neat cut.

CHAPTER 3

"Does Jacqueline realise her betrothed is as fruity as a pineapple?" The question asked, I raised the tumbler to my lips and took a healthy sip of tonic water and gin, double measure. Ice cubes clinked reassuringly in the glass.

After dinner's endurance, Theodora had raced us back to her house in Wilkington Mews, a stone's throw from Fitzroy Square Garden. She was very fond of her sports car – dark green in colour like the door to her home and priced at over five hundred pounds (not that I'd asked her, I'd looked it up in a magazine). We were upstairs in the master bedroom with no intention of engaging in any heterosexual activity. Instead, Theodora was going through a most wondrous transformation as she swapped her feminine attire for his masculine one.

"How does that look?" she asked.

"Decidedly flat."

"Good."

Theodora had just spent a number of minutes rearranging her breasts within his corset to ensure they were suitably compressed. Our friendship lacked an alarming number of inhibitions. We had met the autumn prior in a big house on Hampstead Heath. She'd been engaged to a man I rather fancied at the time, and suffice it to say, I hadn't taken to her at first. But after multiple glasses of champagne, numerous cups of tea and the solving of a double murder, we'd clicked. Our acquaintanceship had deepened since then, and amongst other activities, we'd rowed on the Serpentine, perused a number of galleries and shared a little of our burdens – living spiral lives in a doggedly angular city. She kept me at one remove from her other social circles, but my world spun a little faster with her in it.

There's nothing like a kindred spirit. It lightens the soul and lessens the Stygian gloom. Thanks to Theodora, the fogs of loneliness were lifting, allowing me greater ease in forging other connections. A new chap had joined Childs & Co., the bank at which I clerked, and he'd proved much friendlier than my other colleagues. Meanwhile, over the summer just past, I had taken to more regular bathing at the ponds. I'd carried on with my chum Arthur and promptly made the mistake of falling for him (again). He very kindly let me down, and as a consolation prize, invited me to events with some of his other pals – many of whom I also suspected of nursing broken hearts. London can be a cold and lonely city, but three years after moving from Horsham the ice was starting to thaw.

"How about that?"

He turned to face me in a buttoned-up white shirt, jade-green cummerbund and half-done bow tie of the same colour.

His walnut hair, mannishly short as Theodora, was now verging on womanishly long. He also sported a trim moustache and the shadow of recently shaved stubble.

"Theo, you look stunning."

"I do, don't I?"

I always found my attractions most confused when Theodora transformed from an eye-catching woman into an attention-grabbing man. I was not the only one. Theo went down well at the River Styx, a club we liked to attend.

"What of Jacqueline?" I asked again. "Surely she's aware Lance is an omi-palone."

"It's not as simple as that," said Theo, sitting on the end of the bed and taking another swig of gin and tonic. "She *was* aware, yes."

"*Was*? Has she suffered from your aunt's second-favourite plot device – amnesia?"

His aunt was the famed crime writer Octavia Stubbs who wrote under the pseudonym Oscar Trolloppe and had a predilection for ghosts. I'd met her in the same mansion on Hampstead Heath and hoped never to repeat the experience.

"Nothing of the sort. It's Lance that has changed."

"I'm still not following, dear chap."

Theo smiled; he liked it when I used masculine terms for him.

"Ever since Hector saved my father's life, I've become rather too acquainted with the travails of the Fortescues."

"Was that the near-drowning off Whitstable?" I asked.

"That was my cousin Bertie. Father had a heart attack on the links near Orpington. Fortunately, Doctor Fortescue is also a keen golfer. He hastened from hole three and thrust some smelling salts under Pa's nose. That woke the old brute."

I'd never met the seventh Baronet of Etherley, nor the rest of the Smythe family, and I didn't think Theo had any intention of facilitating an introduction. Family photographs were conspicuously absent from the mews house and I did my best not to enquire into the details, as Theo did of my family.

"Pa wouldn't normally socialise with a doctor but he felt he owed the chap. And over a pint of ale, Fortescue revealed the exact nature of his work, which is when Father concocted a nasty little punishment for me."

"A four-course meal plus cheese at their house in Belgravia."

"Exactly. Fortescue is a doctor of diseases of the mind, specialising in cases just like ours."

I took another glug of my drink, the bitterness a suitable distraction from the familiar feeling of dread.

"He cures people like us. Rids our minds of morbid passions and gets us back on the straight and narrow. Me in a dress, you married to a woman, children on the way, the social order corrected and the Empire saved."

"Your father is trying to have you cured?"

Theo laughed bitterly. "Pa knows well enough mine is a fatal peculiarity, but my ongoing connection with Doctor Fortescue associates me with those of moral fortitude."

"To stop others asking questions?"

"And to protect the Smythe family name from further scandal."

"That's beastly of him."

"Think of it as the rent I pay for this place."

I had long been jealous of Theo's affluence – the car, the house, the parties – but over time I'd learned of the price of membership to a family with such wealth. A high price that had left many scars on their daughter-son's heart.

"What does this have to do with Lancelot and Jacqueline?" I asked.

"Who do you think is Hector's most prized case?"

My lower lip parted from the upper one and remained that way for a moment. I couldn't believe it. Yet I could believe it all too easily.

"He cured his own son of his homosexual proclivities. And the treatment was so successful Lance ended up engaged to a woman his social superior."

"The poor bugger," I said, contemplating downing my drink or hurling it against the wall. "Jackie's from wealth?"

"Tinned goods, I think, or one of those new chocolate bars."

"I do like a Crunchie."

"Positively sinful!"

We laughed, the shared laughter of those who danced close to the edge of the abyss.

"Like Lance's homosexuality, it would seem."

"Except now he's cured," said Theo solemnly.

"You can't think all that works?"

"Of course not, but *they* do and that's what matters."

This explained some of the peculiar behaviour at dinner. How the other family members had waited on Lance's responses with more eagerness than was necessary. Whatever the efficacy of Hector's treatment, Lance had to present himself as cured, hence his disavowal of the Servants' Ball.

"It must be awful for him, living in that house," I said.

"It is."

"There's plenty of temptation as well. I bumped into Reginald downstairs."

Theo cocked an eyebrow. "I bet you did."

"He's dancing the waltz, all right."

"And off to the buggers' ball."

"Having bought more tickets than he should."

"An accident?" asked Theo.

"I doubt it. He clearly wants that other servant, Max, to go. I caught a glimpse of him – quite good-looking."

"Selby! You're so predictable."

"I'm simply stating a fact. Still, Max shan't be at the ball, having been punished for bad behaviour."

"Even though it was Lance who knocked him over."

"He did say it was an accident," I replied. "Unless there was more to it? Where's Max from?"

"Liverpool, like his mother. And his father is from India, I believe."

"You don't think Lance could be a racialist?"

"I hope not, but it runs in the family."

"What of the mystery of the fourth ticket?"

"One can only speculate."

Theo downed his glass, rose from the bed and went in search of his trousers. He navigated the obstacle course of dog-eared paperbacks, including the latest from his aunt – *Read to Death*, about a series of grisly murders in a remote Cornish bookshop.

"Come on, Selby, we need to get you spruced up."

"Aren't you concerned?"

"About what?"

"About the Fortescues. Couldn't you sense the tension at dinner?"

"I sense tension at every family dinner."

"I think there might be more to it than that."

Theo's trousers paused halfway up his legs. He looked me directly in the eye. "How worried are you, Selby?"

"Someone slit Lance's portrait."

The trousers rose slowly up his thighs. "Max perhaps, in revenge for being shoved?"

I shrugged, genuinely unsure.

He buttoned the trousers around his waist. "Is there a bullet in the barrel?"

I shook my head. I simply didn't know. This was not the first time Theodora and I had encountered intrigue, and over time, we had come to appreciate that intrigue works on a scale. There's good-natured trickery on one end, which might conclude with someone choking on salty rather than sugary tea; somewhere in the middle was hugger-mugger of a more menacing sort, often involving ill-natured muck-spreading or petty theft; but on the far end lay conspiracy to murder. Fortunately, we'd only encountered that once so far, excluding the gruesome death of a librarian's cat (the result of a series of poison pen letters, but that was a story for another time).

"I really couldn't say," I replied finally. "Family Fortescue might not be a happy one but it's hard to imagine assassination is on the horizon."

"I'm inclined to agree with you," he said. "Which means it's time we dressed you up."

"I beg your pardon."

Theo, trousers now belted, pulled me to my feet and led me to his dressing table.

"What will it be, a little rouge on the cheeks, some scarlet on the lips or perhaps a lavender eye?"

"What are you talking about?"

We stared at one another in the mirror – confusion on his face, shock on mine.

"Darling, we're going to the ball, you must look the part."

"I… I think my suit sufficiently dashing."

"This isn't any old ball."

He reached for a compact but I batted his hand away. "I'll go like this, if you don't mind."

"Mary, Mary, quite contrary," he said with a big grin.

"I'm not being contrary."

"How does your garden grow?"

"Perfectly well, thank you very much, plenty of radishes."

"I never had you down as antithetical to a little slap on a man."

"I'm not, as you well know, but said slap being on this man is quite something else."

"Oh, is the great Selby Bigge scared of some lippy?"

"Stop it."

"Petrified of powder?"

"I said 'Stop it.'"

My voice had risen and my tone become more aggressive. Theo stepped back from the looking glass.

"I suppose this isn't a conversation we've had before," he said quietly.

It was not and I'd be buggered if I was going to explain myself to him. My fears were my own matter and not to be joked about.

I knew all too well the overworld's nasty habit of punishing men who ventured too far from the trenches of masculinity. The further one went, the greater the risk and the more severe the punishment. Sometimes having sex in a bush was safer than walking down the street in lipstick.

"I know it can be difficult," he said.

"What?" I replied curtly.

"Keeping our secrets. It's a second occupation."

"You don't have a first," I replied tartly.

"I'll take that in good humour."

"Look, old chap, you attend to your appearance and I'll attend to mine."

"If you wish."

I excused myself for the adjacent bathroom and turned the sink's cold tap on. The gin had reddened my face and I was feeling rather hot. I dabbed some water on my cheeks and swilled some around my mouth. Clashing with Theo was nothing new and it was typically followed by a brief cooling-off period, a shrug of our shoulders and moving on as if nothing had happened.

I looked at my unpainted face in the mirror above the sink and, of all things, I thought of Macbeth. My father had taken my mother and I to a West End matinee in London – my sister left at home in the care of a nanny – and we'd been thrilled by the witches and the bloody spot. But during the interval, we encountered a man at the bar. He spoke with a high voice, and to our horror, had a painted eye. My mother gripped my wrist and dragged me away and the things my father said after I preferred not to recall. But at the time, and much to my shame, I'd agreed with him. Back then I was a thirteen-year-old foot soldier in the war against effeminacy – a family upbringing and an all-boys' education will do that to a chap.

I tried a smile in the mirror, but I didn't like it. In time, I unlearned the lessons I'd been taught and quit the trenches altogether. I crossed No Man's Land and defected. These days I fought for the fairies, fruits and queens. It was liberating. It was exhausting. The human can adapt to all sorts of hostile environments, but there was only so much of it I could take. The fear remained a constant, background hum, like the artillery fire of the enemy, or tinnitus. It required nerve to defy a society so hellbent on war. Nerve that many queens had in ample supply, whereas myself…

"Come on, Selby," I whispered, "tonight of all nights you cannot let them win."

The fronts of the battle were many – the streets, offices and drawing rooms – but the one on which I'd gained most ground was the home front. My heart knew ceasefire more than it ever had and upon occasion I felt almost happy. But there were times when I was reminded that the war still waged within. I placed a hand on my cheek and held it there. No one had ever taught me how to be kind to myself. Peace might be a distant destination but perhaps tonight I could take one more step towards it.

"Fine," I said, returning to the bedroom, "I consent to a spot of rouge."

"I say!"

"And don't for one moment think you've scored a victory over me."

"Oh, but I have. If not my Waterloo, it's certainly a Trafalgar."

I glared into the mirror as Theo dabbed at my cheeks with

a brush. I soon acquired a blush that even I had to admit was quite becoming.

"It was those Fortescues," I said. "They got under my skin."

After another round of gin and tonics, my companion was all spruced up in his dinner jacket, looking every part the gentleman, and I remained just as dapper with the addition of a light pink handkerchief in my jacket's top pocket and a carnation through my buttonhole. I already knew I was dreadfully underdressed for the ball as many of the guests were renowned for the fantastic costumes they wore. Theodora had regaled me of the tiger she'd seen last year, the medieval knight with a very long sword and the entire cast of the Commedia dell'arte. I hoped to see such delights tonight. Down in the hall, we checked our hair in the mirror and donned our thick coats, scarves and hats. I was a homburg chap while Theo favoured the trilby, which suited him well.

"You missed a spot," I said, gently rubbing my finger against the tip of his moustache, where a dab of glue remained visible.

"Gloves?" he asked.

"Bugger!"

I dashed back into the kitchen and retrieved them from on top of the bread bin. I was forever forgetting my gloves. Theo held the green door for me to pass through. I checked the hall clock as I left – half past nine.

The night was just as nippy as it was before, if not a little nippier. I shivered despite my layers. Our breaths misted in front of us, like the smoke wafting from the many chimneys and the clouds crowding the sky. No stars tonight. Attached to the mews house was a small garage in which he kept his pride and joy: the Crossley Silver.

"Shall I take us up to seventy miles per hour tonight?" he asked, as we climbed into the beast.

"I'd like to get to the ball in one piece, preferably breathing."

"But there are some divinely straight roads around Hyde Park."

"It's the divine we'll be meeting if we drive them."

"Do mind the upholstery. Can you just feel the spring in the seat?"

I rolled my eyes but chuckled despite myself.

"I won't praise the motor car again if you don't mention the Ancients."

"I haven't mentioned Heracles once tonight," I protested, "or Zeus for that matter."

Theo was referring to my love of the Greeks and Romans. I had studied Classics at the University of Oxford – Fitzalan College, as it happened.

"But it must be said, these seats are heaven for the posterior."

"A veritable Mount Olympus," I replied. "Perhaps tonight my posterior will find heaven elsewhere."

On that note Theo fired up the engine.

CHAPTER 4

More a bosom than a phallus, the Royal Albert Hall of Arts and Sciences proudly claimed its space in the city of smokestacks and spires. Layers of red brick offset those of sandstone, topped with a miracle of engineering – the domed glass roof. Apparently, it had been given a trial run in Manchester and then the individual pieces escorted to London by horse and cart. Almost a giant birthday cake, but one baked to commemorate the passing of Queen Victoria's husband. Not all of us could afford to honour our loved ones with such splendour, but upon occasion, we were allowed to visit. And tonight the Hall was playing host to an entirely different sort of royalty.

The steps leading to our destination were alive with anticipation. Scores of well-dressed servants chattered energetically as they ascended, lit by a number of burning torches that lined the balustrades. Men wore impeccably pressed suits with tailcoat jackets and handkerchiefs in the pockets. Some even dared to wear brightly coloured bow ties. Many a breast was adorned with a red poppy in anticipation of Tuesday's Armistice services. Women wore gay dresses, some sparkling, some satin, most quite beyond their wearers' means but lent by mistresses. Beyond the blacks and greys of their uniforms, they were finally allowed to indulge in a little colour and it was a joyous scene caught in torchlight and the weak glow of the occasional gas lamp. There were also those in fancy dress. I spied a Viking king, a jester and a peacock of indeterminate sex, trailing a great plumage of turquoise and sapphire tails. A gentleman in alarmingly revealing tights and a high powdered wig sauntered past.

"I wager that will have fallen off before the night is out," I said.

We reached the top of the steps and soon arrived beneath one of the many grand statues. It was good old Prince Albert, surveying the Empire upon which the sun never set – good job his stone eyes were unseeing, given some of the company his Hall was entertaining. We were overtaken by a group of men dressed in what they clearly believed to be some form of tribal dress. Grass skirts, completely topless and their skin darkened by brown paint and burnt cork. I wondered what Max would have made of all this. Perhaps it was best he'd been forbidden from attending.

"Virginia boasted she made a very convincing Emperor of Abyssinia," said Theo.

"Virginia?" I asked.

"Woolf. You may have heard of her."

"*To The Doghouse*, was it?" I replied acidly. Theo, and Theodora for that matter, enjoyed regaling me of their glamorous friends to whom I was never introduced. I was just as bright and young as any other thing.

"She boarded the HMS *Dreadnought* with some of her pals and they even spoke a made-up dialect. The Captain and his crew were completely fooled." He paused to look at yet another pale, young man with painted skin, this time dressed as an Egyptian Pharaoh. "I do wonder when our race will tire of this unfortunate pastime."

We joined the orderly queue heading for the southern entrance – a predictably grand affair with huge wooden doors framed by a sandstone arch. A few burning torches hung from sconces and I marvelled at the effort Lady Malcolm and her entourage had put in to ensure tonight would be one to remember. I must confess, my heart was beating a little faster.

"I'm looking forward to a drink," I said, fishing in my jacket pocket for my cigarette case.

I lit two cigarettes in my mouth and passed one to Theo. We enjoyed a good puff as the queue progressed, pulling us ever closer to the Hall. Snatches of conversation batted to and fro as the excitable guests anticipated the pleasures to come.

"Biggest one yet," said the chap in front of us.

"First time at the Hall," replied his companion.

"Last year was a good one."

"A corker."

"Poor Harry though, almost drowned in that fountain."

"*I am most disappointed*," said the first in a mock posh accent, presumably imitating one of his employers. "*You have brought shame upon our household, young Harold. What would your father say?*"

The pair laughed as Theo and I suppressed our smiles. It must be a joy to escape the drudgery of domestic servitude, if only for a night. Lord knew, clerking at a bank was hardly the world's most stimulating of professions, but it paid enough that I could rent a room in Pimlico, treat myself to the occasional fancy dinner and afford the doctor. I'd had a brush with a rather nasty urinary infection in spring, the details of which I needn't provide, but I'd paid the doctor's fees, received my medicine and all was well downstairs. We finally reached the front of the queue as a gruff-looking man took the tickets from Theo's proffered hand, tore off the stubs and promptly returned them.

"Good turnout?" asked Theo, his voice appropriately low.

"Too bloody many," huffed the doorman.

"Don't worry, we'll behave."

"It's not men like you I'm worried about," he said, giving him the once-over. "It's those men in frocks. Should be banned."

He turned his attention to me. Comprehension dawned slowly but inevitably as he spotted my rouged cheeks. I longed to look away but I forced myself to hold his gaze. So, the briefest of battles commenced – imperceptible to most but felt deeply in my chest. My forces were few while he had a whole nation onside. But tonight I would not let him win. He rearranged the silk poppy at his lapel then grunted. On that note, we crossed the threshold and the festivities began. As outside, so inside the corridors surged with folks bustling this way and that. Somewhere a champagne cork popped followed by a round of applause.

"I could do with some of that," said Theo.

"Me too," I said, sounding a little flustered.

"I'm sorry if you felt strong-armed into rouge," he said, which surprised me given neither of us were particularly fond of apologies.

"I think a little powder on my cheeks a slight risk in comparison to the ones you're taking."

"A risk nonetheless."

"Don't they say something about how sharing sorrows halves them?" I remarked. "While sharing risks quadruples the fun!"

The pull of partygoers streamed on and we went with them, our path heralded by gold and silver ribbons and balloons. The peacock jostled past, affording me a closer glimpse of the long turquoise and teal dress she wore, her slender arms and the brilliant tail she trailed.

"I say, Theo!" twittered the bird.

Theo's eyes widened in delight. "By Jove, Lady Splendid."

They reached across me, their fingers momentarily touching, as we carried on along the corridor.

"Who's your friend?" she asked, eyeing me most unashamedly.

"This is one Mr Selby Bigge."

"A pleasure, I'm sure," she said, reaching out a hand, which I briefly took. "Your first time?"

"Is it that obvious?" I asked. Damn my nerves!

"You're not in fancy dress."

"But I am in disguise," I said.

"Oh yes, what as?"

"Someone relatively unassuming."

That got a laugh and what a lovely smile she had. Her skin was a pale brown but lighter than Max's and I presumed a family history somewhere far from Great Britain, but where exactly, I couldn't tell. Her long black hair came down past her shoulders and shimmered in the light. Theo had such dazzling friends. And there was something else about her, something I couldn't quite put my finger on.

"The man on the door wasn't very friendly," I said.

"Grumpy old bore," replied Lady Splendid dismissively.

"Do you think the police are here?"

"Oh no," she said, "the Met don't have jurisdiction here. Tonight, the world is ours!"

The river of guests rushed us towards one of the doorways, bordered with more gold and silver. I took a deep breath as the current pulled me through.

"Bloody hell!" I exclaimed.

The auditorium of the Royal Albert Hall was enormous. No, bigger than that – gigantic, colossal even, like a number of cathedrals and castles and palaces had been rolled into one. Before us stretched a vast dancefloor filled with revellers, many arm in arm, many smiling. A band played somewhere on the far side, a lively number for now. The seats of the stalls had vanished beneath us – the Hall had raised the floor but it was our job to raise the roof. Around the edges was the first row of boxes, already filled with happy servants. These had been engaged by their employers – from Dukes to Marchionesses, and even the King, generosity was not wanting tonight. Above the three tiers of boxes were rows and rows of seats, affording a good view of the crowds. And finally, all the way up top, was the expanse of domed roof. I couldn't bloody believe it, I was here! Lady Splendid gave us a flirtatious wave as her plumage was swallowed by the throng. That was when the penny dropped.

"I say, there's more to her than meets the eye."

"Much more," said Theo. "She's like me, two spirits in one soul."

London had done much to challenge and expand my attractions. Once upon a time I might have pined only for a broad-shouldered man in a suit, but nowadays the suit could be a dress and the man defined quite differently.

Theo and I followed cautiously in her wake and soon we were amongst the festivities. We did a slow circuit of the dancefloor, passing endless smiles and dancing couples. I saw the group of tribal men again and one or two chaps in long robes, clearly thinking dressing as a Muslim the height of fancy dress. A packet of cigarettes waddled past and a bottle of Brasso. Eclectic was a polite term with which to describe the crowd and it wasn't long before I was heating up.

"I say, it's Susan!" said Theo.

"Who?" I asked.

"Susan Goodley, you remember?"

I remembered a number of anecdotes concerning Susan's expensive possessions, raucous parties and glamorous holidays, but that was about it.

"I must say hello. You will be able to look after yourself?"

"I should be able to manage," I replied. "I'm gasping for a drink."

"Good-o. Thirty-one."

"I beg your pardon?"

"It's our box number, darling. We can meet there later."

Off he went, ever the socialite, as I circled back through the crowds. A disarmingly handsome young man sidestepped around me, followed by his dance partner, another chap, in a dress. Here was just the sort of rascal the doorman was worried about, flaunting all the codes of fashion and muddying the waters of Great Britain's racial superiority. The sort of person Doctor Fortescue would cure. We looked at one another, big grins spreading across our faces. He fingered his pearls before departing with a wink.

I left the heaving auditorium and wound my way through the labyrinth of corridors and up a flight of stairs until I found a bar. I queued behind a group of men gaily chattering away. Some of their number wore colourful silk blouses and tight-hipped trousers, affording me a pleasant view until I finally acquired a chilled glass of champagne. Finding a seat at a recently abandoned table, I took my first sip and enjoyed the dry taste of nectar. It was good to take a moment's reprieve. Crowds could easily prove overwhelming.

A programme lay on the table, which I briefly perused. The Ball was raising money for the West End Hospital for Nervous Diseases and Billy Mason was the one conducting the Café de Paris Orchestra downstairs. Many a waltz was to be danced, not to mention the foxtrot – a personal favourite. Lady Malcolm was addressing the crowds from the Royal Box later and the fancy dress competition would be judged after midnight. From Humorous to Home-Made there were all sorts of classes, and I hoped Lady Splendid would win one. The judges were a who's who of the stage and music hall – if I were lucky I might bump into Prudence Bourchier or Amber Ensleigh!

"Excuse me," came a voice. "Mind if I join you?"

I looked up into the smiling face of a mask.

"Not at all," I said, motioning to the empty chair.

"Jolly good."

He took the other seat, glass in one hand, champagne bottle in the other. As well as the mask, which covered his entire face, including his ears, he wore a voluminous one-piece costume of coloured diamonds.

"Bottoms up," he said, his voice distorted by the mask. His other hand went to push his mask back but then stopped. The two brown eyes stared at me. I looked away, feeling a mite uncomfortable, only to look back and see him still staring at me.

"Is everything all right?" I asked.

"It's Simon, isn't it?" he said. "Simon Bigge?"

"Selby."

"That's the ticket."

"And who might you be?"

He placed his glass on the table then reached around the back of his head. Slowly, he untied the ribbon that held the mask in place. It was a very beautiful piece, expensive-looking too, most likely the product of skilled artisanship. The ribbon untied, the mask was removed.

"Well I never," I said, utterly failing to hide my surprise. "Lancelot Fortescue!"

"The very same," he said with a roguish smile, patting his gelled chestnut hair back into place. "Although you must call me Lance."

My mind rushed back to the dinner, endured only hours ago, and that strange, po-faced family rife with opinion on the decline of the Western world and the best ways to save it.

"Then one of those extra tickets was for you," I said, recalling the servant Reginald and his scolding at Hector's hands.

"My, you are quick," said Lance, with an approving nod.

"I do like an Agatha Christie."

"I prefer *The Birds of the British Isles*," he replied. "But you will keep mum?"

"You have my word."

"Thank you," he said, saluting me with his glass again. This clearly wasn't his first glass as he appeared somewhere between half-cut and dismemberment.

"May I?" I said, motioning to the mask. He nodded as he quaffed on his drink. I held it up in front of me: it depicted a simple, smiling face painted with bold colours. A large white diamond covered the nose and mouth, a black diamond the right eye, a red one the left, and the forehead was golden.

"Harlequin," he explained, "one of the characters from the Commedia dell'arte."

"We all need a bit of colour in our lives."

"I was in Venice not long ago. Found this wondrous little shop down a side street not far from the Piazzetta di San Marco. I was spoilt for choice. I could hardly have just one!"

"It's beautiful," I said quite honestly as I placed it back on the table.

An awkward silence fell between us, neither one of us sure of the protocol for such an encounter. Rather unexpectedly, Lance made the first move.

"I hope you don't mind me saying, but I'm not particularly surprised to find you here."

"Oh really?"

"And I saw Theodora downstairs."

"I'm sure you're mistaken."

"I'm sure I'm not."

"Perhaps you spotted her brother, Theo."

"I wasn't aware either of her brothers had that name."

Evidently not too half-cut, then!

"We're all being a little naughty, aren't we?" he said.

"What makes you say that?" I asked cautiously, wondering if a threat was looming on the horizon.

"This ball isn't for people like us."

"It's not?" I replied, trying to keep my tone neutral.

"You, Theodora and I, we're none of us servants!"

He laughed and took another swig. I took rather a large gulp.

"Don't worry, Selby," he said, "if I can call you that."

I nodded.

"I can keep mum too. Besides, I believe we have a mutual acquaintance."

"I find that hard to believe."

"His name is Arthur."

"Oh." Yet again the surprise was mine. "Were you two close?"

"Briefly. Foolishly. But I wouldn't have had it otherwise."

This time I couldn't restrain my grin. Many of us had fallen for Arthur's charms, we the hapless sailors heading for the rocks, he the largely unwitting and largely endowed siren.

"Arthur has many friends," I agreed.

"He's broadened many a man's horizons."

"Amongst other things."

Lance snorted as he refilled his glass and offered to top mine up. Why not? Conversations like these were always a fine dance between secrecy and disclosure, but it was clear Lance, albeit in a drunken state, wanted to open up. He might even have been flirting with me.

"I met him at the River Styx," he added, referencing the delightful little club in Soho that catered to chaps of our sort.

"I don't believe I've seen you there," I said.

"I haven't been for some time. Need to keep a low profile."

"I see," I said, not seeing at all.

"It's my father. If word got back to him, he'd have my guts for garters."

"He wouldn't approve?"

"I think you already know the answer to that. As far as he's concerned, I'm cured." He drained his champagne, wiping a hand across his lips. The bitter look on his face wasn't because of the drink.

"I am sorry about all that," I said. "Some of the things he said at dinner, and your mother for that matter, were truly beastly."

He regarded me through tired, harried eyes, and I wondered how often he received sympathy for his situation in life. My family was a void of such understanding, one of the many reasons I'd long fled Horsham.

"How did you know?" he asked.

"It takes one to know one."

"Was I that obvious?"

"No. You played the part of the dutiful son very well," I replied carefully. "It's a part I play as well."

"It can get very fatiguing."

"Exhausting," I concurred. "Does Jacqueline know?"

The question pained him, and while that was regretful, I still wanted to know the answer.

"I do feel beastly," he said, shaking his head. "Poor Jackie doesn't deserve to be caught up in all this but I was desperate. Cold baths and flaked corn are one thing, but if it weren't for that engagement it would have been chemical therapy."

"That sounds dreadful."

He poured himself another glass and began to drink. This wasn't the first time I'd played confessor but that usually happened in the early hours of the morning after a night of intimacy. I barely knew this man from Adam.

"Lance, forgive me for being rude," I said. "Why are you telling me all this?"

"Because it doesn't matter any more."

"I beg your pardon?"

He tried for another smile but achieved only a frown.

"I wish we'd met sooner, Selby. I think we'd have been good friends."

"What's stopping us?"

"Time. I have to go soon."

"But the night is still young."

I looked around the bar and saw a small clock hanging above the bottles of wines and spirits – it read twenty minutes past ten.

"It will all be over tonight," he said solemnly.

"What will?" I asked.

"Everything."

An uncomfortable lump formed in my throat.

"You're not planning on doing anything silly, are you?"

"That depends on who you ask," he said.

Before either of us could say any more, someone else

appeared at our table.

"There you are," said Lance, rising to his feet.

I looked up as Lance hugged the man. Lo and behold, it was Reginald the manservant. He looked a veritable dish in his white tie.

"You might remember Mr Bigge," said Lance, ending the embrace.

"I do," he said. "Evening, Mr Bigge."

"Please do call me Selby."

The look he gave me was far from friendly; most unlike the look he'd given me outside the Fortescues' water closet. But surely my prior suspicions had proven correct – if Lance were a pineapple, then Reginald must be, at the very least, a pear.

"Are you enjoying the ball?" I asked.

"Yes, it's a gay affair."

"They'll be judging the fancy dress later."

"I'm sure that will be fun," he said. "But I have to be off."

"So soon?"

"Reggie has work to do," said Lance, slurring his words. "Such a busy boy."

What a life. The one night of the year when a servant could let loose and still he had chores.

"Perhaps we have time for one more dance?" asked Reginald hopefully.

"If I have to face any more music my ears shall fall off," replied Lance.

I could tell something wasn't quite right between them. They seemed on edge, as they had done at dinner. It was probably best I left them to it.

"Well," I said, trying to rise steadily from the table, "time I returned to the auditorium."

"Time for some drama," said Lance, glancing down at his mask of colourful diamonds.

"Only of the proper sort."

"Do say hello to Theo from me."

"I will," I said, with a wink. "Goodnight, Lance."

"Farewell, Selby."

"Goodnight, Reginald."

He nodded his head in return but did not smile. His change in temperament struck me as odd – I couldn't tell if he was annoyed at my presence or if something else was worrying him. I sensed the pair was eager for me to move on but there was just one more thing I had to say.

"Your portrait," I said to Lance, "that seemed a nasty thing."

He shook his head wearily and I wondered on the many thoughts that jostled in his skull. Here was a man of multitudes and I worried many of them were unhappy.

"It doesn't matter."

So I left them to it. And what a pair they made – the drunken master and the ever-vigilant servant. Perhaps it was as simple as that, the latter tasked with keeping an eye on the former or perhaps, as was invariably the case, there was more to it. Curiosity got the better of me, and just before I left the bar, I looked back. The two men had retreated to one of the corners and were standing very close to one another. It was hard to miss Harlequin in his gaudy costume of coloured diamonds. Reggie produced a silver hip flask from his jacket pocket and took a quick sip. He offered it to Lance, who declined. The hip flask vanished. Lance cast a furtive glance about the place before quickly placing his hand on the other's cheek. For the briefest of moments Reginald closed his eyes and his manner transformed. On his face appeared a look I recognised with ease – bliss.

CHAPTER 5

Downstairs the auditorium continued to heave. There must have been thousands of us. The veleta had given way to the Paul Jones – a lively dance number of circles within circles and much partner swapping. The fancy dress added to the gaiety as a swan ended up with a packet of Capstan cigarettes and Queen Victoria a nun. Apparently Lady Malcolm had even danced with her butler – class be damned (for an evening). I thought it would be a good idea to find Theo so I returned to the corridors in search of box number thirty-one. Map reading had never been my strong suit but I got there eventually. Inside were a handful of seats, all with a spectacular view of the hall, but the only occupants were Theo and Lady Splendid. They were both sipping sidecars.

"Have a nip," said Theo, holding out his glass.

"Don't mind if I do."

That was the ticket: sweet, sour and the perfect amount of brandy. I took the seat on Theo's right.

"Do save me," said Lady Splendid dramatically. "Theo's been regaling me of his new Crossley."

"You said you liked motor cars!" my chum protested.

"I said I liked men with big engines. Perhaps Mr Bigge knows what I'm talking about?"

I had the decency to blush but found myself warming to this peacock. Perhaps I should ask her to dance.

"You'll never guess who I bumped into at the bar," I said.

"Lancelot Fortescue," replied Theo promptly.

"How on earth?"

"I saw him on the dancefloor with Reginald and Grace."

"Is she here too?" I asked of the maid.

"Looking rather splendid in one of Helena's gowns."

An angel passed overhead as we gazed out on the multitude of merrymakers. The young men I'd seen at the bar were merrily dancing together. Tonight they were not valets or footmen, they were free. Two danced arm in arm, looking every bit in love.

"There have been complaints about us undesirables," observed Lady Splendid. "Apparently the ball committee has suggested a Board of Scrutineers be established."

"Whatever for?" I asked.

"To check our costumes at the door. God forbid someone with a penis wear a dress."

"I dread to think how they'll go about that," observed Theo sourly. "I bet Constable Clod is simply dying for an excuse to put his hands up someone's skirt."

Despite all their protests and objections, the normals were

simply obsessed with us rouged rogues. Heaven forefend anyone be allowed to have more fun than them (and more sex for that matter).

"I'm off to make the rounds," announced Lady Splendid. "There's a Scotsman in a kilt I'd rather like to introduce myself to."

"I'm sure we all know why," retorted Theo.

"Drink this for me, would you," she said, passing me her glass.

"With pleasure," I said.

"And buy me another one later."

There was no subtlety to her flirtations, which suited me just fine.

"I suspected you two would get along," said Theo, once the peacock and her plumes had departed. "She performs at some of the clubs every once in a while."

"We should go."

I sipped on the remains of the sidecar as Theo finished his. The minutes passed in bursts of colour and cheer, all to the sound of trumpets and strings. We enjoyed watching those in fancy dress, offering our own opinions on the efforts. We both agreed the packet of cigarettes was rather nifty but the bollard less so.

"What's the time?" I asked, now that my drink was empty.

"Just gone quarter to," said Theo, checking his slim wristwatch. "We should get another." But neither of us moved, too comfortable on our posteriors. "Look, there's Lance."

I followed Theo's pointing finger, and sure enough, there he was in his colourful mask and costume. I spied Grace with him, in a beautiful sapphire ballgown. She looked every part the aristocrat.

"They look like they're having fun," I said.

"They do."

"A funny pair," I added.

"No funnier than we."

"Do you think everyone here has secrets?"

Lance and Grace weren't aware they had an audience and it proved fun to watch them free from the oppressions of the household. They talked freely with one another and Grace laughed openly. It wasn't long before a young chap dressed as a soldier asked her to dance and off they went into the crowd. Lance made his way towards the steps, heading for one of the exits. As he went, he looked amongst the boxes and eventually saw us. He gave us a little wave, which we returned.

"Do you know him well?" I asked.

"Only from those intolerable dinners. We run in different circles."

"He's not acquainted with Susan Goodley, then?"

"Now, now, green doesn't suit you."

"He didn't sound too gay when I spoke to him," I said, ignoring the jibe. "Do you think he'll be all right?"

"He's lasted this long," mused Theo, "so presumably he has one or two tactics for survival."

"One of which may well be Reginald."

Our concerns were answered ten minutes later when Lance reappeared, this time ignoring us as he returned to the melee of dancers. Soon after came a rather formidable plague doctor dressed in a dark suit and a long flowing black gown. He wore a black hood that covered his head and a top hat. His mask was terrifying with dead, empty eyes and a long beak. He resembled an overgrown carrion bird – a giant vulture perhaps.

"I say, I must visit the lavatory," I said, suddenly aware of how full my bladder was.

"Lovely. I'll locate more sidecars."

"Meet back here or the upstairs bar?"

"The bar."

We returned to the corridor and went our separate ways: Theo upstairs for more alcohol and I further along until I found the gents. Every urinal was taken and the three cubicles were all locked. Oh dear, I was close to bursting. Eventually the far urinal freed up and I was relieved to relieve myself. It was only then I appreciated quite how much I'd drunk. I concentrated on not swaying, lest I dampen my footwear, or the chap's next door for that matter. An involuntary smile came to my face – this was proving a decidedly good evening. And it got better the moment I returned everything to its proper place. As I stepped away from the porcelain trough, the door of the cubicle opposite opened a crack.

"Psst," came a voice from within and I saw a pair of turquoise eyes. It was Lady Splendid and she was beckoning me over. Never one to miss an opportunity, I made sure no one was watching – all too busy attending to their own bladders, the washing of their hands or, in one chap's case, combing his hair in a hand mirror – and confidently strode to the cubicle. The door gave way and soon I was inside, pressed close to the stall's other occupant.

"I was hoping to get you alone," she said.

"That makes two of us."

As she had made the first move, I thought it appropriate I make the next, so I leant forward to kiss her. Our lips acquainted themselves with one another; hers were soft and warm. Then our mouths opened to allow our tongues an introduction. She tasted of orange and lemon. We pulled one another closer and pressed our crotches together. My cock was quick to stiffen, as was hers. It wasn't long before her hand was at my crotch, rubbing my erection through the fabric. I had to stifle a moan lest I give the game away. I didn't have the first clue how to navigate her dress nor the undergarments I presumed were underneath, so instead I put my lips to the side of her neck, which she seemed to enjoy. Soon she had the buttons of my fly undone and was reaching inside. My buttocks tensed as she grasped my member through the fabric of my elasticated underpants (a most marvellous invention). Then someone knocked at the door.

"Hurry up in there," shouted a man. "Got to use the crapper."

"Bugger," I whispered as we pushed apart.

"One minute," I said out loud, panicking, Lady Splendid too slow to cover my mouth with her hand.

"I haven't got a minute!"

Sorry, I mouthed.

She rolled her eyes as she straightened her dress and I tucked everything back.

"What should we do?" I whispered.

She leant forward and put her lips to my ear, sending a jolt from my neck to my tailbone.

"As far as he's concerned," she said, "I'm every inch the woman. Simply exit the way you entered – with confidence."

Getting her gist, I coughed loudly and unlocked the door. The man was waiting impatiently on the other side, but before he could enter, he had to make way for a resplendent peacock.

"Bleeding hell," he exclaimed. "You old dog!"

"Woof," was my response as Lady Splendid giggled.

"Perhaps we should find somewhere a little quieter," I suggested, once we were back in the corridor.

"Maybe later," she replied. "I want to see the view from up top."

"Shall I accompany you?"

She shook her head and quietly turned away from me. I tried not to feel too rejected even if our dalliance had been very spur of the moment.

"By the way," I said as she departed, "did you find out what the Scotsman was wearing under his kilt?"

She turned to bat her eyelashes at me. "Exactly what I was expecting."

I grinned all the way to the bar upstairs, looking forward to another cocktail, perhaps something with vodka this time. I scanned the drinkers, trying to find Theo, only for my grin to vanish. He was seated at one of the tables and someone was with him, someone decidedly unhappy – Jacqueline Bosanquet. She looked both angry and distraught. I made a beeline for them, thinking it best to come to Theo's aid.

"Miss Bosanquet," I announced, "what a pleasant surprise."

"No, Mr Bigge," she said quickly, "the surprises this evening are far from that."

My encounter in the lavatory was evidence to the contrary, but I kept that to myself.

"Selby," said Theo, his voice decidedly more feminine now, "Jackie found me at the bar and I've had to explain our little ruse."

"You have?" I asked, no clue as to where this was going.

"She's quite clever," said Jackie. "I would have been fooled if it weren't for her lovely brown eyes."

"I'd hoped to go undetected," said Theo, who I now assumed to be posing as Theodora. "You see, I have a wayward butler to catch."

"Of course," I said, my eyes widening in surprise. "The wayward butler!"

Theo glared at me. "I was explaining to Jackie how I'm here at Father's behest, on the tail of one of our butlers who might just be thieving the family's silver."

"Which explains your disguise," I added, cottoning on.

"Staff these days," said Jackie, "simply cannot be trusted."

"Indeed," I said, pulling up an empty chair to the table. "What brings you to the ball, Miss Bosanquet? A misbehaving maid, perchance?"

"A misbehaving fiancé, more like it."

"Oh," I uttered, offering my best approximation of a sympathetic smile.

"Jackie is convinced Lancelot is here tonight."

"Surely not?"

"I fear the worst," said Jackie. "You haven't seen him, have you?"

"Neither hide nor hair, I'm afraid," I lied.

"He came last year, you see," she said, "and it caused no end of problems."

"Then let us hope he's learned his lesson."

"I do hope so," she said. "But it was the affair with all those tickets. I fear one might have been meant for him."

"Surely he wouldn't steal the fun from a deserving servant."

"You have," she shot back.

"That's because Selby is here to help me find an undeserving servant," said Theo.

"You must have a ticket too," I said, trying to get my own back.

"Most certainly not," said Jackie. "I simply told the man at the door that there was a family emergency."

"An emergency?"

"I didn't specify it was my fiancé's disease."

An obdurate silence blocked our conversation. I was drunk enough that I had to attend more carefully to my tongue, lest I say what was really on my mind. In the end, it was Jackie who relented.

"I'm sorry for my foul temper," she said, "but my nerves are strained to tatters."

"I bet Lance is tucked up in bed," suggested Theo.

"No, he said he was off to his club after dinner."

"And you've doubtlessly checked there," I said.

"It's not for women."

"A telephone call perhaps?"

She shook her head slowly. "I know my fiancé, I know his illness."

"But Doctor Fortescue has cured him," I said, even though it pained me.

"His contagion has deep roots."

"Look, Jackie," said Theo soothingly, "there's no use you being here, I'm sure Lance has fallen asleep in front of the fire at his club. Let me take you outside to find a taxi."

"I should search the upper galleries."

"That will only strain your nerves yet further," he said, gently squeezing her hand. "You need a warm glass of milk and sleep. You look dreadfully tired."

"I… I haven't been sleeping well as of late."

"All the more reason to see you home," said Theo, rising to his feet. "Selby, I will look after Jackie and then I'll find you in our box."

"Right you are. Goodnight, Miss Bosanquet, and let me assure you – your fiancé cares for you deeply."

"Thank you, Mr Bigge." She was about to turn away but paused. "I say, your cheeks are rather red."

"It's very hot in here," I said, which conveniently was true.

"Indeed. Goodnight, Mr Bigge."

She cut a frail figure as Theo led her away from the clatter and merriment. Frail but determined. That had been a close shave for Lance. I debated alerting him to the perils, but given Jackie was on her way out, why spoil his night? I checked the clock above the bar, twenty minutes past eleven, still plenty of time for fun.

I opted to go upstairs this time and soon found myself at the gallery. Many others had had the same idea as me, and the dancing and drinking continued even at this great a height. The view was both vertiginous and marvellous. I looked down at the matchstick merrymakers and tried to find recognisable masks and costumes, but the movement was too quick for my quarter-cut eyes. The acoustics were quite incredible as the band played a jazzy American number. I enjoyed the view for a while before walking a little way around the gallery, admiring the many marble pillars and the diamond pattern of the floor.

I passed a group of young women all talking animatedly together, although quickly realised not all were women in the conventional sense. Further along a butler and a maid were having rather a lot of fun in the shadows. I wondered if Lady Splendid was still up here, displaying her plumage to another gentleman. Lucky blighter. Her attentions had proven easy to catch but hard to hold on to. Besides, if I were to find her in flagrante delicto she wouldn't appreciate it. I took one last look at the view and briefly let my tipsy mind wander to a place where every night could be like this – men free to be women, women free to be men and all gentlefolk free to let loose. A silly wish for a drunken fool.

En route to box thirty-one, I purchased a gin and tonic and asked a topless chap for a light. He gave me more besides and let me squeeze one of his decidedly pert nipples. Theo was nowhere in sight and I worried for his handling of Jackie. Who knew what the aggrieved fiancée would do if she found herself betrayed yet again? Sir Walter Scott's tangled web came to mind.

Once I was comfortable in my seat, I let my gaze roam the dancefloor. All was a blur of movement and colour until a few familiar figures came into focus. But where I had expected to see gaiety, I saw conflict. The smiling Harlequin faced off against the plague doctor, both gesticulating at one another. The foreboding bird reached out and took a hold of the clown's shoulder, gripping him tight. It didn't look like an intimate gesture and soon Lance was shoving at the hand.

It was at this moment that Grace appeared, her look of content quickly becoming one of frustration. She pushed the plague doctor's hand away and stood between the two men. She looked just as angry with Lance as she did with the masked stranger, but soon enough the fearsome bird was turning on his tail and storming off. I watched him part the crowds as he left the auditorium, his cloak billowing behind him. If the plague didn't kill one of those doctor's patients, his looks would. Back on the dancefloor Grace was remonstrating with Lance. I quite pitied the chap. A few moments passed before she calmed down, Lance placing his hand over his heart. She sighed and then she too departed, leaving Harlequin alone.

"Got a light?" asked Theo, dropping himself down in the seat next to mine.

"I thought that's against the rules," I replied, reaching into my pocket and producing a snazzy little zippo – one Theo had given me for my birthday back in May. He leaned towards the flame and soon his cigarette was glowing. He inhaled deeply and let out a long stream of smoke.

"Everything all right with Jacqueline?"

"She cried for a bit then nearly fell down the steps. I got her into a taxi eventually."

"There's been drama on the dancefloor. Young Lance has been having a number of arguments."

I turned back to the Hall, but the masked clown was gone, swallowed by the sea of dresses and suits. Instead, the waves had another offering as the sparkling peacock appeared, making her way towards us.

"I must wish you both goodnight," said Lady Splendid, leaning into the box, her cheeks flushed.

"Off so soon?" asked Theo.

"Always leave them wanting more."

She gave us both a kiss on the cheek. Her lips were very cold.

"I'm singing at the Styx on Thursday," she said. "Maybe I'll see you there?"

With a saucy wink she was gone.

"She's not one for attachments," said Theo.

"But still nice to look at."

The band's tempo dropped for a waltz as the happy couples danced slowly arm in arm. Many of the pairs were to be expected – the clothes matching the presumed appendages – but there were those that didn't – masculine bodies in dresses pressed tight together and feminine bodies in suits, arms around one another's waists. How I longed for my own dance partner.

"How about some fresh air?" I suggested. "It's getting a bit stuffy in here."

"A turn around the park?"

"Jolly good."

Off we went, this time circumnavigating the corridors until we reached the doors for the northern exit. The hallway was busy, as with everywhere else, and I found the chap in pearls again. He plucked the carnation from my buttonhole, stuck his nose in it and sniffed.

"I smell even better," I said as I carried on my way. The clock above the doors read midnight as we pushed through. The November cold was just the tonic. It felt delicious against my hot cheeks. There were a few burning torches to light the scene and one or two gas lamps. The orange glow was romantic, the perfect scene for a lovers' tryst. A taxi rumbled past on the road in front of us. The passenger in the back had his face glued to the window and looked horrified at our open displays of joy. Another taxi came and then some snazzy-looking motor.

"Quick, quick," I said, making the most of the empty road and hoping to distract Theo from a long description of the car we'd just seen. Soon we were in Kensington Gardens overlooked by yet another giant statue of Prince Albert. This one was by far the more resplendent as the man himself was embossed in gold and housed under an enormous pavilion in the Gothic style. Surrounding him, in white stone, were the various peoples and animals of the Empire – from elephants to camels, Albert had the world at his feet.

"I do sometimes wonder if there's such a thing as too much decadence," I said as we passed around the monument.

"No, you don't," said Theo.

Off we went, laughing, until we found a wrought-iron bench not too far away. Bottoms down, it sent a cold chill along my spine, just what the doctor ordered. I could feel my blood quickening and my head clearing.

"This is awfully fun," I said.

"I concur."

"Thank you for my ticket."

From deeper within the park, a match was put to a fuse and a rocket went screeching into the sky. It exploded in a shower of red sparks. Beautiful. A few people applauded as another firework blasted into the sky. This one was golden, illuminating the surrounding trees and bushes. It was the 8th of November so these fireworks may well have been tardy offers for Guy as well as Lady Malcolm's guests. Another explosion. The gilded silhouettes of park dwellers flashed briefly in the light. I assumed them to be other ball-goers or late-night strollers with other pursuits in mind. I had visited Hyde Park upon occasion; it was a favoured spot amongst men of the armed forces.

"I'm catching a chill," said Theo.

"Off we go then."

We got up and headed back for the monument, heralded by a shower of green bursting across the dark sky. Not far from us a pair of young women drunkenly staggered from the path and onto the grass, giggling as they went. I doubted either of us were under any illusions as to what they were up to. The gloom of the park was the perfect place for all sorts of misbehaviour. A whole orgy could be underway, for all I knew, and if it were, it probably involved Lady Splendid! I let out a cherished sigh of contentment and put my arm through Theo's. Another firework burst red, then off we went, ready for another bat at the ball.

CHAPTER 6

"More kedgeree, Mr Bigge?"

"I'm really not sure I…"

Another generous spoonful of the yellow rice dish was transferred from the serving bowl onto my plate. My insides, comprised of a toxic cocktail of the many alcohols I had consumed the night before, were not prepared for hard-boiled eggs and flaked fish. They yearned for something simple like unbuttered toast or a bowl of flaked corn with no milk. A glass of water would have been nice, but for now, I was working my way through a pot of Assam.

"I couldn't find parsley for love nor money," explained Miss Wickler apologetically. "Nor lemons for that matter. And I'm afraid the cream was off so that is lacking."

In essence, most of the things that gave the dish flavour were absent, for which my stomach was grateful but my tongue less so. I thought better than to ask for salt lest I offend my ever-attentive landlady. Up at the crack of dawn, Miss Wickler had long ago eaten her breakfast but she liked to ensure I was well fed. The upside of this was I didn't have to do my own cooking and while savoury dishes were not her forte, her desserts were prizeworthy. The downsides were numerous and included rarely eating alone, meaning I was bombarded with a litany of questions between mouthfuls and a catalogue of unwarranted advice during. I also had to eat according to her timetable, and on a Sunday, that meant breakfast at half past seven before she left for church. On occasion, I slept through this meal, usually under the pretence of a head cold, but today I felt duty bound to act the well-behaved lodger.

"You were out very late, Mr Bigge."

"Did I wake you? I'm most frightfully sorry."

I had, honest to God, tiptoed the moment I'd reached Pimlico, let alone passed through the front door, and I could avoid every creaking floorboard with my eyes closed. Experience suggested that she kept herself awake to give her something to complain about the next day.

"To be forced to work on a Saturday and so late into the night, I think it improper."

"As do I, Miss Wickler, but things are rather difficult at the bank."

"And in every bank, according to the vicar. He says God has punished the Americans for their wayward spending and now he looks to punish us."

"I wouldn't quite put it tha—"

"Such gross speculation should be a sin."

"I do admit one must take care when taking on credit bu—"

"Will man never learn? Were the scandals of Clarence Hatry not enough?"

She referred to the notorious financier and fraudster who'd fooled the Stock Exchange, Wall Street and investors the world over. His business empire had crumbled in September of 1929 – the canary's swansong before the whole coal mine collapsed a month later. Due to my working at a bank, my landlady regularly chastised me for the industry's woes. That I lacked the power to topple national economies was by the by.

"We will be knitting after the service, gloves and hats for the wounded and poor. It's one thing for those in banks to gamble with a country's future, but it has very real-world consequences, Mr Bigge."

"I am aware—"

"And it is so frightfully cold."

I agreed with a shiver but was glad for the fire in the small grate. Central heating was an ongoing concern for the English and Miss Wickler preferred never to turn hers on, due in part to a Christian aversion of pagan indulgence as well as the sheer cost of it.

"It is my duty as a God-fearing woman to help those in need."

"Doubtless the vicar is most grateful."

"Just last week he praised my floral presentation and said my Victoria sponge was verging on a sin."

She released a titter of laughter as I tried to subtly remove a haddock bone from between my teeth.

"Will your group be knitting at the church?" I asked tactfully. The thought of putting my feet up in front of the fire and having a snooze was very tempting.

"I have invited the ladies back here. I trust you will be on your best behaviour."

The latter comment she made lightly and I smiled in return.

"Perhaps they could spare some woollen socks for my chilly toes."

"Now, now, there are many far more deserving of warmth. Need I remind you that you have a roof over your head and a bed to sleep upon."

She didn't but she enjoyed doing it nevertheless. Unfortunately for me, the bed was incredibly close to the roof because my room was in the attic, ensuring ice on both the inside and outside of the window in the colder months.

"I say, who could that be?"

Our familiar breakfast conversation was interrupted by the ringing of her telephone.

"Do excuse me," she said, hurrying out of the room.

I allowed myself a moment to close my eyes – hoping my spinning head would ease its velocity. For someone still experiencing the after-effects of last night's drinking I was proving a most passable breakfast companion. I still longed for Miss W's departure, so I could return to my bed. Fortunately, she had provided me with an extra eiderdown and a number of rugs to withstand the worst of the chill. My thoughts briefly flashed back to the ball, the memories a blur of colour and fun, and a passing moment of pleasure in a toilet cubicle.

"I say," said Miss Wickler, sounding flustered, "it's for you. Your esteemed friend, Lady Theodora Smythe."

This last comment was made entirely free from irony and based on a number of misunderstandings on Miss W's behalf regarding Theodora's importance and the correct address for a baronet's daughter. I'd long ceased trying to correct her.

"Perhaps we are to church together," I said, as I rose from the table, glad to be free from the pungent aroma of smoked fish. I entered the hall and went to retrieve the telephone. It was stationed on a table not far from the front door which itself was not far from the sitting room door, should Miss Wickler wish to take a ringside seat.

"Hullo," I said. "Frightfully early for a morning call."

"Selby, I'm calling on a serious matter."

"Is everything all right?"

"My mother rang me this morning."

"Oh dear."

"To tell me that Helena Fortescue had rung her this morning."

"Oh dear times two."

"We have been summoned."

"Where to?" I asked, secretly hoping for my first invitation to the Smythes' Surrey pile.

"To 42 Pendragon Rise."

"You're pulling my leg, Theodora. One meal with them per annum is more than enough."

"I'm not joking," she said, her tone grave. "Helena doesn't have my Wilkington Mews number, which is why she called the family home. Mother was most put out and Helena was most insistent: you and I must return at the earliest convenience."

"What's happened?"

"I don't know. Are you dressed?"

"Yes, I'm breakfasting with my delightful landlady." This last part I said a little more loudly.

"Then expect my arrival shortly and I'll motor us back to Belgravia."

She'd rung off before I had time to ask any more questions. Just when I was starting to get my bearings, off went my head again, spinning like a merry-go-round. A polite cough issued from behind.

"Is everything quite well, Mr Bigge?"

"I am to be collected," I said.

"For church?"

"Sadly not."

It was not long until the dark-green Crossley honked its arrival outside the house. Even I knew it was too early for such noise but Theodora was a law unto herself. Miss W followed me down the short path that led to the gate, heedless of the cold, while I had wrapped myself in scarf, gloves and coat. I rearranged the drooping, silken poppy in my buttonhole. It resembled its wearer – worse for wear.

"Hallo, Miss Wickler," called Theodora from the driver's seat.

"Lady Smythe," she replied, peering to and fro to see if any of the neighbours were watching. "What a pleasant surprise. Would you care for a plate of kedgeree?"

"No time, I'm afraid. Although Selby tells me how scrumptious it is."

I glowered at her as I passed through the gate – something which I regularly oiled with regards to Miss W's light sleeping and my nocturnal habits.

"Hurry it up, Selby," Theodora muttered to me before increasing her volume. "A cup of tea another day!"

"That would be lovely," trilled Miss W. "Do drive carefully."

She waved us off from behind the little gate and soon we were away.

"One day," I said, "I'm going to lock you in a room with her and a bible open at the book of Leviticus."

"Detestable shellfish, is it?"

"Lobsters are the least of her concerns."

As ever, Theodora was well put together in a smart dress and a natty cloche with a feather, presumably a jay's as it was blue-and-black striped. I wore my usual Sunday suit and my ever-trusty homburg. Fortunately, time's somewhat premature march across my scalp was a slow advance and I still had plenty of hair to keep my crown warm, just not quite as much as before. Nevertheless, three years in the City of the Plain had proven that most men didn't care tuppence about that sort of thing – it was other things they had their eyes on.

"What's the matter?" I asked as we zipped through Pimlico.

"In between calling you, starting the motor and arriving, I'm afraid I haven't acquired any further information."

"Don't be sharp," I said. "It's not even eight o'clock."

"I'm sorry, Selby, but I'm worried."

"You are?"

She nodded solemnly.

"Then so am I."

The car slowed as we fell behind a horse and cart filled with coal. Early morning pedestrians made their way up and down the pavements; most looked chilly, some glum, and many were intently heading for church. Red poppies glistened on lapels and buttonholes, like splashes of blood.

"I do hope Helena Fortescue hasn't learned we were at the

ball," I thought aloud. "We feigned ignorance at dinner."

"The thought crossed my mind," said Theodora, concentrating on overtaking the cart. "But I have a horrible feeling it's something far worse than that."

CHAPTER 7

"I know where you were last night."

Helena Fortescue was not one to tarry on her way to the point. She would have made a frightfully good headmistress and had the greatest claim to being Cleopatra in a past life. Upon arrival at the Fortescue household, we'd been ushered upstairs by Grace and led into a parlour that overlooked the street.

"Would this be in reference to our respective beds?" replied Theodora, who'd instructed me to let her do the talking.

"No," replied Helena coldly.

The simplest word with which to describe the parlour was brocade – the settees, chairs and even the poufs, were tastefully decorated in floral and leaf-like patterns of muted blues, silvers and greys, while the curtains and their valances combined cream and gold. The effect served only to emphasise the mistress's importance and to further disorientate my addled mind. Mrs Fortescue was seated in the middle of a large sofa, the windows behind her, while Theodora and I perched on small, upholstered seats opposite. The sun had made a reluctant appearance, haloing the mistress of the house.

"It would be in respect to your attendance at the Servants' Ball."

Bugger! How on earth did she find that out? Had Lance ratted on us or perhaps Grace, which might explain the harried look on the maid's face.

"What makes you think we attended the ball?" asked T.

"Because I was told."

Who needed Wimbledon when one could listen to these two converse?

"By whom?"

"Jacqueline."

So, she was the guilty party!

"Then I'm sure Jacqueline will have told you why we were at the ball," replied Theodora, volleying the shot.

"She didn't, as a matter of fact."

"The wayward butler."

"Who?"

"For some time now, silver has been vanishing from the family home and my father suspects one of the butlers. He asked me to undertake a little detective work."

"Dressed as a man?" asked Helena. A marvellous backhand.

"I can hardly go dressed as myself, people would ask all sorts of questions."

"Surely they'll be asking even more questions now."

"I had no intention of being recognised."

"And I hear Mr Bigge wore rouge."

"Selby is prone to excess perspiration," said Theodora with disconcerting ease. "He's of a nervous disposition."

Bloody marvellous.

"I'm surprised you weren't tempted to dress as a maid," said Mrs F, skewering me with her all-seeing gaze.

I was never much of a tennis player but lying was another sport entirely.

"I haven't met the butler in question," I replied calmly (miraculously cured of my nervous disposition). "So there was no risk he might recognise me and, besides, Theodora needed protection. Underneath that stiff exterior lies a fragile heart."

I sensed her bristling irritation. Advantage Bigge.

"You were her bodyguard?"

Helena's tone had changed; no longer cold, it was now sincere, verging on concerned. Was it match point to us?

"I was."

"Then... then, I must apologise."

Game, set and match.

"I must apologise..."

Victory proved bitter as Mrs Fortescue utterly lost her resolve and began to sob. Tears fell from her eyes as she produced a clean, brocaded handkerchief.

"Helena, whatever's the matter?" asked T.

More sobs and more tears as Theodora crossed the room to sit next to her on the sofa. She patted tentatively at the older woman's shoulder. I felt it improper to watch, so I shifted my gaze to the elaborately patterned carpet, trying to make sense of the matriarch's crumbling resolve.

"There, there, you can tell us what's happened," said Theodora gently.

"It's Lance... he's..."

She blubbed and my heart sank. Like Cassandra the unheeded priestess who foresaw the fall of Troy, like Tiresias the blind prophet who'd foreseen the fall of Thebes, so I knew exactly what she was going to say next.

"He's dead."

"Dead?" echoed Theodora weakly.

With a great effort of will, Helena Fortescue straightened her back, stifled her sobs and wiped away her tears. Neither lower nor upper lip wobbled as she spoke her next words.

"Last night Lancelot was killed."

"Oh Mrs Fortescue," I said, "that is quite... quite..." Words escaped me as I exerted a great effort of will to suppress my shock.

"Utterly devastating," said Theodora. "I can only begin to imagine the pain you must be feeling. To lose a child is a cross no mother should bear."

Dead. Lance was really dead? It hadn't even been twelve hours since I'd spoken to him at the ball. How vital he'd been then, quaffing champagne and chatting with Reggie.

"Was it some awful accident?" asked Theodora.

Mrs Fortescue shook her head. "It was murder."

"My God," I exclaimed.

The two women looked at me – Mrs Fortescue surprised at my exclamation of shock but Theodora's eyes wide in recognition of the feeling.

"I cannot begin to express my sorrow," my friend said soothingly. "This news is beyond awful, for you and the family."

"The police called just after six o'clock this morning. I was still asleep but Hector went downstairs. They told him everything."

It was at this moment that a knock came at the parlour door. Helena bade the knocker entry. A head appeared through the gap, belonging to a young man I hadn't met before. He had sandy blond hair combed in the middle and a neat moustache of the same colour beneath a strikingly small nose.

"Mrs Fortescue, your husband has requested your presence in the drawing room."

"Do come in, Cyril, I would like to make an introduction."

The young man stepped across the threshold. He was quite short in stature but held himself politely. Perhaps this is what became of cherubs once they'd reached adulthood. As far as I was aware, he wasn't one of the staff but nor did he look like he belonged to the family.

"Miss Smythe you know and this is her acquaintance, Mr Selby Bigge."

"Good morning," he said, his voice nasal and polite.

"This is Cyril Blanford, my secretary."

We looked at one another, and for a moment, he squinted, as if he couldn't make me out properly, then he blinked. He acknowledged my presence with a brief nod and I did the same.

"How do you do?" I asked, offering him my hand. He approached slowly and we touched only briefly. I noted his eyes were red and puffy, which I put down to a lack of sleep or a surplus of squinting rather than a bout of crying like his employer.

"I shall be down shortly," said Helena.

He bobbed his head and retreated through the door. As he went, he cast me one final look. Perhaps he recognised me, but from where, I hadn't a clue. Strange. There was a man that would take some fathoming.

"The very epitome of reliability," said Helena. "He assists with my work for the National Vigilance Association and my other endeavours."

"Helena, I do not wish to be insensitive," said Theodora, "but you called us here to discuss our presence at the ball. Is this of import?"

"Yes," she replied solemnly. "I telephoned Jacqueline the moment I'd heard the news. She's now upstairs in one of our guest bedrooms. This has thoroughly broken her."

"I can imagine," said Theodora sympathetically, "but I still don't see why our being at the ball matters."

"It's where they found him," she said gravely.

"Where?" I exclaimed before I could stop myself.

"In Kensington Gardens, not far from the Albert Memorial."

The tennis match was definitively abandoned as the thunder-clouds opened, the rackets broke and the balls burst. The very spot Theodora and I had gone for some air was now the site of a murder.

"Let us help," I blurted.

"I beg your pardon."

"Theodora and I were there last night, as you know, doing our own detective work. We may have seen something."

"Well, did you? Did you see Lance?"

"I… I don't believe so."

Typically, it was Theodora who liked to drive fast, but for some unfathomable reason I'd put myself in the driver's seat. She gave me the briefest of looks, and if telepathy had been a shared skill, she may well have told me to put the brakes on. Helena rose to her feet.

"Come, Hector and Percy need to hear this. They're downstairs awaiting the return of the police."

"Right," I said a little uncertainly.

We left the brocaded parlour, following in Mrs Fortescue's wake. Her resolve had returned. Gone was any trace of the distraught mother. She was a woman of business once again. Theodora took hold of my arm and gave it a very tight squeeze.

"Lance promised he'd never return to that ball," said Helena. "And now it's killed him."

CHAPTER 8

Our reunion with Doctor Fortescue and Percival was an expectedly sombre affair. We were shown into the grand drawing room on the ground floor with equally expensive furniture and upholstery as the parlour. Logs and coal roared in the grate, so at least the temperature was warm. Theodora and I offered our condolences to the grieving father and brother, both of whom looked drained but reserved. It was the lot of any Englishman that his education should involve the stiffening of the upper lip and the ironing of the brow. What the two men felt on the inside I could only but surmise.

"He promised us," repeated Helena. "He promised us he'd never return."

She sat next to her husband on one of the settees. He'd taken the pocket square from his jacket and was wringing it between his hands. Percy had positioned himself behind them, standing sentinel.

"For all we know, he kept that promise," said the doctor. "They found him in the gardens, not the Hall."

That their late son had very much been at the ball, thoroughly enjoying a bottle of champagne with one of the staff, was something they would never hear from my lips.

"I didn't see him," lied Theodora reassuringly.

"Then why was he there at all?" asked Helena.

"Perhaps it was a test," suggested her husband. "To prove to himself he could resist temptation and that the cure had worked."

"In the same way a reformed dipsomaniac might enter a bar?" said Helena.

Her husband nodded and looked to me. "My son was very ill, you see."

"I'm sorry to hear it," I replied.

"It was an illness of the mind."

"Father," interrupted Percy, "is it appropriate to share this information with our guests?"

"They can help us," said his mother. "They were there."

Theodora had repeated her story of the vanishing butler and the missing silverware (which sounded like the premise of one of her aunt's novels), and the Fortescue men had appeared to believe her. Only I knew how little it would take to reveal her lie – namely another telephone call to her mother. But in a society such as ours, everyone knew the daughter of a baronet was beyond reproach.

"With all due respect, Theodora," said Percy, "the problem is precisely that you were at the ball and not outside in Kensington Gardens watching someone cosh my poor brother."

My insides roiled and Theodora gasped, raising a hand to her mouth. I knew her well enough to know she wasn't acting this time.

"I had spared them those details," said Helena.

"Coshed?" repeated Theodora.

"With a heavy, blunt instrument that remains missing," said Hector.

"That's dreadful."

"It was one of those degenerates," said Helena, her voice cracking. "The ones that sneak into the ball and ruin it for everyone else. Perhaps one of them saw Lance outside and attacked him."

"Mother, we can hardly presume," said Percy. "It's just as likely to have been a drunkard or a thief."

"Was anything stolen?" I asked.

"The police are yet to confirm that," he replied, eyeing me sceptically.

"Perhaps Theodora or Mr Bigge saw one of them leave the ball," said Helena hopefully.

"Them?" I asked innocently.

"One of the perverts."

"Was he also brandishing a candlestick?" said Percy.

"Now, now, be civil," said the doctor. "The police are doing their job and we will know more soon. Besides, Grace has confirmed she saw nothing, so it's most unlikely our guests will be able to add anything."

He looked at us sympathetically as I thought on Grace the liar – she had clearly seen something because she'd spoken with Lance not long before he'd died. It appeared we were all united in saving our respective skins.

"What about Reginald?" I asked.

The question was met with utter silence. It seemed harmless enough, given we had all discussed his purchasing of ball tickets at supper, but the quiet persisted. Helena's pale face seemed to whiten a fraction more, Hector crushed the pocket square within a balled fist and Percy shifted from one foot to the other. Theodora looked to each one of them and I could see the strain beginning to show at the corner of her eye. The answer, when it arrived, came from Percy and shocked the both of us.

"He's vanished."

"Vanished!" said T. "But he went to the ball?"

The only remaining son of family Fortescue nodded gravely.

"You don't think…" Theodora left her sentence purposefully unfinished.

"Absolutely not," shot Helena. "He was devoted to Lance, simply devoted. If anything, he saw what happened and was silenced for it."

"After having made off with Lance's motor," said Percy.

"His car's been stolen?" I asked.

"It has," he replied bluntly, clearly not warming to me.

"Was that the Bentley?" asked Theodora.

Percy nodded.

"What a shame. You think Reginald stole it?"

"I think it a distinct possibility."

"He'd never do a thing like that," protested Helena. "Reginald's always been so good to us, like one of the family. So loyal, especially to Lance."

"And if he was at the ball, he'd hardly have had time to steal Lance's car," I added.

"Exactly," said Helena, tapping the air with an approving finger.

"Then the swine must have come back to the house," said Percy.

"Did you hear anything?" asked Theodora.

"Nothing," said Helena. "I was in bed not long after supper, but you two remained up. Did you hear the servants' door?"

"Of course not," said Hector. "We were drinking in here. We were hardly listening for the sound of footsteps below stairs."

"Drinking until when?" asked Theodora.

"Around half past ten, if I recall correctly. Then I took myself to bed."

"And yourself, Percy?"

"Theodora, you are asking an awful lot of questions," he said.

"Anything to help you get to the bottom of this."

Well, well, this was a turn up for the books! One minute she was digging her nails into my arm and raising her eyebrows in silent protestation. Now here she was trying to take the wheel from my hands.

"That's the job of the police," said Percy frostily.

"They're only trying to help," said Helena. "If we can find Reginald, we might be able to find whoever…" Her voice cracked.

"There, there," said Hector, taking a moment to stroke his wife's shoulder. "Did you hear anything, Percy?"

"I wish I had," he said. "But I drifted off not long after you left, Father."

"In here?" I asked, lest everyone forget I was still present.

"I'm afraid I had rather too much brandy."

"Then perhaps someone else has stolen Lance's car," said Theodora.

"I can't think who," said Percy. "Far more likely it was Reginald."

"Maybe it was part of a silly drunken game," said Helena,

clutching at whichever proverbial straws were presented to her. "He may well come back today."

"We can only hope," replied her son.

"What of the extra tickets he purchased?" I asked.

This time mother and son looked to the doctor – his pocket square a crumpled mess.

"Gone, I'm afraid," he confessed. "I left them on my desk but someone must have pinched them."

"And Lance's portrait?"

"It fell."

Onto a conveniently placed sharp object!

"Stolen tickets, Reginald missing and dear Lance murdered," said Theodora, summing things up most alarmingly. "Selby and I are so very sorry."

Flashes of the night before came unbidden to my mind as the Albert Hall loomed high in the cold November evening; as revellers danced and danced around the auditorium in blurs of colour; as cigarette smoke and bodily odour fused. Then there was Lance, removing his colourful mask to reveal that handsome face of his, and Reginald arriving not long after. Lancelot and his loyal manservant. If only I hadn't been so squiffy, I might better have understood the meaning of his words. Then black and gold and red as fireworks burst in the night sky.

"Excuse me," I said, rising swiftly to my feet. "I shall return in a matter of moments."

Everyone looked politely shocked at my sudden ejaculation. Theodora's look was less polite, but my head was spinning so fast it might just fall off. I retreated across the carpet and let myself back into the hall. Fortunately, no one was to hand as I took in one long, shuddering breath and slowly let it out. Lancelot and Reginald, was I truly the last person to have seen them alive?

I planned to lock myself in the water closet, inwardly scream and wait for my head to cease whirling. But just as I was straightening my cuffs, I heard a sound issue from below stairs. It was something between a sigh and a sob. Then came another. I walked quietly towards the top of the stairs and peered over the banisters; one flight below was a woman, a hand pressed to her mouth and a silly little hat on her head. It was Grace. Hoping my head would remain in place a little longer, I quietly descended, thinking it best to catch her unawares.

"Grace, I say. Whatever's the matter?"

"Mr Bigge!" she said accusingly, no trace of anguish in her voice.

"I'm sorry to startle you."

"You didn't."

"The news is tragic," I said, positioning myself between the bottom of the stairs and the corridor that led deeper into the servants' domain. "The ball was meant to be a dream but now it's a nightmare."

"You're right, sir," she said, unable to get past me.

I felt something of a brute trapping her, but if she was capable of lying to her employers, what else might she be able to hide?

"The Fortescues are asking whether myself or Miss Smythe saw anything last night, but alas, we were busy on the scent of a thieving butler. Did you?"

"Did I what?"

"See anything of Lancelot?"

"Of course not," she said.

"Even though I saw you dancing with him."

"I was being friendly."

"Perhaps you'd care to tell Doctor Fortescue that?"

Her eyes flickered, her jaw tensed. "I saw nothing. I was back by midnight."

"By which time Lancelot may well have been murdered. What of that plague doctor?"

"I'm not sure what you're referring to." She paused. "Sir."

"The chap with the beak-nosed mask I saw quarrelling with Lance. You intervened in their argument."

Surely now I had her!

"Perhaps your eyes deceived you, sir."

"I think not."

"Maybe you saw another woman in a similar dress and mistook her for me."

Gosh, she wasn't going to budge an inch. She peered over my shoulder as footsteps tapped along the corridor.

"What's all this?"

I turned to see another servant approaching. It was Max. He wore his formal servant's attire and looked thoroughly concerned.

"Mr Bigge is lost," said Grace tersely.

"Lost. Wherever are you going, sir?"

"The water closet," I replied. "And you would be?"

"Galloway, sir. Max Galloway."

Up close I saw his dark hair was cut short and his cheekbones pleasingly prominent. Theodora had told me his mother was English and father Indian – I couldn't believe that made for an easy combination in a house such as this, or a country such as this for that matter. He smelled of silver polish.

"I'm very sorry to hear of your master's death," I said.

"Thank you, sir, it's a great loss."

"Had you worked for him for long?"

"Long enough, sir," he replied.

"And Reginald's disappearance – yet more bad news."

"Yes," he affirmed sadly.

"That damned ball."

"I curse the day Lady Malcolm ever thought to put it on."

He spoke the words with true feeling and I was briefly afforded a glimpse of the man underneath the servant's calm demeanour.

"Perhaps you know of some disagreement between Master Lancelot and Reginald?" I asked.

"I don't. We like our employers very much."

"Come, Mr Galloway, were you not arguing with the master only recently? I believe you called him a brute."

Oh, how I liked to dance near the edge! Max looked far from happy.

"The water closet is upstairs," said Grace.

Max held my gaze for a moment. It was a nice face to look at, with deep brown eyes, but I felt decidedly uneasy for trespassing and these two were fast closing ranks.

"Thank you," I said, beating my retreat. I felt their eyes on me as I climbed the stairs, but once I was out of sight, I slowed my pace.

"You shouldn't talk to him," said Max with a hiss.

"I didn't," snapped Grace. "He trapped me unawares."

"What did you say?"

"Nothing."

"Are you sure?"

"Yes. Now leave me be."

There was a rustling of fabric and a pattering of feet as the two departed. I sped on down the corridor in case one were to mount the stairs and quickly locked myself in the loo. I hurried to the sink and dashed some cold water against my cheeks. This wasn't the first time Theodora and I had been near-witnesses to a murder and something told me it wouldn't be the last. Despite our many protestations, the thrill of detection was like no other. I pulled the chain of the toilet and waited a moment as the water flushed. Rearranging my tie, I re-entered the corridor and prepared myself for another round with the family. I'd barely walked one step when the doorbell rang.

Grace hastily appeared from below stairs just as the doctor and his wife emerged from the drawing room. The maid opened the front door and there, standing at the threshold, was a man I'd hoped never to see again. Average height, a little over middle age, greying temples and a bushy moustache good for tugging at, it was one Detective Chief Inspector Lisle of Scotland Yard. Behind him, just a few steps down, was his all-too-familiar, square-faced lackey, Detective Constable Stovell. My head, long having threatened to spin off its axis, now seized the moment to absent itself of my neck. I thought it best to step back inside the water closet.

CHAPTER 9

Unfortunately, English law and I disagreed as to whether or not I was a criminal. I considered my attraction to other men quite natural – that I admired the curve of their cheek, the shape of their jaw and the fall of their hair (if they had any) was neither here nor there. That I also admired the naked male body and its various accoutrements was certainly a little more exciting for me, but still all rather quotidian. The laws of the land disagreed. That I could spend time in prison for kissing a man on his cheek, let alone his lips, was an unfortunate fact of my existence, and one I had to contend with on a daily basis.

I pretended to wash my hands in the basin for a second time. The man in the mirror looked calm enough, his hair in place, his cheeks and upper lip freshly shaven, but I knew the signs to look for. The slight twitch in the corner of my left eye was absent, reserved for times of extreme stress, but I was clenching my jaw, a dead giveaway. I opened and closed my mouth a few times, trying to relax.

"Come on, old man," I said, "get yourself together."

As a young boy, deportment had always been a concern. I was careful to hide the scratches from the bramble thickets I'd entered to find blackberries. Likewise, I would wipe any mud from my shoes after my jaunts across the fields. Preparatory school proved even more dangerous, where untied shoelaces and loose shirttails might be met with corporal punishment. I was also taught a new lesson, repeated at boarding school and that fated West End matinee, one that connected carriage with nature. A high voice or a limp wrist was not merely considered girlish, but also peculiar. And peculiarity was as equally abominable in a man as girlishness.

I left the lavatory and walked as slowly as I could down that long corridor. I paused to admire a painting of a dramatic swathe of moorland, upon which a shepherd attended to his flock under a foreboding sky of grey and purple storm clouds. As for Lancelot's torn portrait – it was gone. In its place hung a picture of some ancient-looking maiden aunt type of the Victorian era. She wasn't smiling and wore a white bonnet and a big white ribbon. I wondered if the thought of engaging in heterosexual activity had ever crossed her mind.

Bashed to death. It made me queasy just to think of it. I hoped Lance's suffering had been brief but I doubted it. Back in the hall, I placed my hand on the gilt doorknob of the drawing room and remembered to straighten my back and unclench my jaw. I had every right to be here. I turned the knob. I had every right to be here.

The first person I saw was Constable Stovell – an irritatingly handsome man who I'd first encountered in a public convenience a few years ago. He'd have been sent there to lure unsuspecting men into acts of gross indecency for which he would promptly arrest them. As tempted as I had been by his pleasing features, good fortune had appeared in the form of a coughing commuter, and I'd fled the urinals after passing water. Nowadays his features pleased me less because I knew what sort of man lay underneath. There was no space in his heart for my kind. The second time I'd encountered him was shortly after someone had been murdered. History had a knack for repeating itself.

"Ah, Mr Bigge, there you are."

Doctor Fortescue had spoken from his position next to his wife. Percy remained to attention behind them and Theodora on the settee opposite. Jackie was still upstairs, resting in the guest room. That left the final member of the gathering who, like some presumptuous usurper king, had claimed the high-backed chair between the two settees.

"I believe you're acquainted with Detective Chief Inspector Lisle," said the doctor.

The man in question rose to his feet and fixed me with his stare. "That's right," he said. "Mr Bigge and I have met."

"Chief Inspector," I replied, walking as calmly as I could around the settee and sitting myself next to Theodora. She didn't look at me; presumably as anxious as I was.

"How surprised I was," he said, reseating himself, "to learn of your presence."

"The surprise is mutual," I replied. "How I long not to be meeting you again under such unfortunate circumstances."

"You have a habit of being proximal to murder."

"A habit I wish to break, I assure you."

"Chief Inspector." This time it was Helena's turn to speak. "Miss Smythe and Mr Bigge have proven most obliging in offering us what little information they have regarding my son's death."

"Indeed," said the chief inspector, "but having listened to Miss Smythe's account, there really is so little information as to be none whatsoever."

The smug so-and-so!

"We must leave no stone unturned," she implored.

"I'm inclined to agree," he said. "Have you anything to offer, Mr Bigge?"

He looked straight at me. I should have flushed myself down the bowl.

"I'm afraid I don't."

Damn it! Lying to the police was fast becoming a habit of mine these days, but in a houseful of liars I was hardly the only one. Lance had lied to his family about the suppression of his desires and I wasn't going to snitch on the chap now he was dead.

"As I suspected," said Lisle. "Still, it's not as if Mr Bigge fancies himself an amateur detective."

"Perish the thought," I said through gritted teeth.

"That sort of work must be left to the professionals and we're making good progress."

"Already?" asked Helena hopefully.

He nodded but said nothing. We all looked on expectantly.

"Such as?" prompted Percy.

"For starters, we know that your son's body was found in Kensington Gardens at five o'clock this morning, by a young guardsman."

"What else?" said the doctor impatiently.

"He was last seen leaving this house at half past nine, which narrows down the time of death significantly."

"Between half past nine at night and five o'clock in the morning is hardly narrow," complained Helena.

"Surely you can be a little more specific, Chief Inspector," said Theodora.

"Surely," I echoed, simply to rub salt in the wound.

"The coroner is working on that," he said defensively, "but there was a frost last night, which makes things rather difficult."

"Rather," protested Percy.

"At least that timeframe includes when the ball was underway," said Helena.

"That's correct, Mrs Fortescue, but I'm of the inclination your son was attacked by a chancer. The crime speaks to a spur-of-the-moment incidence. Perhaps an attempted robbery?"

"You've confirmed he was robbed?" asked Doctor Fortescue, running a hand through his neatly trimmed beard, ever the Freudian.

"That we have not."

"If nothing was taken, then it's unlikely to have been a robber," I said, receiving an approving look from the grieving parents and one of barely restrained ire from Lisle.

"What is likely," he said, "is that the thief was interrupted and fled the scene of the crime before he could finish the job."

"Have you found the weapon?" asked Percy.

"Not yet," mumbled the policeman. "But we are looking for a blunt instrument – a brick or stone, perhaps."

My stomach churned. No one had anything to say to that.

"What of Reginald?" Percy again.

It has to be said, I might not have warmed to family Fortescue, despite their loss, but we were teaming up rather well against London's finest.

"I think there we have a second thief."

"I simply will not believe it of him," said Helena.

"He did take Lance's car," said Percy.

"We can't be sure it was him," she retorted.

"These things are often an inside job," said the chief inspector knowingly. "He'll know where the family silver is kept."

"None of the servants have reported any missing silver," said Helena.

"Perhaps a small suitcase?" asked Lisle. "We found an empty one not far from where we found your son."

"I'll ask Grace to search below stairs," said Helena. "So far, only Cook has complained."

"Your cook?" asked Lisle with a raised eyebrow.

"Ashes all over the floor in front of the oven, an utter mess."

"Maybe a pigeon flew down the chimney?"

"The only pigeons that enter the kitchen, Chief Inspector, are plucked."

Here was a woman who took no prisoners – a quality I admired, providing I wasn't the one facing execution.

"It could have been a strong gust of wind." This suggestion came from Constable Stovell, allowing me a chance to look over my shoulder. He had a notepad in hand and a pen in the other, looking ever the Platonic form of a diligent subordinate keen to impress his boss.

"Thank you, Sergeant," said Lisle. Evidently the blighter had been promoted since the last time I'd endured his company. I wondered what for – misdirecting traffic, arresting queers, tying his shoelaces?

"So, you think Reginald stole the car but didn't kill my brother?" asked Percy.

"Precisely," said Lisle. "I'm inclined to believe there's no connection between your brother's death and Reginald's disappearance."

"Chief Inspector, I do so hate to interject," said Theodora, relishing her interjection, "but are you really suggesting those two things are unconnected?"

The chief inspector grunted his assent.

"That strikes me as a most remarkable coincidence."

"Having more experience of these things than you, Miss Smythe, I don't find it remarkable at all. In my line of work, I happen upon a coincidence at least once a day."

"But surely Chief—"

He held a hand up to silence her – the cheek! How she'd be fuming inside, but the show must go on. Currently we were on stage, sweating in the spotlight and playing the parts of the law-abiding family acquaintances.

"We must at least find Reginald," implored Percy.

"Of course, Master Fortescue, and it's for this reason I have returned. I want to know the sorts of places we might find him – if he had any relatives nearby, the pubs he frequented on his time off, that sort of thing."

I expected each of the Fortescues to rush to answer but the question was met only with silence. Percy took to walking the length of the settee and Helena looked cautiously at her husband, who, in turn, reclaimed the pocket square from his pocket and dabbed his forehead.

"We'd be happy to provide this information," replied the doctor eventually. "His mother lives in Shepherd's Bush. Our maid will be able to assist further."

"And will you assist?" asked Lisle, surprisingly perceptive for a change.

For once the doctor was lost for words.

"There is another side to all this," said Percy, filling in for his father, "concerning Lance's illness."

Lisle merely nodded. It was a good trick – silence. People so often rushed to fill it.

"And his cure," said Helena. "But sometimes an illness can return, no matter how watchful the patient. That's where Reginald comes in."

"He keeps a close eye on my brother," said Percy. "Follows him all over town."

"To ensure he doesn't stray," added the mother.

The pair now looked to the doctor. His face had reddened, not just from the heat of the fire, and his brow had acquired a sheen. He looked almost angry. "I did everything I could," he said quietly.

"You did, darling, none of us are in doubt."

"But you know what that ball is like, Father," added Percy. "Almost as bad as those places in Soho."

"Sinks of turpitude," said Helena.

I knew exactly of the places they were describing – the sorts I enjoyed frequenting of a Saturday night.

"Young men like Lance are vulnerable," said Lisle. "And those places prey on vulnerability."

"Lance was in good health," said the doctor, shaking his head. "He was testing his resolve."

Helena turned her gaze to rest on Theodora and I. She offered us a kindly, tired smile, little knowing the tumult in our breasts.

"Theodora, Mr Bigge, I must explain. The chief inspector has proven an invaluable ally in my work with the National Vigilance Association."

"Is that right?" said Theodora, her voice a shade quieter than usual.

"It was thanks to our collective efforts we were able to close one of those awful sinks earlier this year – Frank's Goldmine."

The sink in question had been a cavernous Soho cellar available for rental from a man called Frank. From Communists to ballerinas, all sorts had hired the space, including a chap who'd organised some dances. Neither a Marxist nor a ballet dancer, I'd ventured into that subterranean den for comfort. The musk of damp walls and the flickering light of dim lamps had provided the backdrop for a passionate evening with a young tailor from Basingstoke. Fortunately, that wasn't the night it had been raided and shut down, back in February. Four had been arrested, including Frank. The newspapers had gleefully reported another dance hall scandal, when all we wanted was a fun night out (or the end of capital for those with Communist leanings).

"You think Reginald might be connected to these places?" I managed to ask.

"Only because he was forced to visit them when Lance strayed," explained Percy.

"He hadn't done that for a year," said Doctor Fortescue. "I'm sure of it."

"Your son may well have avoided those places," said Lisle, "but that wouldn't stop them avoiding him."

"What do you mean?" asked Helena.

"Perhaps Lancelot encountered one of those unsavoury sorts at the ball, or outside it. Someone he'd met on a previous occasion. They might have assaulted him."

Bingo! Just as Helena had done, now it was Lisle's turn to blame that most infamous of chaps for the crime – the deranged pervert. He was a scapegoat in near constant employment (unpaid, of course).

"And the altercation may have proven fatal."

"And if Reginald were there," I said, "he might have seen all this happen."

"You're right," piped up Theodora. "He might even have gone in pursuit of the attacker."

"And if things came to blows," I continued, "he—"

"He may have ended up a second victim," finished Theodora.

"Now, now," interrupted Lisle, openly irritated by our suggestions. "Let's not get carried away."

"But it's a possibility," said Helena, clawing at the straws we'd offered.

"Many things are a possibility," replied Lisle.

"Which is why you should consider them," commanded Hector.

I heard Stovell suppress a cough as I suppressed a grin.

"I can assure you," said Lisle, his assurance already sounding flimsy, "that we will explore every avenue."

"Not just the avenues," said Percy enthusiastically, "but the alleyways as well. We should write a list."

"Quite right," chimed Helena, "a list of all those detestable places Lance might once have visited."

"The River Styx will undoubtedly be on it," said the policeman.

She nodded. Of course he'd have to bloody mention one of my favourites – much loved and much reviled, depending on one's predilections. On Peter Street in Soho, it catered to all sorts, and despite all the slings and arrows of an outrageously bigoted society, it remained open. One of the doormen had heavily implied the local police were on the take and that one of the top brass liked the male appendage as much as I did.

"What was that particularly dreadful one?" said Percy. "The Parrot?"

"The Pigeon?" offered the doctor.

"The Parakeet," corrected his wife.

They referred to a bar which had closed last year, although this time I believe said closure was due to financial mismanagement on behalf of the proprietor rather than police involvement. Apparently, the owner had invested unwisely and liberally, and then Wall Street had crashed (taking some of my own savings with it). Rumour had it, he'd never even wanted a queer clientele but a few bohemians had taken to the place. Nevertheless, despite their patronage (or because of it), the Parakeet had fallen from its perch.

"Soho is in need of further drainage," said Helena.

"That it is," replied Lisle.

A look passed between them that implied a strength of

shared opinion verging on the fervent. These two would make for a formidable pairing.

"Lady Malcolm attended one of my meetings not long ago," said Helena.

"Your meetings?" I asked.

"Of the Vigilance Association. We gather here on occasion and at Regus Hall. Lady Malcolm was quite adamant that her ball was only for servants. She said perverts were not welcome."

Had it not occurred to her that servants could be just as perverted as the middle classes, not to mention aristocrats? I'd bumped into a number of working-class fruits last night and they'd been having a whale of a time.

"They should be banned," said Helena.

"Then imprisoned," chimed the chief inspector.

"Or treated," said the doctor, finding his voice again. "We mustn't give up on those able to change. Homosexuality is an affliction that can be treated."

If something is believed strongly, however untrue, and by enough people, however deluded, and if it is repeated over and over again in sufficient drawing rooms, newspapers and courtrooms, it has a nasty habit of becoming the truth. I needed a stiff drink, a long cigarette and some toast. The little of Miss Wickler's kedgeree I'd ingested had long been digested.

"Theodora, you look ill," said Helena.

I turned to look at my friend and she didn't look well. It wasn't just the pale cheeks and sullen lips that concerned me but the familiar look of pain in her eyes. Despite appearances, her armour of erudition and good manners was not impenetrable, and underneath beat a human heart as fragile as mine.

"Just a little faint," she said. "I'm yet to breakfast."

"Oh, my dear, I'm so sorry. I summoned you to my home without any regard for your stomach. I can have Cook make you something."

"No need," she said. "I have a prior appointment."

She rose with as much dignity as she could muster, given the circumstances.

"Hector, Helena, Percy, may I reiterate my sorrow. Lance was such a bright young man. Chief Inspector, I hope you find whoever is guilty of this terrible crime."

"I'm under no doubt I will."

"Come, Selby, it's time we left the family to their private grief."

I followed my orders and offered my sympathies once again. I was thanked but the faces that eyed me were bemused, given how little any of them knew me.

"I do have one more question for you, Chief Inspector," I said. "What was Lancelot wearing?"

All heads turned to the policeman. It was fun to put him on the spot.

"Why do you ask?"

"Many people were wearing costumes last night. Perhaps Lancelot was as well?"

"You're right," he consented with evident displeasure. "He was wearing a clown's outfit covered in coloured diamonds."

"Oh God," exclaimed Helena, clutching at her husband's hand. "Then he really was at that ball."

I'd assumed that was obvious by now but clearly the family matriarch had been clinging to her denial with a tight grip.

"He was testing himself," said the doctor, as equally subscribed to denial as his wife.

"Was he wearing greasepaint?" I asked.

"No," came the gruff reply.

"A mask?"

"No," said the chief inspector. "Good day, Mr Bigge, Miss Smythe. I believe you have a disobedient butler to apprehend."

"You're right," said Theodora, quickening her pace as she made for the door.

"If a butler is not to be trusted," he said, "then who can be?"

It was on that note Theodora and I made our exit. I cast one glance back across the room as I closed the door – at the grieving doctor and his wife with their one surviving son close at hand. I pitied them their loss but they grieved a different man to the one I'd met. None of them had ever known who Lance truly was. No. They had known and they hadn't liked it, so they'd forced him to change. Family – how often that word was employed to permit all manner of harms.

CHAPTER 10

My fork skewered the head of the sausage as my knife cut it off. I dipped it in the fried egg, piercing the film and causing the yolk to run. This delightful concoction I put into my mouth along with a bite of hot buttered toast. After a few chews, I washed it all down with a big sip of milky tea. It was approaching ten o'clock, and after the early morning summons, the shocking news and the distinct lack of tea and biscuits, my body was perking up.

Theodora and I had alighted at a café not far from Mornington Crescent. For all intents and purposes, it was closed to the general public, but Theodora was on good terms with the proprietor who, for twice the asking price, had fried us up breakfast. We sat at a small wooden table right at the back, so as not to attract undue attention. Besides the tea, there was also a pot of coffee and an ashtray slowly filling with our butts.

"Well," she said, raising a severed mushroom into the air, "are you going to explain yourself?"

We had remained silent in the car, our hunger leaning dangerously close to anger. I'd let her focus on the driving and she'd let me stew. With filling bellies and lungs, she wanted some answers.

"Clearly Lance's death and Reginald's disappearance are connected," I said. "To suggest otherwise is sheer lunacy."

"That's not what I meant, Selby, and you know it."

"What is it then? You want an apology?"

"I want you to explain why you volunteered my services for solving yet another murder."

"I thought you'd jump at the chance. You leapt last time."

"I chose to leap. I was not pushed."

"Please, there was no pushing this time either."

"Yet, thanks to you, the surviving members of the Fortescue family, a number of their staff, a detective chief inspector and his recently promoted sergeant all know of our attendance at the ball."

"It was Jacqueline who snitched. You can't blame me."

"What if Bile," she said, employing her pet name for the chief inspector, "were to phone my family home? Did you think of that?"

"No... I, er... didn't."

"Liar!"

I was for it now! I'd evidently misjudged Theodora's appetite for mystery-solving. She sipped her coffee and eyed me critically, rivalling Helena Fortescue for the role of headmistress.

"Fortunately for you," she said, "if the chief inspector

employed more initiative than I credit him for, he'd find my mother would corroborate my story."

"Because there really is a thieving butler?" I asked, quite confounded.

"No! Forget the damned butler. My mother would lie for me."

"She would?"

"Of course," she said defiantly. "It's called family loyalty."

"It's called minimising a scandal."

"The two are often synonymous."

She withdrew another cigarette from her silver case and lit it with my lighter.

"Now, back to business," she said. "Who killed Lance?"

"What? You really don't mind being involved in all this?"

"As a matter of fact," she replied smugly, "you pipped me to the post by a matter of moments."

"You were going to volunteer *my* services!?"

"We were there, Selby! We as good as witnessed the thing."

"My thoughts exactly."

"Great minds."

"You think I have a great mind?" I asked, my heart dangerously close to my sleeve.

"Now, now, let's not get ahead of ourselves."

"You really are a brute," I said, affecting as remonstrative a tone as possible. "You could have told me you didn't mind."

"You still jumped the gun and I hadn't breakfasted." She forked a piece of bacon and some of her fried egg. "Let's get to it," she said after swallowing her mouthful. "We have pieces of the puzzle the police never will."

"Pieces which prove incriminating for the both of us," I

replied, reaching for another slice of toast.

"We know how to play it close to our chests."

I bit into the toast and leant back on the rickety wooden chair. The café was nice enough but Mornington Crescent was known for its mixed reputation. How tolerant the usual clientele would be of a chap like me I didn't know. There was one time at a bistro near Charing Cross… No, best not to think on that.

"Grace was acting suspiciously earlier," I said.

"I knew it! You went downstairs?"

"Briefly. When in Rome, do as the Romans do."

Theodora's face lit up with a big grin. It suited her.

"She's hiding something, that's for sure. And I bumped into that fellow Max."

"Who'd been forbidden from going to the ball," she said.

I nodded. "Ever the Cinderella. He'd had that altercation with Lance."

"Which could make him our number-one suspect," she said.

"Lance accidentally knocks him over, thereby inciting a lethal grudge," I replied dramatically, "and last night he sneaked off to the Albert Hall and hid in the bushes."

"The trouble is all number of people could have been hiding in those bushes. And we have to work out exactly where those bushes were, who was in them and at exactly what time."

"Elementary, my dear Theodora," I replied, pausing to wipe the remains of my toast through the dregs on the plate – sausage grease, egg yolk and the sauce of the tinned baked beans. This beat Miss Wicker's breakfast any day of the week. "Let's start with what we know."

"Let's," replied Theodora drily.

"First of all," I said, ignoring her sarcasm, "we know Lance spent most of the evening dancing in the auditorium until he left close to midnight."

"Just before we went to watch the fireworks."

"Precisely."

How close had we been to his body? How fresh the killing blow as we'd craned our necks to watch gunpowder explode in the sky? The thought made my viscera quite unhappy.

"If only we'd left a moment sooner," I said.

"It's too horrible."

"We might have seen who attacked him. Or even stopped them."

"You can't think like that, Selby," she said. "It's too late."

How often in life it was too late, and now one life was lost. Beyond the grubby glass windows of the café front, city life continued as usual. People in Sunday best returned home from church, walking quickly to avoid the biting wind. A few buses rumbled past, the clouds grey above, threatening rain, or snow if the temperature dropped.

"Assuming Chief Inspector Bile to be wrong..."

"A good assumption," I interjected.

"... then it's logical to think Lance's murderer is someone who knew him to be at the ball."

"That discounts most of London, aside from the thousands of guests at the Hall."

"Yes, yes, but let's go with what we've got. Murder is invariably personal. Who else was there before midnight?"

"Reginald," I replied. "I spoke with him and Lance at the bar."

"What time was that?"

"Oh dear, now you're testing me." I thought back to the brief encounter. "I found them at twenty past ten, I think. And Lance said Reggie would be going back to the house shortly thereafter."

"Easy for Reginald to pretend to leave and hang around until lights out."

"It's a possibility," I mused, "but I'm still not sure about Reginald. His disappearance is certainly suspicious, but when I saw him with Lance they were so close."

"Lovers?"

"I'm no gambler but I'd be inclined to put money on it."

"Leading to a lethal lovers' quarrel?"

I shook my head, unable to commit.

"Then I bumped into Jackie about an hour later," continued Theodora, "and fussed about trying to get her into a taxi."

"She definitely got into the taxi?" I asked.

She nodded. "I saw it drive away."

"I had a stroll around the upper gallery then returned to our ringside seats," I said. "I had a good view of Lance and Grace, and the mystery plague doctor who knew Lance well enough to have a big row with him."

"A disgruntled lover?"

I shrugged my shoulders. "The plague doctor left first, then Grace, leaving Harlequin alone. That's when you reappeared."

"At about ten to midnight, I think."

"Giving Lance sufficient time to slip away from the ballroom, exit the Albert Hall and…"

We left a moment of respectful silence for the departed. My coat was draped over the back of a nearby chair and I looked at the red poppy in the lapel. I let myself imagine it was also for

Lance – a victim of peacetime. As I wished for all the dead, I hoped wherever he was now was better than this. Somewhere with less misery and more bliss.

"Which means we have rather a large list of suspects," she concluded, "all lacking in alibis for midnight."

She took another drag on her cigarette and offered the case to me. I was glad to take one. Too much of the morning's distress was lingering in the pit of my stomach, only partially submerged by grease and toast.

"We also know that both Reginald and Lance's Bentley are missing," she said.

"You sound more cut up about the car than the manservant."

"Don't be tiresome, Selby." She puffed her smoke in my direction. "What might have induced Reginald to flee?"

"I can think of a number of things," I replied. "Firstly, he did indeed return to the ball to kill Lance and has subsequently evaporated."

"The incurable homosexual coshed by the thieving valet. The press will like that."

"Don't remind me," I said. "A second option is that Reginald returned to the ball, saw Lance get killed then fled the scene to protect himself."

"Or pursued the murderer?"

"With fatal consequences."

"Or not so fatal," she said. "He may well be in hiding."

"With all this to-ing and fro-ing, there is one thing we need to ascertain."

She raised a quizzical eyebrow.

"How long it takes to get from the Fortescues' house to the

Albert Hall."

"That's a good point," she said. "By car, it's a matter of minutes I'd say, and by feet, well, maybe ten to fifteen, depending on one's pace. We should test that for ourselves."

"How methodical," I said with a patronising wink. "Nevertheless, if your estimates stand, it really was feasible for Reginald to return to the house then head back to the Hall."

"But why bother trudging back to Pendragon Rise when it wasn't suspicious for him to stay at the Hall as a ballgoer?"

This was a good question and I pondered it a moment. I had a strong feeling that ascertaining Reginald's precise movements would prove vital to solving all this. I stubbed out the cigarette and eyed my empty plate forlornly.

"We have an awful lot of haystack but no needle," observed T. "It's a shame the chief inspector wasn't more forthcoming. That was clever of you to ask about the costume."

"Oh, Theodora, a compliment."

"Which I'll retract if you're not careful," she said. "Come to think of it, we don't even know what killed Lance."

"Presumably because the police don't either."

"My, my, do we know anything else at all?"

"We know an unidentified plague doctor forms part of the evening's events."

"Who could have been Reginald in disguise," she mused.

"We know that Grace is hiding something, and Max is aiding and abetting her."

"What of family Fortescue?"

"You did well on that front," I conceded.

"I did rather," she said with a self-satisfied grin. "They

answered my questions most readily and we know they were asleep in bed or on a settee long before the bells tolled twelve."

"Without alibis."

"Therein lies our problem," she said, tapping a fingernail against the rim of her coffee cup. "We need to find out which of them have proof of their midnight whereabouts and which do not. Tell me, Selby, what are you doing tomorrow?"

"Working."

"Oh, I've heard of that. Do you think you could feign stomach troubles of some variety around four in the afternoon?"

"I could try. Why?"

"I want to meet outside Fortnum's."

"Is that really necessary?" I asked.

"Naturally."

Unfortunately, I was not the scion of a baronet nor Lord Peter Wimsey for that matter. Like so many Londoners, I had to concern myself with earning a salary and paying the rent, tiresome as that was.

"What about the squinting blond chap?" I said, suddenly remembering Helena's secretary.

"Cyril Blanford? I certainly wouldn't put him down as a ballgoer, let alone a murderer."

"Discount no one," I offered sagely.

"In that case, let's not forget the cook," she replied dismissively, flicking the end of her cigarette. For a moment her eyes were fixed on the ashtray. "Ash."

"I beg your pardon."

"We also know the cook complained of ashes all over the kitchen floor."

"Someone below stairs treating themselves to a midnight cup of cocoa," I mused. "Surely that's not of import?"

She retrieved her gloves from her handbag and slipped them on. They were satin and impeccably clean. Appearances were everything to Theodora, Theo and I.

"Dear Selby," she said in a tone as cold as the weather, "if you think it wise that no one, not even an unremarkable secretary, be discounted, then may I suggest we discount no *thing* either."

"You may certainly suggest that," I replied, standing from the table, "but only time will tell if I think it a worthy suggestion."

CHAPTER 11

Monday morning arrived with fated inexorability. I travelled the Underground to the bank, marvelling at how many of us could fit into cramped compartments in rickety carriages of noisy trains that ambled unceremoniously from stop to stop. I was seated between two suited men, both of whom had their broadsheets broadly opened, affording me a good look at the morning's news. While Wall Street had crashed over a year ago, its impacts were still being felt the world over as workers united in protest against poor wages and even poorer working conditions, as Britain struggled to maintain the Gold Standard and America's rise to power wobbled.

The 24th of October 1929 had come to be known as Black Thursday. I'll never forget it. An unsatisfactory lunch of a fatty ham sandwich sat heavy on my stomach as I'd joined the crowds outside the London Stock Exchange. Hundreds strong and predominantly male, we stood in our bowlers, trilbies, flat caps and homburgs, umbrellas up one minute then down the next as the weather toyed with us. We refused to believe New York was crumbling but the numbers spoke for themselves as did the rising number of poor chaps throwing themselves from skyscrapers. The Western world shook that day and I finally saw how fragile the whole system was.

It was as if money were a religion. The temples were the banks – those buildings of such haughty architectural splendour – and the devout those of us crowding the cold autumn streets – the bankers. We were dressed in our ceremoniously drab garb, desperately praying that our idol would not fall – the god of capital. Then there were the men like Clarence Hatry, the high priests, who'd convinced us they could turn base metal into gold. How faithfully we'd followed them! If Hatry's confession to fraud the month before had been the first gust of the storm, then Black Thursday was the hurricane. Still, a job was a job, and Miss Wickler's attic room wasn't free.

I alighted at Bank station and spent thruppence on *The Times* at my usual newsstand. I flicked through the pages until I found what I wanted: *Body Found in Kensington Gardens.* The title was lacking in sensation and the piece lacking in information. Lance's name was given but there was little else on family Fortescue or even Lady Malcolm's Servants' Ball. Instead, Detective Chief Inspector Lisle's initial assumption had been parroted – a mugging gone wrong with deadly consequences. I wondered if strings had been pulled to keep information back from the press or if they simply didn't care. The death of a doctor's son was no high society murder, after all, and a missing manservant didn't even warrant a mention. For now, Britain's economy and the demise of global capitalism remained front-page news along with updates on the country's growing public electricity supply.

I attended to my ledgers, cross-checked various figures, and at a quarter to four, excused myself for the WC and returned with a sheepish look upon my face. I spoke with my immediate senior who offered little sympathy for my dicky tummy but suggested I take the rest of the afternoon off nevertheless. I thanked him and left the building with my tail between my legs and didn't release it until I was well away from Childs & Co.

A few stops on the Central London Railway followed by a few more on the Piccadilly line took me to the Circus. Despite myself, I revelled in the bustle of London – the big red buses, the black taxis and the busy pedestrians. We were an eclectic mix as we circumnavigated the ceremonial fountain topped by Anteros, commonly mistaken for his brother, Eros. Both were Erotes, a group of seven winged gods of love, which also included Hedylogos – god of flirting (I was well acquainted with him) and Hermaphroditus – a god of many things. The Classics had proven a refuge for me, whether as a bullied boy at boarding school or an overworked undergraduate at Oxford. As for Anteros, he was the god of requited love, who blessed those matched unions (of which I hadn't had enough). He was also the avenger of unrequited love – punishing those who scorned an offer of romance. I'd turned down a few lovers in my time, but fortunately, none of them had skewered me with an arrow. Eros, on the other hand, had fired whole volleys in my direction. One had even penetrated me not far from here. If London's statues could talk!

I crossed the Dilly, dodging a tall woman with a wide-brimmed hat and a young newspaper seller flogging his periodicals. Up above, vast advertisements encouraged me to buy their wares, including one for Bovril and another for Schweppes' tonic water. Truth be told, I did quite like Coca-Cola; the Americans were more reliable with their carbonated drinks than they were their financial products. I left the Circus behind me and headed down Piccadilly.

My musings on Anteros and his brother made me think of Lance. He'd struck me as a man in love but more likely with a chap rather than his poor fiancée. Reginald was top of my list for being the object of his affection – or perhaps it was the other way around and Lance was the object. Had Reginald's love proved unrequited and been subsequently avenged?

"There you are!"

And there she was, Theodora, as splendid as ever in a dangerously pointy hat and a long coat with fur collar and sleeves – a decidedly feminine look with a few dashes of masculinity to appease Hermaphroditus. Naturally, my chum was acquainted with the one and only Vita Sackville-West, and doubly naturally, had never facilitated an introduction. Corduroy trousers, bow ties and unadorned hats were proving increasingly appealing to the modern woman, despite the diagnoses of Doctors Freud and Fortescue.

"I do hope you're hungry," she said.

"Certainly peckish."

"Good. We're to have afternoon tea."

"Are you saying I lied to my boss for the sake of a scone?"

"And finger sandwiches and an assortment of small yet

delicious cakes. And…" she continued, holding up a hand, "… before the lady doth protest any further, we will have company."

"Who?"

"Jacqueline Bosanquet. This way."

Almost as tall as it was long, Fortnum & Mason's was one of those comfortingly solid, red-brick buildings that dated back to the time of the Stuarts. I had a distant memory of my paternal grandmother taking me there for tea not long after the death of my grandfather, an act which had outraged my parents. My father's father was lovingly remembered for his frugal approach to finance (and fun for that matter), the fruits of which my grandma had decided to enjoy in her final years. And quite right too! Inside, it was reassuringly British and expensive with thick red carpets and grand displays of tea, coffee and all varieties of biscuits. Smartly dressed men and women perused the wares while Theodora led me swiftly to the stairs, all gleaming mahogany and tasteful wallpaper.

"You're sure this is a good idea?" I asked, a few steps behind.

"Sceptical Selby strikes again. We must start somewhere."

"She knows I'll be with you?"

"She does. I've explained we're making discreet enquiries on behalf of Helena and the family, and wish only to ensure the course of justice runs smooth."

"Which we do, even though it rarely does."

We continued our ascent up a few more flights before Theodora paused on the landing. She turned to face me, her superior position lending her a haughtiness that much suited the surrounds.

"On Saturday night I escorted Jackie to a taxi shortly after we'd conversed with her in the bar," she said. "For all intents and purposes, she remained in that taxi until it arrived at her home but…"

"But," I continued, climbing the few steps to join her, "there is every chance she left the taxi as soon as your back was turned and went in search of her late fiancé, found him and…"

"Exactly. We mustn't discount any possibility. Now's our chance to assess its probability."

"I never took you for a mathematician."

"Ascot demands it. Shall we?"

I nodded and she slipped her arm into mine as we crossed the threshold into the dining room. A well-groomed waiter guided us between the tables of happy customers busily consuming their teas. Gilt-edged teapots were in abundance as were all variety of sweet and savoury treats from miniature chocolate éclairs to delicately prepared finger sandwiches, not to mention a hen coop's worth of devilled eggs. My stomach rumbled at what I hoped was a quiet volume.

Then there was Jacqueline, dressed in black and sitting at one of the elaborately bedecked tables. We made our introductions and I offered my condolences. She presented herself with poise but her eyes belied the calm. The poor woman had just lost her fiancé in a most brutal fashion.

"Thank you so much for meeting with us," said Theodora, as we took our seats. "I'm terribly sorry we're slightly late. Selby struggles with stairs."

I restrained my rolling eyes.

"You should have taken the lift," said Jackie kindly.

"Selby struggles with those too."

Theodora enjoyed being tiresome.

"Shall I order?" she said.

"I will have a pot of Earl Grey," said Jackie.

"Nothing to eat?"

"I have no appetite."

"I understand," said Theodora.

Without wishing to be insensitive to her grief, I worried this meant I'd have to go without a scone, but much to my relief, T ordered all the trimmings. She'd already promised it would be her treat, much to my bank account's relief. Afternoon tea at Fortnum's was a very delicious form of daylight robbery.

"It must be so difficult for you," she said, removing one glove. "If there's anything we can do."

"I want you to find the man who killed my husband."

"We hope the police will achieve that," she replied, removing the other glove. "But we also hope our parallel – and tactful – investigation will assist."

"Good, because you were there. You must have seen something."

Jackie's composure almost faltered but she kept her tone in check and blinked back any threat of tears. Whether she wished to scream or cry, or some combination of the two, we'd never know. We were civilised animals, after all, and kept noise to a minimum.

"What about you, Mr Bigge? Did you not even briefly see Lance?"

"Please do call me Selby, and I'm afraid I didn't."

Theodora and I had spoken about this at length – for the time being we were going to honour Lance's lie, knowing it might have been something he died for. Trust was a rare commodity for people like us, traded with exquisite delicacy.

"Perhaps you saw something, Miss Bosanquet?"

"Me?" said Jackie defensively. "But I'd left before..."

"Indeed you had," I said encouragingly, "but you may have seen something without even realising you'd seen it."

It was the sort of thing I thought detectives were supposed to say, like Hercule Poirot or even Inspector Glover (the sleuth Theodora's aunt had created).

"If I hadn't realised it at the time, I'd hardly realise it now," she replied sharply.

"What I think Selby is trying to say is that perhaps something struck you as odd or unexpected."

"Asides all those men in dresses," she said. "What if one of them had followed Lance out of the Hall and chased him into the park?"

"Why?" I asked.

"Why not? If they're mad enough to don woman's apparel, then who knows what else they might do."

Comments like these were such a common feature of my life that the blow was barely glancing. Sometimes my skin was thick enough to deflect bullets.

"Did you see anyone from the Fortescue household? Reginald perhaps?" I asked. "I know Grace was there."

"I didn't see them."

"Or someone dressed as a plague doctor?"

"Nothing of the sort. Although I do remember seeing a pair of goats waving for a taxi."

Driven by Noah, perhaps.

"Remind me what time you left," I said.

Jackie paused to recollect and I wondered if she was also stalling for time. "I think it was some time after half past eleven, but how much I can't remember."

"You drove straight home?" I asked.

"I did."

"Maida Vale?"

She nodded.

"Was there any word from Lance upon your return?" said Theodora, picking up the thread. "A message with one of the servants?"

"I asked my maid, but there was nothing, so I went straight to bed."

"Assisted by your maid?"

"What difference does that make?"

"My dear, no difference at all," said Theodora. "I'm just glad you were well looked after."

It must be said that Theodora had very few tells as a liar, but I had begun to notice the phrase *my dear* appearing before an untruth. The other day I'd asked her if she liked my new tie and was promptly referred to as her dear – an otherwise rare occurrence.

The teapots arrived along with a pyramidal structure of increasingly small and decreasingly large gold-rimmed plates, each carrying a delicacy my stomach yearned for. If the situation had permitted, I would have taken a scone at speed, lathered it in jam and cream, and wolfed it down. Instead, I had to politely wait as Theodora helped herself to a slim cucumber sandwich and then the egg one – both ones I'd had my eye on.

"Are you sure I can't tempt you?" she asked Jackie.

"No, thank you," she replied, her voice suddenly wistful. "Lance loved a fruitcake."

"He did?" I said, trying not to spill the tea I was pouring.

"He had such a sweet tooth."

"You must miss him terribly," said Theodora.

"Not yet, it hasn't sunk in. Sometimes when the telephone rings, I think it's him. We used to have such long conversations."

"Oh, Jacqueline, you poor thing."

"It was all arranged, you see," she said with a small, self-conscious smile.

"What was?"

"Our first meeting – by our mothers, no less."

"Mothers can be so interfering," said Theodora sympathetically (and I felt rather earnestly).

"How glad I am of it. We were holidaying in Torquay last summer, during that exceedingly hot week in August. Do you recall?"

"I think I was on the Riviera," said Theodora, "with Susan Goodley."

"Dear Susan, how is she?"

"Very well."

"I was at work," I said, vividly recalling sweating at my desk.

"Remind me what you do, Mr Bigge?"

"I work at Childs & Co., the bank."

"That must be hard work these days."

Bankers had never been the most beloved members of the human race, but these days everyone and the butcher's son had an opinion on our profession, and a typically negative one at that.

"Things are rather turbulent," I replied, "but back to Torquay."

"I remember it like it was just last week," she replied. "We were there for a fortnight and Mother soon befriended Helena Fortescue. They bonded over their love of cribbage and their moral integrity."

"Fine upstanding women, I'm sure," said Theodora as I shuddered to think of Helena's moral integrity.

"Mother can be a little forthright in her views. It comes from a deep love of the Almighty. Not long into the second week, they insisted Lance and I join them for a rubber of bridge. Helena played a sharp hand."

"I bet," I said.

The two women glowered at me and I quickly retreated behind my teacup.

"Lance and Helena made mincemeat of us. It was all good fun. I remember thinking how handsome Lance was and how wonderful his smile. He caught my eye across the table and I blushed, like a schoolgirl really."

Love as well as money was something that bonded many of us, and despite Jackie's views of my kind, I couldn't help but feel for her. True love was truly rare.

"Our mothers suggested coffee but promptly retired to the library, leaving Lance and I alone. We were both shy, having fallen foul of their matchmaking, but little by little we began to talk and found we had so much in common – a love of birds, the Conservative Party and the occasional trip to the theatre. Lance told me of his hopes to follow in his father's footsteps as a doctor. I was smitten."

"It sounds so delightful, my dear," said Theodora, taking the second and final cucumber sandwich. "I always thought you and Lance were so well matched."

"We were. He was my second knight."

"I don't quite follow," said Theodora.

"I had a childhood sweetheart, you see. A whole happy life had been charted for us with a house, a garden and children. He was older than I and was called up in 1917. He never returned." She paused to stir her untouched tea with the silver teaspoon. The steaming ochre liquid spiralled and swirled. "It wasn't until I met Lancelot that I thought perhaps the broken pieces of my heart could be mended. He was my knight in shining armour and I his Guinevere."

"I thought Guinevere married Arthur," said Theodora with purposeful tactlessness.

"But Lancelot was her true love, as he was mine."

Neither Theodora nor I said anything, our silence filled by the background din of chattering customers and clinking crockery.

"Mother was so pleased for me," she continued. "She says a respectable woman should be married by twenty-two and have her first child the following year. I tried my best. Our courtship was sporadic, you see. Lance was reticent at times. Mother worried he might be questioning my womanly virtues, which is why she took me to Italy."

"When was this?" asked Theodora.

"This summer – another conspiracy of the mothers. We met with the Fortescues in Palermo. I ate spaghetti for the first time!"

"What was it like?" I asked, my hunger unabating.

"Slippery." She looked rather repulsed by the memory. "I

finally mustered the courage to tell Lancelot what I really felt for him."

"That was very brave of you," I said, and I meant it. Theodora had often told me of the freedoms she lacked as herself and the ones he gained as Theo. That a man could place his heart first and all a woman could do was follow. This was the natural order, or so we were told. "And you found those feelings returned?"

She nodded, lost in memories of happier times.

Theodora swallowed her mouthful of sandwich. "Did you ever have any inkling about Lance's other… inclinations?"

Jackie tapped her teaspoon against the cup, with some force. "We went to the Cotswolds this September to watch the tits. On one of our rambles, he said there was something he had to tell me. I thought he was finally going to propose."

The finger sandwiches forgotten, I awaited the next part with bated breath.

"He told me there was a peculiar side to his nature – one that had almost got the better of him. It had made him do all sorts of terrible things, all of which he regretted. Eventually, he'd turned to his father for help. Our walk had taken us to a great oak tree and I can still see the look of fright on his face as he unburdened himself. He was so worried but I just laughed. I said it didn't matter – it was behind him now, and besides, love was the best of medicines. I would have loved him with all my heart."

"And he would have loved you," I said with enough ambiguity that it might have been a question.

"Of course he would," shot Jackie and for the first time her composure slipped and I witnessed a brief flash of anger.

Theodora saw it too. "He was cured, you see, and if he ever tripped it was because *they* pulled him."

"They?"

"The sodomites. I've seen the way they fawn and paw at one another, like animals."

I nearly choked on my tea.

"Of course!" she exclaimed, her eyes widening.

"Is everything all right, Jackie?" asked Theodora.

"I do remember something at the ball. Or someone. That strange woman with the long, dark hair."

"Someone you knew?"

"No, someone who claimed to know Lance. She'd once approached him during the interval of a play, an Ibsen if I recall, and he'd looked most uncomfortable."

"When was this?" asked Theodora.

"Earlier this year, I think."

"You saw her at the ball?" I asked.

"Dressed as a peacock of all things!"

"How… How do you think she knew Lance?" said Theodora, as surprised as I was.

"I don't know. I asked him after the play, but he was reticent, said she was from a different time in his life, one he wanted to forget. I can't even begin to contemplate what her occupation might be."

A singer, I didn't say.

"This is where I disagree with Doctor Fortescue," she said.

"How so?" said Theodora.

"I appreciate his promotion of heterosexuality is to benefit the smooth-running of a good marriage, but I'm my mother's daughter. Marriage is to promote the birth and raising of children, not wanton pleasure-seeking."

"You think married adults seeking pleasure in the privacy of their own bedrooms such a bad thing?"

"I think it is a weakness to give in to one's baser instincts. This may be easier for women than men, but we aren't animals. It is a wife's job to perform her womanly duty when her husband requires. But that is all." She blushed. "We must be the ones to set an example for the lower classes and I worry that the doctor's approach will permit all sorts of depravity."

"Are you implying Hector and his wife are animals?" asked T, treading close to dangerous terrain.

"Of course not. I find Hector a little eccentric and Helena very loyal."

"You think she might disagree?"

"I think she might not agree as fervently as she says she does. Still, it is a wife's job to stand by her husband even if his views are unconventional. As far as I'm concerned, the dictionary is very clear in its definition of heterosexuality."

"It is?" I asked.

"A morbid sexual passion for one of the opposite sex."

It wasn't long after this tirade that Jackie departed, her cup of Earl Grey full and cold. Theodora gave me permission to tuck into the scones, which I did with relish – raspberry to be precise. I also tried one of the small éclairs, which was just as rich and creamy as it looked.

"Did you not have lunch?" asked Theodora drily.

"Half a cheese sandwich," I said. "It's not healthy to repress one's passions."

"We don't all have appetites as big as yours."

"It is good though," I said, wiping cream from my lips.

"Worth every penny, I'm sure."

"I shan't ask how many."

"Don't."

We laughed.

"Now, to business," she said. "Jackie recognised Lady Splendid at the ball, who, it transpires, knew Lance."

I nodded between mouthfuls.

"Jackie also thinks Lady Splendid is a prostitute."

"Is she?" I asked.

"I find discussing work tiresome. Still, we should talk with her next."

"She'll be singing at the Styx on Thursday, remember?"

"I do have a functioning brain, thank you. I suggest you head there."

"And you?"

"I'll be booking you a doctor's appointment for Friday."

"Why does that worry me?"

"Because the doctor will be Hector Fortescue."

"Theodora, you mustn't tell him anything!"

"I won't, I promise. I'll say it's for a check-up – to make sure everything's in working order."

"Honestly!"

"You get him talking about his treatment of Lance and I'll talk to Helena – to discover what she really felt about her son's alleged malady."

"Fine," I replied, a little tetchily, "but aren't we forgetting the look on Jackie's face. Her hackles were raised at the merest hint that Lance's love might not have been genuine."

"Go on."

"When I spoke with him at the ball, he as good as said the engagement was a sham. You yourself are familiar with that sort of thing."

"I am."

"I can believe he wanted to change and actually thought it possible. I can even believe he cared for Jackie and presenting her with the ring wasn't an entirely hollow gesture. But we both know he it did it primarily to convince his parents and the world at large that he was cured."

Theodora nodded. "He may also have been trying to convince himself."

"Meanwhile, Jackie is head over heels – thinking that, because he shares a name with a character from Arthurian legend, he truly is a knight in shining armour. Her love for him burns with an ardour of mythic proportions."

"Selby the poet," said T. "Although the description is apt – I remember all the fairy tales my nannies read to me. The princess was nothing without the prince. Marriage gave her life meaning."

"Precisely. But what if a few months after the proposal she learns it's all a lie? I can only imagine the betrayal she must have felt – worsened if she were to discover the true object of Lance's affections was one of the servants."

"You think Reginald?"

"I do. Imagine the fury she would have felt. All those repressed passions finally erupting as she confronts the man who'd deceived her. The man who'd promised to give her all she'd ever wanted."

Theodora took a long, slow sip of her Earl Grey with a slice of lemon in.

"It's certainly an idea. I'll try and facilitate an encounter with her maid," she said, placing the dainty teacup back in its saucer. "To see if she can give Jackie a midnight alibi."

"What if she can't?"

"Then it may well be possible that Jackie killed her fiancé."

"Probable?" I asked.

"That we shall have to find out for ourselves."

CHAPTER 12

There's a club off 42nd,
I joined up last September,
it's full of booze and full of boys,
the perfect place for a bender.

If the road to Hell is paved with good intentions, then the river to Hades is awash with the peculiar. On Tuesday I'd returned to work, my dicky tummy miraculously healed, and we observed the two-minutes silence for the fallen. Wednesday was for keeping my head down and anticipating Thursday evening, which proved a busy one at the River Styx. The reason why stood not far from me on a small raised stage.

Now, if you have a daughter
to this club I wouldn't send her,

for the liquor here is very strong
and half price in December.

Her long hair cascaded down her back, done in curls like the crests of waves, and she wore a slinky satin dress that plunged from the neck. The club was full and the audience rapt. She sang a jazzy number imported from the United States of America, as most jazzy numbers were. Her accompaniment was an occasionally out-of-tune piano and the clinking of glasses. We tapped our feet to the rhythm.

So come on chum, don't be glum,
be gay and pay our vendor,
just don't forget our club's motto:
the bigger the better the member.

She swept the room with her painted eyes, and for a fleeting moment, ours met. Quite unbidden, a feeling stirred in my nether regions as I thought back to our brief liaison at the ball. As for Lady Splendid, her voice faltered for just a moment and I wondered if she was surprised to see me, displeased or something else entirely. On flew her gaze.

Short or tall, thin or fat,
hirsute, hairless, round or slender,
the only preference that we have:
the bigger the better the member!

The final line was repeated a number of times as more and more of us joined in. Then the pianist finished the tune with a flourish and the room erupted in a thunderous round of applause. Lady Splendid promised us more but first had to wet her beak. She stepped down from the stage and took herself to the bar, where she was surrounded by a flurry of men offering to buy her a drink.

The River Styx first burst from its source early last year and swiftly acquired a loyal following amongst those with tastes like mine. Located in and amongst the labyrinth of Soho behind an innocuous door of peeling blue paint, it soon attracted the morality brigade and their complaints. However, the club's first closure, last summer, was for fire safety reasons. We held our breath as the necessary building works were undertaken and, much to our relief, the waters were flowing by autumn. Unfortunately, this January, the river froze after a visit from one of the higher-ups at Vine Street police station. For a while, it was used only for storage. But the ice broke in spring and the swimmers returned. That the club was still going was a minor miracle, and an indicator of corruption amongst the local police and councilmen, happy to turn away for the right price. The underworld was forged on a multitude of unlikely alliances, prone to rupture.

Tonight's Charon, the ferryman of the eponymous river, was a beefy doorman called Seb. We'd flirted a little in the past but I'd never got further than feeling his tensed bicep. I'd asked him if everything were that hard. The club proper was up a flight of stairs and decked out in dusty Turkish rugs and frilly lampshades, suffused with smoke from our cigarettes and the occasional hookah pipe. The clientele was predominantly male. Most wore suits, some wore make-up and a few were in dresses. Not all places would have admitted the latter and some would have asked those wearing lipstick to wipe it off. The skin was predominantly white but not exclusively, another rarity given the state of race relations in Albion's capital. The class bracket was mainly middle but also working. A few sailors and stevedores mixed with the clerks and accountants. While our world beneath the waters usually distorted the light from above, sometimes it was merely a reflection. I wondered where Lancelot had placed himself amongst our ranks.

"Is this seat taken?" asked a sultry voice.

My heart rate quickened from a saunter to a canter as Lady Splendid looked down at me.

"I was reserving it," I replied, trying to sound nonchalant.

"For me, I presume."

She delicately lowered herself onto the stool next to mine, the satin of her dress shimmering in the low light. How I wished to loosen those thin straps and kiss the smooth flesh of her shoulder blades. She took a hefty gulp of her white wine and I couldn't help but thrill that, of all the men here, she'd chosen to sit with me!

"I didn't know you were a regular, Mr Bigge."

"Not as regular as I'd like but I'm glad I caught you. You're dazzling."

"I know," she replied matter-of-factly. "Why did you want to catch me?"

"For your singing, of course."

"Please, Mr Bigge," she said, after taking another glug, "I'm on again soon, so if you have anything to say, I suggest you say it."

"Where were you at midnight on the night of the ball?"

"What?"

Her glass slipped in her hand, some of its contents spilling over the rim, but she didn't drop it.

"The night of Lancelot Fortescue's murder."

"I beg your pardon?" she said. "I thought you were going to invite me to dinner."

"Oh."

I could have slapped myself on the forehead. Perhaps I wasn't as good at this gentleman detective business as I'd thought.

"Instead, you're trying to connect me to that awful murder."

"I… I… I'm just trying to ascertain what happened that night."

"I tend to avoid drinking with the law."

"I'm not a policeman. I simply want to find the truth."

"Why?"

"Because the police have already reached their conclusions."

"What if they're right?"

"With people like us," I said, taking in the club with a wave of my hand, "it doesn't much matter to them."

"And what do you know of a person like me?"

"Um… well… actually very little."

I didn't know where she was from; whether she was Lady Splendid every day or only upon occasion; how she coped with it all. I barely knew her from Eve. She eyed me over the top of her glass. The scrutiny both scared and thrilled me.

"I suppose you are a friend of Theo's," she said. "Did he send you?"

"Theodora suggested I come."

At that she laughed, which only heightened her good looks.

"In case you've forgotten, I was with you and Theo at midnight, kissing you on the cheek."

"That was a bit before twelve actually."

"Then I was in the back of a taxi cab," she said, flashing me a look of irritation, "reminding myself of what the Scotsman had on under his kilt."

The lucky jock! "Nothing, if I recall correctly. He must have been chilly," I said, a shade unkindly.

"I warmed him up."

"And his Loch Ness Monster."

"Do I detect a hint of the green-eyed one?"

"No," I lied.

"Don't despair, Mr Bigge, I have many admirers but I'm generous in my affections."

At that the blood rushed into my cheeks and another part of my body. If only there wasn't the subject of a murder to discuss. Perhaps when this nasty business was over I could do more than loosen her straps.

"But I did hear something," she said.

We leaned towards one another, the din of the room verging on a racket.

"When you were swimming in the loch?" I asked.

"Earlier, when I was contemplating a paddle. I saw him."

"Who?"

She was about to answer but quickly stopped herself and offered something else instead. "The man who was murdered."

"Lancelot Fortescue?"

"Him. I'd been kissing the Scot near the back entrance."

"I beg your—"

"Of the Hall," she added, wetting her lips. "We'd only been outside a few moments when I heard raised voices. I pulled away and looked over to see Lancelot. He was most striking. I can still picture his colourful costume."

"He was Harlequin. Did he have his mask on?"

"No, because I saw his profile caught in the gaslight – such a high forehead. The Scot was quick to pull me back but I do remember hearing part of the argument."

My heart was galloping now, and despite the din, all I could hear was Lady Splendid's voice.

"*How could you betray him?*" she said.

"You're certain that's what you heard?"

She nodded.

"And it was Lancelot who spoke?"

"I can't be sure because I was no longer looking. The voice certainly sounded masculine but that's neither here nor there."

"Quite. You didn't see who he was arguing with?"

"I only saw Harlequin, and soon after, heard those words ring out. Angus laughed, calling it a lovers' tiff, but we were only momentarily distracted."

"What time was this?"

"Earlier in the night, around eleven I think. Maybe before. Or after."

"Can you be more precise?"

"No darling, I'd been drinking."

"It must have been just before eleven," I said, racking my brains. "After Theo and I saw Lance leave the dancefloor, but before he returned."

"If you say so."

At that she raised her glass and downed its contents. She got up from her seat; the expectant audience was hooked on her every move.

"One more question," I said.

"Go on."

"Was that night the first time you'd seen Lancelot?"

"Yes."

Her answer was quick and calm, and could easily have resembled the truth.

"And you'd never met his fiancée, Jacqueline Bosanquet?"

"If I hadn't met him, I'd hardly have met her." She gave me another groin-quivering smile then looked above my head. "Darling, you made it!"

"Sorry I'm late," came the reply.

I turned to see Max, the manservant from the Fortescue household. He looked strikingly different out of uniform, dressed instead in an evening suit with a white rose in the buttonhole.

"Have you met my friend, Mr Selby Bigge?"

He looked down and didn't even bother to hide his annoyance. "I have."

"Marvellous, you should have my seat. Cheerio, boys!"

Off she went, wending her silken way between the tables and seats. Her buttocks were most suggestive beneath her dress and I couldn't be sure if she was wearing anything underneath. Max gave me another dismissive look and was about to turn but I reached out and gently clasped his forearm.

"Can I offer you a drink?" I said, thinking on my feet. "And an apology?"

He stared at me for a moment, sizing me up. "Vodka soda, double."

"Right you are."

"With two slices of lemon."

I swam my way through the soup of smoke and bodies, and waited in the queue at the bar. Unfortunately, I'd positioned myself next to a lovers' tiff. It was impossible not to overhear and I soon ascertained one chap had found photographs of the other stark naked. The latter defended his actions and said the photographer had paid him handsomely, prompting his mate to ask him how he'd been paid. I pushed forward to avoid having to hear the rejoinder and was greeted with a knowing smile from the bartender. He took my order and quickly relieved me of a small fortune. Prices in London had never been good, but with the recession bedding down, things were only getting worse.

"Here you go," I said, returning to my seat at the table. We took our sips as Lady Splendid began to sing a sultrier number.

"How do you two know one another?" I asked.

"It's a small world."

"Do you come here often?"

"Unlike some, I can't throw away two shillings whenever I wish."

I felt suitably reprimanded and tried a different tack. "Any news of Reginald?"

"No."

He looked past me to watch Lady S instead. I noticed a few of the guests were watching him – some with looks of approval but some without. Many places didn't serve men of colour, or made them drink in separate rooms. He appeared not to notice and I assumed that was an art he had perfected over time. His guard would be up but I knew now might be my only opportunity to talk with him far from his place of employment. Something was afoot downstairs at the Fortescues', and I'd bet good money it linked to Lance's death.

"Were…" I began but quickly corrected myself, "… Are you and Reginald close?"

"That's none of your business."

"I'm sorry. I just got the impression that he was one of us."

"One of what?"

"One who likes swimming in the Styx."

"You're very nosey for a stranger."

"I assure you I'm only trying to help."

"Why you?"

"Because I've done it before."

"What? Solved a murder?" he asked dismissively.

"Yes."

That finally got a reaction that was neither disdain nor indifference as he regarded me with surprise.

"You a private dick then?"

"Something like that."

"Waiting to put the so-called *swimmers* in prison."

"I have as much desire to avoid prison as any other customer here."

"Who do you work for then?"

"Those whom justice tends to ignore."

"Ha, a bleeding Joan of Arc is it."

Despite his bitterness, I continued – let it not be said that I'm anything if not persistent. "Did Lance come here?"

"I wouldn't know."

"Would you know if he had any enemies?"

"Nor that either."

"Your friend," I said, indicating Lady Splendid, "said she overheard him arguing with someone outside the Royal Albert Hall the night he was killed. Any idea who that was?"

"Nope."

"Somebody else said he was seen arguing with someone dressed as a plague doctor," I persisted, slightly tweaking the truth.

"I don't know about that," he interrupted, "or that damned ball. The closest I got was hearing Grace crashing back at midnight."

"At midnight?" I asked, noting the time.

"I heard the chimes."

"Had she walked back?"

"Yes," he said, although immediately looked to regret it. "I think."

Given I'd seen her leave the dancefloor at around ten minutes to midnight, she must have walked at a considerable pace. Nevertheless, if what he said were true, then that had Grace and Max as one another's midnight alibis, far from Kensington Gardens. But one was wise to distrust information freely given by those who had hitherto expressed only animosity.

"Doctor Fortescue forbade you attending the ball, didn't he?"

"Bloody right he did."

"You don't like your master?"

"Ha, I'm hardly going to deign that with an answer. But it's not just the likes of these swimmers he wishes to cure."

"What do you mean?"

"You're not blind, Mr Bigge. A man of my race is to be civilised by the doctors of this country."

"I see," I replied, slowly nodding my head. "That must be difficult."

"And that must be an understatement."

He drained his glass.

"How about you fetch me another?"

That surprised me. If anything I'd expected to get the lemon slices slapped against my cheeks. "Tell me this first," I said. "Doctor Fortescue said he stopped you attending the ball because you'd argued with Lance. About what?"

"Maybe I'd prefer a bottle of champagne," he said with a wry smile.

"But Lance said his father was being overly harsh."

"When did he say that?"

"At dinner. He clearly had your best interests in mind. So, what was your dispute?"

Max brought his face close to mine. It was a nice face, cleanly shaven, with an elegant nose. The look he gave me was anything but.

"First you're sniffing around downstairs. Now you're sniffing around the Styx."

"Talking of sniffing, did you smell the burning?"

"What?"

At least that one had caught him unawares.

"The cook complained of ashes all over the kitchen floor."

"Trying out new recipes, for all I know."

"In the early hours of the morning?"

"Got it in for Cook too, have you?"

"Not forgetting that slashed portrait," I added, pushing my luck.

"Why can't you stop hounding us servants?" he said, his tone somewhere between angry and afraid.

"I'm not hounding anyone. I simply want the truth."

"If I were you, I'd leave the truth – and us – well alone."

Even Sherlock had to admit defeat upon occasion. I offered Max a goodnight and left him at the table. I glanced back at Lady Splendid. She was busy singing to a man seated directly in front of the stage, whose head was more or less in line with her crotch. Had Jackie really recognised her at the ball or had she mistaken her for someone else? If it was the former, then Lady Splendid was lying about not knowing Lance. And if she were lying about that, what's to say she wasn't lying about overhearing an argument? And who could say whether Max had really heard Grace returning at midnight?

People told lies as easily as spiders spun webs, and I would know. Nevertheless, a web of lies wasn't entirely useless because it still required spinning, and if someone were to spin a lie, they had to have a reason for it. And if I could unravel the lies, however arduous a task, I might just be able to uncover what truth the web concealed.

I reached the hole in the wall and asked for my belongings. The little chap in the round glasses, who I always thought resembled a mole, went off to burrow amongst the coats. I surveyed the club from my vantage point near the stairs. I spied the couple from earlier – the amount of petting and posterior squeezing suggesting they'd made up after their row over the nude photographs. Had Lance known a tumultuous love affair like that? *How could you betray him?* Had it ended fatally? My eye was drawn to a man sitting alone by one of the hookah pipes. While everyone else was watching Lady Splendid, he was staring dead at me. He looked of similar height and build to myself, but his face was covered by a big bushy beard and moustache, and he wore a pair of thick spectacles. He quickly looked away.

"Who's that?" I asked when the mole returned with my coat.

"Bearded one?" he replied peering through the haze. "Think I've seen him here once before."

"Not a regular?"

"Oh no. Think he was alone last time as well. Perhaps you could offer him some company. They say a bristly beard can prove most stimulating."

"I've had enough stimulation for one night," I said with a grin.

"You take care then."

"You too."

I headed for the stairs, ready to cross the river and return to the land of the living. At least on this side the spirits were stronger.

CHAPTER 13

My trousers and underpants were around my ankles. With the blunt end of a pencil, Doctor Fortescue lifted the shaft of my penis. He held it at a right angle to my body before lifting it a fraction higher. After a moment's inspection, he nodded then gently cupped my scrotum and testicles in the palm of his hand. The former was slightly shrivelled given the nature of the situation, but that didn't stop him giving it a jiggle. Under different circumstances I might have enjoyed this experience, and I certainly knew one chap who'd have paid good money for it. My genitals were finally released with a satisfied harrumph.

"You may dress," he said, turning away to allow me a moment of modesty. I lowered myself from his examination table, my buttocks cold from the leather, and bent down to retrieve my garments. He approached a small sink in one corner of his study and began to wash his hands with strong smelling soap. I surveyed the domineering bookshelf as I dressed myself.

Naturally, Freud's works were in pride of place, outlining in great detail the course of *normal* sexual development – from overcoming a desire to murder at least one parent, foregoing an obsession with various orifices and attaching permanently to one's first lover. It was quite the obstacle course rife with hurdles I hadn't even bothered to jump. Nearby was an edition of Richard von Krafft-Ebing's *Psychopathia Sexualis.* Much as Darwin had done for the finches of the Galapagos Isles, so Krafft-Ebing had painstakingly catalogued all manner of perversions. It was a veritable bestiary of sexual diseases, of which I'm sure I suffered from many. I spied a copy of *Spermatorrhea and the Dangers of Masturbation* and a dog-eared *How a Good Husband Can Satisfy a Worthy Wife.* With these tomes to hand marital bliss was a mere wedding vow away.

"I have good news, Mr Bigge," he said, drying his hands with a small towel. "Everything is in working order."

"Marvellous," I said, my voice a little squeaky.

"Please do take a seat."

I took the wooden chair with leather arms as he took the much grander one on the other side of his desk. The space in between was ordered neatly with a fountain pen placed in its holder next to a full pot of ink and a small jotting pad. A number of scientific periodicals were stacked to one side and in pride of place stood the phrenologist's ceramic bust. From destructiveness to hope, all the relevant lumps and bumps had been delineated and labelled. I refrained from scratching my scalp.

So it was I found myself in the doctor's study a little after five o'clock on Friday afternoon. The physical aspects of my appointment (or should that be ordeal) were over and now I would be submitted to an examination of the mind. Theodora had booked me the appointment under the pretence of a simple check-up rather than the insinuation I might be suffering from anything worse. The suffering was having him fondle my privates. As for Theodora, she was calmly sipping tea with Helena Fortescue in the adjacent drawing room. I hoped they hadn't heard me cough.

"I note your left testicle hangs slightly lower than your right."

"Is that normal?" I replied.

"Perfectly," he said, brushing a hand through his neat, Freudian beard, "and your penile shaft is of average length and shape."

Average!

"Shape?" I asked.

"Yours is sufficiently tubular from base to tip."

"Is that also normal?"

"It is. There's evidence to suggest the phallus of the diseased is conical in shape having adapted to enter the..." He paused and I was pleased to see he wasn't the only one suffering discomfort. "I hardly need go into the details and I can't say I agree with that particular hypothesis, but one must remain open-minded. Some even say that the degenerate anus is more akin to a vagina than a healthy male's anus."

I thanked the God I didn't believe in that he hadn't asked me to bend over.

"Deviancy has many symptoms."

"I do hope your examination hasn't revealed any of those."

"We will come to that," he replied ominously. "Tell me, what do you eat for breakfast?"

"Oh..." I was briefly lost for words having expected another probing question pertaining to my anatomy. "I'm partial to the odd slice of toast, usually with marmalade. Perhaps a piece of fruit. I do like a pear."

"Butter on the toast?"

"Yes, sometimes jam instead of marmalade, I especially like raspberry. My landlady also makes delightful porridge to which I might add a drizzle of honey."

"Bacon and eggs?"

"Oh yes! At weekends, sometimes with black pudding and kidney if I'm lucky."

"Oh dear, oh dear," he said, shaking his head slowly from side to side. "This will never do, Mr Bigge. To think what you are doing to your body."

"Which is what exactly?"

"Over-stimulating it, especially at such an early hour of the day. Jams and fruits strain the nervous system. What you need is something bland. Have you heard of Kellogg's corn flakes?"

I nodded. From the shape of my penis to breakfast foods, my afternoon had taken quite the turn.

"Then I suggest you eat them for six days of the week, with milk, and treat yourself to toast and fruit on the seventh day. I do know the importance of pleasure, after all."

"Do I have to eat them for every meal?"

He shook his head with a kindly chuckle. "Just breakfast! To ensure the regularity of the bowel. Constipation excites the nerves of the pelvis."

I found other ways of achieving that.

"I had the good fortune of meeting John Kellogg on one of my trips to America."

I settled back into the chair, preparing myself for a lengthy anecdote regarding the immoralities of jam and pelvic excitation.

"There's much to be commended on his approach to biologic living, especially flaked corn breakfast cereals and drinking multiple glasses of water every day. How many do you drink?"

"I'm afraid I don't keep count." If I were honest I drank far more tea than water and rather too much gin.

"I don't go quite as far as Kellogg on abstention from alcohol, meat and sexual pleasure, as you know."

How I wished he'd stop reminding me.

"But a clean body and a clean mind are worth fighting for lest we succumb to racial degeneracy. Kellogg put it much better than I in a lecture he gave at the Race Betterment Foundation on the advantages of clean living and sterilisation. I'm sure I have a pamphlet somewhere."

Fortunately, the brief examination of his desk drawers proved as fruitless as my future breakfasts and I was spared from reading John Kellogg's views on the superiority of the white race.

"You're a clerk at a bank, is that right?"

I nodded, fearful his advice might stretch to critiques of capitalism.

"We brain workers must be careful," he said, "lest we succumb to psychic impotence. Too much time at desks and not enough outdoors. Do you take the air?"

"Occasionally."

"You should aim for a little more than that. A brisk stroll in nature can work wonders on the heart. Hyde Park or, better still, Hampstead Heath."

"I do like the Heath," I replied truthfully, "lots of nice things to look at."

"And plenty of hills."

"Always pleasant to have something to mount."

"Then providing you take my advice on breakfast cereal, I pronounce you fit as the proverbial fiddle."

"Really?" I replied, having expected him to diagnose me with a number of perverse illnesses pertaining to my lifestyle.

"You're a robustly healthy individual. Although, if I may, I have one further piece of advice."

"Oh yes?" I asked, dreading the mischievous edge to his tone.

"You delay no longer and propose to one Miss Theodora Smythe."

Hitherto my acting skills should have earned me a lesser role on one of the smaller West End stages but now I could only gape.

"Don't worry, Mr Bigge, I married a woman my superior and have made her quite happy. I wooed her with my intellect and views on societal advancement. I've seen the way Miss Smythe looks at you."

Usually with an ironic glimmer.

"Think of all the pleasures you two could enjoy once your wedding vows have been made."

"Pleasures?" I muttered quietly.

"Pleasures!" he said proudly. "I may have been born a little earlier under Queen Victoria's reign than yourself…"

Given he was in his stride, I didn't bother to correct him but my birth year was 1904, which put me under the reign of Edward VII, not his mother.

"… but we are not all a race of repressed, unhappy men,

intent only on the improvement of our minds and the repression of our bodies. My courtship of Helena involved a number of sensual letters, and once we had entered into the holy bond of matrimony, there were all sorts of activities we could enjoy."

I sincerely hoped he wasn't about to tell me any of them.

"You see, as a member of the medical establishment, one of my great contentions is that the erotic sexual attraction between a man and woman resulting in the pleasures of the bedroom is entirely normal. Wouldn't you agree?"

"I… I…" Again, any words I might have had swiftly fled from the room.

"I'm sure you have an ancient maiden aunt who believes sex is only for procreation, but many of us are a little more modern in our views. We believe that the satisfaction of erotic desire is just as valid as the need to procreate. This is a fundamental revolution in our thinking about sex."

He spoke with such passion and I almost pitied the chap. All the mental gymnastics required to justify the pursuit of pleasure when all I had to do was pass through Hampstead Heath of an afternoon.

"Do not mistake me though," he continued, jabbing a finger against the top of his desk, "I advocate a tempered approach to love-making. Sex too early in marriage will produce less healthy offspring and can cause men to become dim of sight and partially bald."

Again I was forced to refrain from touching my scalp. As I'd never made love to a woman, my hair loss required an alternative explanation, which doubtlessly the good doctor would be able to link to my sexual practices.

"And once intercourse has begun, it should not be overdone. Amative indulgence causes severe debilitation. We aren't rabbits!"

Finally, a point of agreement.

"Yet all too often this advice goes unheeded, as many heterosexuals possess an unfettered capacity for degeneracy."

We were back on track. Theodora had expressly told me to get as many clues to Lance's murder as possible, but given the doctor's verbosity and the prior exposure of my penis, I was decidedly on the back foot. Nonetheless, all roads led to the degenerate.

"One of my patients had a fetish for a particular woman's handkerchief. A brief flash of the square of lace and he was at her command, quite like a dog to its master. Then there was the chap who wanted his wife to shout insults at him when they were in the bedroom, heedless of whether the staff could hear. And another who demanded his wife beat him with a riding crop." He took the small handkerchief from his jacket pocket and dabbed at his glistening forehead. "There is pleasure and then there is emasculation."

I'd been beaten with a riding crop before and hadn't cared tuppence for my masculinity. I'd spared my thoughts for my reddening posterior.

"With my help, all these men were able to repress their perversities and gratify themselves normally."

"How did you help them?"

"I changed their minds, as simple as that. The mind is a powerful tool. With it we can curb our carnal impulses and abstain from abnormal practices. A civilised man knows when and how to direct his passions."

I was minded of an organ grinder's monkey.

"Naturally diet, exercise and hobbies all have their role to play."

"Anything surgical?"

"That's not my area of expertise. The jury is still out on whether Steinach's testicle transplant was a success."

"A transplant?" I squeaked, crossing my legs under the desk.

"A healthy heterosexual testicle in place of a diseased one to alter the hormonal balance. My clients never require anything as extreme."

"Their wives must have been grateful."

"They were. You see, there's nothing to be ashamed of when it comes to healthy heterosexuality."

"Indeed," I said, forcing my eyes not to roll in their sockets.

"I know what the dictionary has to say about our so-called morbid passion. But I am far from alone in my campaign to have it redefined. Respectable men and women shouldn't be shamed for the healthy manifestations of their libido. It's our duty to take the teachings of Freud, unread by many, and share them."

As he spoke, I was minded of a great mass of people all huddled together, like commuters at Paddington Station. On the ground was drawn a great circle in white chalk. Those inside the circle had the privilege of being labelled normal. Outside the circle was everyone else – some clamoured to be let in, some asked politely, while others were so abnormal they'd never gain entry. The doctor straddled the white circle, one foot in, one foot out. He wanted its border widened a fraction, just enough to grant him and his kind the stamp of normality.

"What of the homosexual?" I asked, thinking it time to put the degenerate cat back amongst the heterosexual pigeons. "And his sexual appetite?"

"That's a fair question," replied the doctor, wiping at his brow again. "While many would label him a monster, I would say no such thing. I think what he requires is pity."

"Pity?"

"When a man is racked by an illness of the mind he's not in control of all his actions. Aberrant carnal lusts and internal glandular disturbances cause all sorts of chaos. Tell me, have you ever met a homosexual?"

"I think once, a few summers ago, not far from Didcot."

"Then you will know they are not happy fellows. They're usually temperamental in behaviour and dissatisfied with life, chasing one another in the dark to satisfy their lusts..."

Because chasing one another in the light is illegal, I didn't say.

"... skulking at the fringes of society..."

Because we've been pushed there!

"... corrupting children and innocents..."

Said the man who'd corrupted his late son's life beyond measure.

"The homosexual is a deeply miserable man, torn apart from the inside and doomed to sordid affairs riven with jealousy and anger."

I had tried my hand at relationships, and while jealousy and anger had certainly been a part of them, they weren't the defining features. And unlike the doctor, I didn't have the law, the medical establishment and organised religion on side.

"But he's not beyond help. If I can cure him, I can bring him some relief. He might even be able to take a shot at a decent sort of happiness."

"Marriage and children?" I suggested, shuddering internally.

"Spoken like a true heterosexual!"

"I'm not sure I would use that word to describe myself."

"I agree that adopting new terminology can feel awkward at first but it's important we define ourselves. We must solidify our identity, swell our ranks and rally against those who would call *us* perverts!"

"Perish the thought. Have you treated many homosexuals?"

"A number, yes."

"Successfully?"

"Indeed," he replied proudly, "with my care they all returned to lives of good health."

"Did any prove more stubborn than others?" I asked, remembering Lance's words at the ball.

"There was one fellow, married with two children, from Crawley. He came to London on business and found himself at one of those awful clubs off Seven Dials, whereupon he was seduced by a 'man' who insisted on being called the Countess."

I restrained a laugh. I'd met her a few times (much to my pleasure).

"It's the effeminate ones who are the most cunning, affecting the mannerisms of women and powdering their cheeks. My patient proved smitten with the so-called Countess and even confessed to applying lipstick. Can you imagine?"

Most of his comments had hit close to home and this one proved no exception. My thoughts returned to Theo's dressing table as he'd dabbed rouge against my cheeks. A part of me had so struggled in that moment but now another part wished I'd worn lipstick, painted my eyes and donned a dress. Better to be decadently dressed when the Titanic hit the iceberg than stuffed in a suit.

"The Countess believed he possessed the spirit of a woman, which he said explained his attractions to other men. As women take the submissive role in intercourse, so did he, so to speak, while expecting my client to take the active."

"And did he?"

"Fortunately not. My intervention came just in time. I prescribed he cut all ties with the Countess and the club. I was quite plain. If he continued to socialise with effeminate perverts, his health would suffer, and his soul."

"Have you ever treated someone like the Countess?"

"Once, but he was beyond my help. I refuse to deal with cross-dressing men any more. Their deviancy is incurable. I only administer to men who suffer from homosexuality."

"Is that what Lancelot suffered from?"

I knew it wasn't fair to take advantage of his loss, but I had to ask. He bent his head and brushed his hand along the edge of the desk.

"He did."

"Was he cured?"

"Yes," he said, raising his head to look straight at me. There were tears in his eyes. "I believe from the bottom of my heart that I cured my son."

There was an unspoken "but", so I let the silence do the talking until the doctor felt able to continue.

"But he was my first patient and my methods weren't so refined. He relapsed more than once, but each time he did, I was there to support him. When he proposed to Jacqueline, I genuinely believed all was well."

"Do you think his presence at the ball was another relapse?"

"I honestly believe he went there to test himself, like the man who takes small doses of arsenic to achieve immunity."

This was not the first time I and the world I inhabited had been likened to a poison. I doubted it would be the last.

"What if he failed the test? What would the consequences have been?"

"I had suggested a number of alternative treatments worth exploring."

"Such as chemical therapy?"

I pictured Lance's face when we had talked of this at the bar. He'd looked harried, hunted even, like a man who'd spent so much of his life running. But not running from his truth, running from the society that would punish him for it.

"We had discussed insulin shock therapy but its success rate is questionable. Then there's electricity. In principle, it's no more than Pavlov for humans – associate the damaging stimuli with the electric current."

As far as I was concerned, the electric current was the damaging stimuli!

"There are many who believe the stimulation of convulsions with controlled electric shocks could revolutionise the psychiatric world. The Italians are making good headway here."

A distant Pavlovian bell rang in my diseased mind as I pictured Lance's colourful harlequin mask. He said he'd had it made in Venice.

"Have you met any of these Italians?"

He nodded. "I've met a number of physicians at the University of Genoa and the Mental Institute of Milan. Most stimulating."

"Did Lance accompany you?"

"Not to the meetings, but we were holidaying as a family and I wanted to make the most of it."

"Would you have prescribed such an approach for him?"

He looked beyond me, his gaze slowly taking in his study – the tall bookshelves filled with medical books and journals, his educational achievements framed on the walls, the foreboding examination bed, and on the mantelpiece, the right hand of a skeleton.

"It doesn't matter any more what I might have prescribed. My son is dead, unable to marry the woman he loved."

"Poor Jacqueline," I said. "She seems such a principled woman."

"She is. And quite lovely." His tongue briefly emerged from his mouth to lick his upper lip, brushing against the hairs of his moustache. "Quite lovely."

A silence encased us as if he were encouraging me to think on said loveliness. His lip glimmered with the sheen of saliva. If a son fancying his mother was Oedipal, what ancient Greek malady was there for a father lusting after his son's bride-to-be?

"As for you, Mr Bigge, there's still plenty of time for marriage. You are free from the stigmata of degeneration and have a good pair of testes. You must not let that go to waste. On doctor's orders!"

He got up slowly from his seat and bade me do the same. He led me across the study to the door and I was pleased to be putting this room behind me.

Placing an avuncular hand gently on my shoulder he said, "I cured my son. My methodologies are sound. What happened at the ball must have been some terrible accident."

"Any news of Reginald?" I asked.

"Neither hide nor hair."

"Do you think he's all right?"

He opened the door, seeming not to hear me, and ushered me out into the corridor. I regarded the doctor in his three-piece suit and spotted tie – an outspoken heterosexual man so proud of his efforts at curing the homosexual. But his shoulders were hunched and there was a quiet look of pain on his face. Even he couldn't repress that.

"My methodologies are sound," he repeated, more for his benefit than mine.

CHAPTER 14

"I'm an avowed pacifist," announced Helena. "Warfare's wanton destruction is the scourge of society. The Great War shook the very foundations of the civilised world."

"I agree," replied Theodora politely. "All those men dead, it was horrific."

"And thoroughly dysgenic. Why send all those strong, virile men to be slaughtered, leaving the lazy, unhealthy ones at home?"

The drawing room was warmer than the doctor's study, with a merry fire in the grate, and I doubted either Theodora or Helena would ask me to remove my undergarments. But the conversation proved just as chilling. I let Theodora take the lead as I sipped on a cup of tepid tea and nibbled a thin slither of Victoria sponge. The sponge was dry and the jam was tart. Everything was proving a trial this afternoon.

"Eugenics is a much-discussed topic amongst the members of the National Vigilance Association. While we are of accord that Great Britain must retain its racial purity, not all share my pacifist views."

"Some would prefer warfare?" replied Theodora, affecting surprise.

"Indeed! To sort the wheat from the chaff and sweep the leaves from the bower – as our Empire has done across the globe."

"That sounds rather Darwinian," I said, wincing at both the sentiment and the stewed Earl Grey.

"Absolutely," Helena replied. "Survival of the fittest is at the heart of so much eugenic thought. But I don't believe we need war to achieve our goal when greater sterilisation of the lower classes would suffice."

From the vantage point of the fire, the frying pan looked a veritable holiday.

"Sterilisation!" exclaimed Theodora.

"Perhaps in more extreme cases," said Helena with a mollifying smile, "but at the very least we need a better educational system. If more of them learned how to use prophylactics there would be far fewer children littering the East End. Marie Stopes has done wonders for the cause. Have you met her?"

"I'm yet to have that honour."

Well, well, it transpired Theodora hadn't met every famous personage in the country. Any pleasure at this thought was short-lived as Helena continued.

"I've attended a number of meetings of the Society for Constructive Birth Control and Racial Progress. *Babies in the right place* is one of their mottos and I concur – we want the right people having children. Those fitted for parenthood."

Her gaze shifted from Theodora to myself and back again – the progeny of the Bigge-Smythes would be something to behold!

"Stopes disowned her son, you know."

"Oh really, why?" I asked, pretending to give two hoots.

"He insisted on marrying a woman who wore glasses."

My teacup rattled in its saucer.

"You remember Cyril?" she said.

"Your secretary?" I replied, remembering the impressive thatch of blond hair adorning his round head.

"He used to wear glasses but I told him if he wished to work for me he'd have to overcome that weakness. And he did! It shows great fortitude of will on his behalf."

"How it does," I said.

"He's very good at his job. I take him everywhere."

"Is he here, by any chance?" I asked.

"He's at Regus Hall getting things ready."

"Ready for what?"

"Oh, how remiss of me. There's to be a meeting of the Vigilance Association. You must come!"

"Oh dear—" I began, but Theodora was swift to interrupt.

"We'd love to, Helena, and it would be lovely to meet Cyril. Perhaps he may be able to shed a little more light on this awful situation."

"I doubt it," she replied. "Cyril didn't know Lance particularly well. I like to keep him to myself. He's a very fast typist."

"What of the other members of the household?" asked Theodora. "Things must be rather strained."

"They are. Cook has burnt a number of soups and Grace's dusting isn't what it was. They were all terribly fond of Lance."

"Although Max might not have been," I suggested.

"What makes you say that?"

"Didn't he argue with Lance recently?"

She shook her head. "I don't recall. So much has happened this past week."

For a woman of so many opinions and such breadth of knowledge, her sudden forgetfulness struck me as odd.

"Why don't I call for Grace?" she suggested. "She might be able to shed some light on this. Mr Bigge, would you mind?"

My suspicions were briefly dispelled as I was commanded from the sofa to the fireplace, next to which hung a bell cord. I gave it a sharp tug. Somewhere below I imagined a bell ringing, perhaps a brief moment of respite being interrupted, and feet tapping quickly across the threadbare carpet.

"We've done such marvels with her," said Helena.

"What do you mean?" said Theodora as I returned to my place next to her.

"When we employed her, she was far from the maid she is today. Her parents are from the North."

"Whereabouts?" asked my chum.

"I don't recall but she's lost all trace of an accent."

I braced myself for another diatribe but Helena sunk into an unexpected silence. The flames crackled quietly in the grate and even the clock ticked at a polite volume. I typically enjoyed November's progress as the evenings drew in and the final leaves fell from the trees. There was nothing better than warming up by a nice fire – preferably without the company of eugenicists.

"Helena, is something the matter?" said Theodora.

"I do apologise," she said with a weak smile. "I sometimes

forget Lance is gone."

Grace quietly arrived.

"You called, ma'am."

She presented herself neatly and obediently, as was expected of every servant.

"You may not be aware, Grace, but I have asked Miss Smythe here and Mr Bigge to enquire into Lance's death and Reginald's disappearance."

If this fact surprised her, she didn't reveal it.

"We're hoping you could shed some light on the dispute between Lance and Max. Apparently he pushed my son over."

"No ma'am, it was the other way around."

"Lance pushed Max?" She sounded most surprised.

"It was an accident, ma'am, they bumped into one another."

"Where?"

"At the bottom of the stairs."

"Which ones?"

"Leading downstairs."

Arguably all stairs led downstairs, as well as up, but I assumed she meant the ones that led to the servants' domain. I felt a mite sorry for the woman but at least we were finally getting some answers from her. She could evade me as much as she pleased but she couldn't avoid the mistress of the house.

"I believe they exchanged words," I said.

"I cannot recall, sir," she replied drily.

"I can," said Theodora, aiding me in our double act. "I remember Lance saying that Max called him a brute."

"Again, I cannot recall."

"Oh, that's it," said Helena, suddenly remembering. "That

was why Hector banned him from attending the ball. Mr Bigge, you must have another slice of cake."

"Must I?"

"Grace, if you would serve him."

The maid approached the mahogany side table and took the cake knife. I certainly wasn't winning any favours amongst the staff, but whether they liked it or not, I would find out what was going on downstairs.

"Have the police had any luck tracing Reginald?" I asked.

"None whatsoever," said Helena. "It's as if he's vanished."

"With Lance's car," added Theodora.

"It's so unlike him. He was simply devoted to Lance."

Grace approached and passed me the fine China plate. The slice of cake was much thicker than the first. I bet she knew it was dry.

"Reginald and Lance were close?" I asked, making sure to catch her eye.

She blinked and looked away.

"Lance had a simply dreadful sense of direction," recalled his mother. "Send him to the Ritz and he'd end up at the Savoy, and once he drove himself to Godstone when we were meant to be lunching in Godalming." Her voice wavered at this recollection and once again I witnessed the pain of her grief. "That's where Reginald came in – always got Lance to the places he was meant to go." She tried to check herself but a single tear fell slowly down her cheek.

"Helena, perhaps we should leave you?" suggested Theodora softly.

"No, no, it's silly of me," she said, patting at her cheek.

"One mustn't blub. We'll find whoever did this and he shall be hanged."

I took an ill-timed bite of cake.

"What of the empty suitcase?" asked Theodora.

"That turned out to be one of ours," said Helena, "taken from the attic."

"Do you know by whom?"

She shook her head, as befuddled as we were.

"Grace, can you shed any light on that suitcase?" said Mrs F.

"I'm afraid not, ma'am."

"And did you catch that rat?"

"Yes, Cook's arsenic worked wonders."

"Very good, you may go."

"One moment," I said, trying not to spit crumbs everywhere. "Grace, what time did you return from the ball?"

"I was back by midnight, sir."

"Can anyone confirm that?"

"I believe Max heard me closing the basement front door."

"Must have been awfully noisy," I said.

"He's a light sleeper."

"Did you hear anything, Helena?" asked Theodora, catching my drift.

"Heavens, no, I was long abed and fast asleep."

"Did you enjoy the ball?" I asked.

"It seemed a gay affair," said Grace, "but that's all been overshadowed."

"Did you see Lance there?"

"No, sir."

"You're sure?"

"I am."

Finally! Though her delivery was impeccable, I had her in a lie.

"That will be all," said Helena.

Grace bowed her head and left the room as quietly as she'd arrived. Now was my chance to seize the moment and catch her on the back foot.

"Theodora, if you wouldn't mind." I thrust the plate of cake into her hands. "If you would excuse me," I said as I walked quickly from the room. Helena looked most taken aback but Theodora could deal with that.

"Grace?"

She paused at the top of the stairs as I closed the drawing room door.

"I'm aware you just lied to your mistress."

"You must be mistaken, sir."

"I know you saw Lance at the ball."

She said nothing. This time I had her.

"I saw you talking with him in the main hall."

"I believe you—"

"Then someone," I said, cutting her off, "dressed as a plague doctor, appeared and remonstrated with him. You intervened."

She stared hard at me and I briefly saw someone who wasn't an obedient servant but a force to be reckoned with.

"Look, I implore you, someone did Lancelot great harm shortly after you left," I said. "I want to bring his killer to justice."

"I wish you good luck with that, sir."

I was losing her but on I went regardless – it was like running the steeplechase at school, caked in mud and never far from the back.

"There may be things you wish not to share with the police—"

"And I would share them with you?"

"You'll have to share them sooner or later. At least I'm sympathetic."

"Are you?" She crossed the gap between us, keeping her voice low but her feelings clear. "Because all you've done so far is trample on our grief, and as far as I'm concerned, we've suffered enough."

"What of Lance's suffering? Someone must be held accountable."

"Please forgive me if I think you incapable of achieving that."

"I won't stop, Grace. I know suspicious behaviour when I see it."

"You want suspicious?" she said with a restrained laugh. "Then you should talk to the man who was here without invitation."

Only divine intervention would stop me asking my next question.

"Who?"

"Her secretary."

"Cyril Blanford?" I whispered. "When?"

"The night Lance was killed."

The doorbell rang and I almost jumped out of my skin. As calmly as ever Grace passed me and opened the door.

"Good evening, sir," she said.

"Frightfully frigid out there."

It was Percy. Illumined by the porch lamp, he wore a long overcoat, a dapper trilby and carried a closed umbrella. Dark clouds had been threatening rain all day.

"Ah, Mr Bigge, I hadn't expected to find you here."

"Good evening, Mr Fortescue, I trust you're well."

"As well as can be expected."

Grace silently took his coat, hat, umbrella and gloves.

"Miss Smythe and your mother are in the drawing room," I said. "We were just finishing tea."

"Absolutely not, I need something stronger. You a whisky drinker?"

"I am," I lied, but if it meant a moment with Percy then it was worth my throat's temporary displeasure.

"This way," he said with a surreptitious smirk and led me down the corridor to the dining room. Inside Max was laying the table – only two places tonight, presumably for Doctor Fortescue and Percy as Helena would soon be off to her meeting. With a flick of his wrist Percy dismissed Max, who avoided my gaze as he left. I wondered if anyone else here knew he was a frequenter of the Styx.

"I always think a servant would make a wonderful spy," said Percy as he approached the drinks cabinet. "The things they must hear!"

"And see, for that matter."

"I'm a Lagavulin man," he said, pouring out generous measures into two tumblers. "Stronger than Laphroaig."

"Righty-o," I said, girding my loins.

The fire was set but unlit and the only light came from a single standard lamp. The gloom and chill served to exacerbate the household's mourning.

"Bottoms up."

We raised our glasses and I managed not to wince.

"Now, what's all this about Mother asking you to play detective?"

His tone was jolly enough but I could detect the underlying note of disapproval. He reminded me of some of the boys I went to school with.

"Miss Smythe and I will be asking questions the police might not think to ask."

"Such as?"

"If Lance was truly happy, for example."

"Lance, happy?" he asked, surprised. "Of course he was!"

The answer came so reflexively that I assumed Percy must think it true. But the Lance I spoke with on Saturday night had seemed anything but. *It doesn't matter any more* he'd said – hardly the words of a man content with his lot.

"Although perhaps at times he struggled?" I said.

Percy's face turned grave, no longer the good-humoured rugger bugger, now the grieving brother. He drained his tumbler.

"You're right, my brother did struggle, and there were times he was very miserable." He looked down into his tumbler, slowly swilling the whisky around and around. "But I do believe he was gradually approaching a place of greater..."

"Happiness?" I suggested.

"Peace. Lance had experienced his fair share of troubles, but this year, things seemed to be settling."

"What do you think brought about the change?"

"I know my parents would say his engagement to Jackie, but I think it went deeper than that. It was after our holiday in Italy, he seemed quite joyful, as if he'd finally come to terms with his lot."

"During the times he struggled, do you know if he ever tried to..." Now it was my turn to struggle to find the right word. "Did he ever try to hurt himself?"

"Good God, no! Us Fortescue men are made of stronger stuff than that." He poured himself another measure. "Now tell me, Mr Bigge, what does any of this have to do with his death?"

"I'm not sure yet but I want to better understand your brother."

"I'm not sure he always understood himself."

"Therein may lie the key to this mystery."

He gave me the once-over. "Have you really any experience of all this?" he asked incredulously.

"I've solved a number of cases."

"I suppose dicks come in all shapes and sizes. Now, if you wouldn't mind, I'm going to change before dinner."

"One more question, if I may."

A flash of impatience lit his face, but the friendly smile returned, even if it was a little restrained.

"You mentioned you fell asleep in the drawing room on Saturday night?"

"I'm afraid I did. Too much of this stuff."

"Did anyone wake you?"

"The servants know better than that."

"I was referring to your mother's secretary. I have reason to believe he was here that night."

"My, my, you could give Captain Hastings a run for his money."

The mood was far too sombre for celebration, but I inwardly thrilled at the comparison.

"I don't see why any of this is your business," he said.

"Anyone acting strangely that night is my business."

"Why do you assume he was acting strangely?"

"Wasn't he?"

Percy sized me up a moment. I'd been an awful rugby player, usually relegated to the wing or off the pitch entirely. Occasionally I'd managed to hold on to the ball.

"You're right, Cyril was here. A point in his favour, I'd say."

"Why?" I asked.

"Better here than coshing my brother at the Royal Albert Hall."

"Do you remember what time?"

"I do, as a matter of fact. It was a quarter to eleven."

"Can Cyril confirm that?"

"He can, because he was the one who told me!"

"You didn't check one of the clocks?"

"I was too tired and half-cut for that. Besides, I trust Cyril."

"How did he get in?"

"He was tapping at the front door and I was the only one that answered it."

"Did Grace not appear?"

"She was at the ball."

"And Max?"

He shrugged his shoulders. "Either way, I was the one lumbered with looking after our uninvited guest. I could hardly wake Mother."

"Why did he come?"

"He was in an awful state. So, I poured him some whisky and gave him the newspaper."

"Did he tell you what had upset him?"

He shook his head.

"Why didn't you reveal this on Sunday?" I asked, thinking I'd caught him out in a lie.

"I did, to the police. I'm afraid I didn't think Mother was being serious when she said she'd asked for your help. None of us even know you."

I took that in as good a humour as possible.

"What time did Cyril leave?"

"Not too long after midnight, if I recall."

"Can you recall exactly?"

"No. Now it's my turn to ask a question." He fixed me with his gaze. "Why did you lie to us?"

Stunned silence was my immediate answer.

"At dinner on Saturday, you said you knew nothing about the ball, but you had a ticket."

I was rather hoping everyone had forgotten about that. "Miss Smythe and I thought discretion the best way to catch her badly behaving butler."

"Well, I hope you do a better job of catching Lance's killer than you do the Smythes' mysterious butler." He put his tumbler on the dining room table, leaving it for one of the servants to clear away. "My brother deserves justice."

It was almost six o'clock when Theodora and I left the house. The sun had long set and the air smelt of smoke, cold and damp leaves. Max was to chauffeur Helena to Regus Hall. We declined the invitation to ride with her, promising we'd be there for seven. First, we had business to attend to.

I took another long look at the house – 42 Pendragon Rise. It was a lofty, terraced affair of off-yellow brick set back from the pavement. Lights shone in most of the windows. A short flagstone path of around ten yards led to the steps to the front door. To the left of that were the two windows of the drawing room, and beneath them, one storey below, were two windows that looked into the servants' domain. I peered over the low, wrought-iron gate at the little patio below, illuminated by the light coming from the house. It was accessed by a narrow flight of stone steps.

"What are you thinking?" asked Theodora, peering at the house.

"That the house can be entered by the front door and the servant's door down there." I pointed at the humbler entranceway to the right of the basement windows. "Perhaps allowing for unobserved arrivals and departures?"

"Unless someone was looking from the windows."

Theodora pointed upwards at the first floor. There was a narrow balcony with a dangerously flimsy railing that ran in front of all three windows, two of which belonged to Helena's heavily brocaded parlour.

"What's the time?" she asked.

"Six o'clock exactly."

"Perfect. Let's time how long it takes us to get to the Albert Hall. Ready?"

"Steady?"

"Go."

Off we went, affecting the pace of someone keen to arrive punctually at an appointment – they weren't running late, so a light jog was unnecessary, but nor did they have time to spare, so a bummel was out of the question. We settled for a brisk trot, passing through the orange glow of the gas lamps.

"It's a remarkably flat street for one named Pendragon Rise," I remarked.

"Suspiciously so."

"Talking of which…" I said, ignoring her mockery, and went on to inform her of my latest findings.

"The late-night arrival of the suspicious secretary," she said. "We'll have to corner him after the meeting."

"Percy said he was upset about something."

"You think it might have a bearing on the case?"

"I think Cyril being chez Fortescue on the night of the murder is a piece of the puzzle we mustn't ignore."

"I'm fed up of jigsaws," she said.

"I beg your pardon?"

"Let's use a different metaphor," said Theodora.

"What would Her Highness prefer?"

"A crossword."

"Fine," I said. "We've got plenty of letters on the grid, but I've no idea what words they're spelling."

"That's better."

We continued to walk past the grand houses that lined our route to the Hall. The lit windows reminded me of the doors of an advent calendar, a decidedly expensive one, mind. I could only but dream of having sufficient wealth to buy one of these. My best bet would be to seduce an Archduke's errant son and hope he'd invite me for drinks when his parents were away. As the Fortescue household demonstrated, London was a city of many worlds – of class, sex, race and varying pathologies of attraction (if I were to take Hector at his word) – and, more often than not, those worlds collided.

"I need to earn their trust," I said.

"Whose?"

"Everyone's – upstairs and downstairs. They're holding back and I need to discover what it will take to get them to be honest."

"What inclines you to be honest?"

"The truth."

"You must be careful with that," said Theodora. "Your truth can have carceral consequences."

We walked in an amiable silence. I couldn't reveal all of the truth, but maybe a slice of it would encourage the others to open up. They couldn't all be murderers, surely. It wasn't much longer until we were back at the scene of the crime – that great red-brick birthday cake with its candles lit, the Royal Albert Hall.

"What's the time, Mr Wolf?" asked Theodora.

"Sixteen minutes past six."

"A mere jiffy," she said. "We know Reginald left the ball around ten twenty, giving him plenty of time for a nap before sauntering back to kill Lance not long before midnight."

"As for Grace, she'd have to be an Olympic runner."

"Why?" said Theodora.

"Both she and Max say she was back by midnight, but I saw her leave just before ten minutes to."

"I can't imagine her sprinting in those shoes she was wearing. Maybe a taxi?"

"Hailed moments after coshing Lance on the head?"

A cold wind pinched at our cheeks.

"Yet more letters on the grid," said T.

"But a distinct lack of words."

CHAPTER 15

A tall building of grey brick, Regus Hall lacked the splendour of its neighbours but still proved imposing. It wasn't far from Lincoln's Inn Fields, so we had motored over in a taxi, but soon found ourselves caught in traffic. Unfortunately, the cabbie knew all about the place, so spent the journey educating us of its history. It occupied the sight of a former paper factory and its construction was funded by members of the Society of Freethinking Moralists – a group that included anti-abolitionists, Unitarians and patrons of the arts. I wasn't sure what they would make of Helena's gathering, but they'd rented out the space all the same. As we arrived, the clouds made good on their threat and a miserable drizzle began to fall. We rushed the short distance from the pavement and into the sombre entranceway, taking up refuge next to the bust of a grumpy-looking freethinker.

"I need a hot bath and a stiff brandy," said Theodora.

"I could do with something else stiff."

"Not sure you'll have much luck finding that here."

We looked around the entrance hall – austere, grey and poorly heated. A few people dawdled while most of the attendees went through to take their seats in the auditorium.

"Perhaps people have better things to do on a Friday evening than plot the downfall of the homosexual," I observed.

"I wouldn't be surprised if they were put off by the weather."

"Not terribly vigilant of them."

Theodora offered a reluctant wry smile – even in the bleakest of places, I could manage a pun.

"I never asked how your doctor's appointment went?"

"Humiliating."

"I am sorry, Selby."

"No, you're not. You booked it for me!"

"Desperate times and all that."

"He fondled me."

That shut her up for a moment.

"But he did diagnose me with a clean bill of health. I'm as heterosexual as he is."

This time she roared with laughter and I couldn't help but join in. Disapproving glances swiftly found us. Sod them, if I was going down with HMS *Buggeranto* at least let me go down with a smile on my face (and a jolly roger on my poop deck).

"What was your punishment?" I asked.

"Helena educated me on the role of upstanding women in the furtherance of our Empire as I tried to stomach the sponge cake."

"Did she suggest you marry me?"

"Absolutely."

We laughed again and it felt good to find a ray of sanity amongst all the madness. A neatly dressed young woman began to usher the stragglers through into the main hall. It was a large auditorium with room enough for many hundreds of congregants. Fortunately, the majority of the chairs were empty. At a guess, I'd say fifty or so were seated near the stage.

"What's the plan?" I asked, as we walked the aisle.

"Block your ears for the speeches, then make a beeline for Mr Blanford."

We took our seats a number of rows behind everyone else. I spotted Percy sitting up front. We kept our hats and coats on, the Hall more poorly insulated than outside. I was glad for my gloves – dark leather with snug, soft lining.

"There's something about Cyril," said Theodora.

I nodded. "If only I could put my finger on it."

"As long as that's the only thing you put your finger on."

As if on cue, he climbed the wooden steps that led to the main stage and awkwardly shuffled to the centre. His face was sufficiently pleasing to look at – neat moustache, friendly lips, and blond hair liberally oiled and parted in the middle. He coughed a few times as he retrieved a small notepad from his pocket. He rustled through the pages and finally began.

"Good evening, ladies and gentleman, and welcome to tonight's gathering of the National Vigilance Association. We are honoured to have guests from the London County Council, the Public Morality Council and the Council of Concerned Citizens for Britain's Moral Integrity."

"My God," I whispered, "how many councils are there for our erasure?"

"There's much to be said on the matter of our great nation's morality, but I shall let those words be said by a more consummate speaker than I." This received a quiet titter of amusement. "Without further ado, I would like to introduce the chairman of our association, Mrs Helena Fortescue."

Many gloved hands applauded as Helena strode across the boards, far more at home taking centre-stage than her secretary. She placed an affectionate hand on his elbow before sending him on his way. I watched as he very carefully approached the stairs. Was he long or short-sighted? He didn't fall on his descent and I marvelled at the lengths he went to impress his employer.

"Honoured guests," began Helena, "I assume you have all known illness. And when that illness has proven severe enough, I assume you have all paid to see your doctor and bought the medicines he prescribed. This sounds like a sensible course of action, does it not?" She gazed indulgently at those of us gathered and smiled, a much better rhetorician than Cyril. "Then what of our great nation? Her soul is sick and she too is in urgent need of a physician. Perhaps it is those of us gathered who shall be the ones to administer the cure."

"Here we go," muttered Theodora.

Here we went indeed and everywhere else for that matter as Helena's speech spanned the great array of our nation's ills. Prostitution and the white slave trade were the first to be condemned, followed swiftly by photographic and literary pornography. A plea was made for the raising of the age of consent and extra protection for girls and young women from the advances of men. God was appealed to on a number of occasions as were the latest scientific findings. Conspicuously absent were the topics of contraception and heterosexuality. Presumably a broad church had gathered, not all inclined to non-procreative intercourse, and this evening's event was an effort to bring its congregants closer together.

"What we need," Helena continued, "is common ground. We may disagree on many things but there's still much we can agree upon. Which is why I would like to conclude my introductory speech..."

"Only the introduction," I whispered.

"... with a request for your support in the elimination of a vice most decadent and dangerous."

I gripped Theodora's hand (at least if anyone saw they'd reach all the wrong conclusions).

"Gross indecency."

A murmur of accord rippled amongst the congregants – nothing like a good villain to unify a crowd.

"Nowhere is safe these days from those perverted individuals who seek to lead our men astray. One need only walk through Soho of an evening to see them in their pearls and lipstick. And what of the Servants' Ball, an event for the enjoyment of our serving classes, now rife with men in dresses."

She paused, choking a little on her final words. Clearly, she was thinking of her son, his death fuel for her fire. Or perhaps she was still clinging on to the idea that it was a mugging gone wrong, desperate not to have to associate him with the infected. An expectant silence filled the auditorium as she found her resolve.

"This is a war we fight on many fronts, and as vigilance is my watchword, I will see this city cleansed."

The usual terror unfurled in my stomach, a regular companion given the society in which I lived, and now I saw it made manifest as Helena Fortescue and her gathered faithful.

"Hatred," I murmured. "This all rests on so much hatred."

"I know," replied Theodora quietly.

"Could hate be our motive?"

"Whose?"

I nodded in Helena's direction.

"You think her capable of killing her own son?"

"I think her capable of leading a crusade."

"But she was asleep at midnight."

"With no one to either confirm or deny it," I said.

"Unless Hector can. Perhaps they'd been enjoying a brief moment of heterosexuality."

"I dread to think!"

We snickered, despite ourselves, but the point remained – even if Hector and Helena shared a room, there was nothing to stop one of them sneaking out while the other slept. Both struck me as the sort of people who slept very soundly at night and both shared a late son who'd betrayed them. It was often said that those closest to us caused us the most harm – a sad truth I'd learned the hard way.

Helena's tirade eventually ended, to yet more applause, and then she introduced a chap from the Council of Concerned Citizens. He had a bee in his bonnet about the lack of seatbelts in motor cars and the surge of post-war immigration; apparently too many of our jobs were being stolen by men from Eastern Europe. Blessedly, the man from the London County Council had called in ill, leaving only one more speaker – a sonorous old bore from something or other to do with temperance and abstinence. It transpired he hated Communists as much as he did alcohol. I confess to dropping off at one point but Theodora gave me a polite nudge before I began to snore. When all the speeches were complete, we were pointed towards the back of the Hall, where an old tea urn stood next to a few plates of biscuits. Like bees to honey, most of the audience rushed for something sweet and warm.

"Good evening," said Percy. "I'm glad you both came."

"As are we," replied Theodora. "Although I wasn't expecting to see you."

"Mother needed reinforcements. I'm to hand out biscuits," he explained. "Perhaps I could tempt you with a digestive, Miss Smythe?"

"Delicious," she said, placing her arm in his. "Now, Selby, why don't you lend a hand with the chairs."

Suitably commanded, I idled for a moment as Cyril spoke with a few of the guests. Once they'd moved, he attended to the chairs.

"Would you like some help with that?" I asked.

"No, thank you."

He pushed two chairs slightly closer together.

"I'm Selby Bigge, we haven't been properly acquainted."

"You're Miss Smythe's acquaintance."

"I am. And you are Mr Cyril…?"

"Cyril Blanford."

"Mrs Fortescue's secretary."

"I really must get back to this."

What exactly it was he had to get back to I wasn't sure – given he was neither removing nor stacking the chairs. If I were being charitable, I would say he was straightening them, but they seemed quite straight enough to me.

"It must be something to work for such an impassioned woman."

"It's an honour," he replied earnestly.

"Bracing, I should imagine."

He squinted disapprovingly in my direction.

"It's terribly sad about Lancelot," I said.

"Terribly."

He returned his gaze quickly to one of the chairs.

"Might I ask you a question about the night of the murder?"

"I'd prefer it if you didn't."

"I'm afraid I must. Your employer has asked Miss Smythe and I to make our own enquiries."

"The next Tommy and Tuppence, is it?" he shot.

"I beg your pardon?"

"That Agatha Christie crime-solving couple."

"I'm well aware who Thomas and Tuppence Beresford are. It was your tone that surprised me."

"I have a lot on my mind." He pinched the bridge of his nose and blinked rapidly for a few moments. "The association is woefully understaffed."

"They still haven't found Reginald," I said, trying to steer the conversation.

"Evidently."

"Have you any idea as to his whereabouts?"

"No, I hardly knew the man."

"You never spoke with him?"

"I don't associate with riff—" He stopped himself. "With the working classes."

"Not one for socialism, then?"

"I don't have time for politics. I've already spoken about all this with the police."

"Did you tell them why you were at the Fortescues' house on Saturday night?"

"What?" he blurted, bashing his knee against one of the chairs. "How…"

"How do I know? Because someone told me."

"Who?"

"That needn't concern you. What is concerning is your suspicious behaviour."

"Suspicious!? You think I could have harmed…"

He couldn't bring himself to finish the sentence. He looked genuinely anguished.

"I don't," I replied, "but I'd still like to know why you were there."

"That's none of your business."

"What if I were to make it Mrs Fortescue's business?"

For a moment he was speechless and I couldn't tell if I'd angered or wounded him. Chatter from the tea urn wafted towards us and I wondered if anyone was looking our way.

"You wouldn't."

I stared him down, hoping to push home my advantage.

"A friend of mine is unwell."

"I'm sorry to hear it," I lied, not believing him for a second. "Did Percival console you?"

"He handed me a copy of the *Telegraph*."

"Were you hoping to find someone else?"

"That's none of your..." He forced himself to calm down. His cheeks had turned scarlet and he was quite flustered. "None of that matters any more. I wasn't at that wretched ball."

"Was Lance?"

"I... I..." He paused, sensing my trap. "I wouldn't know, but given what's transpired, it appears likely he was."

"Where had you been that night?"

"At home, struggling to sleep."

"Where's home?"

"Hammersmith."

"So, you got up, dressed and went to the Fortescues' in the middle of the night?"

"As you already appear to know."

"What time did you arrive?"

"At a quarter to eleven."

"And when did you leave?"

"Ten minutes after midnight."

"Your timings are very precise."

"That's because I have a watch and a working memory."

That's the spirit, I thought, nothing beats a sassy rejoinder.

"Besides," he continued, "leaving the house that night proved memorable because that was when I saw them."

"Who?"

"The maid and a man."

"Grace?"

"Yes, and before you ask, I didn't see who she was with. They entered via the basement door. He appeared to be wearing some sort of cape."

"A cape?"

"I shall not repeat myself and I shan't answer any more of your questions. I have chairs to tidy."

Off he went to tidy said chairs, leaving the chairs of my mind decidedly muddled – just when I thought I was beginning to put things in order, they insisted on disarranging themselves. I left the front of the Hall, hoping to find Theodora by the biscuits, but as soon as I located her I wished I hadn't – she had company. Not only was she with Helena, but Detective Chief Inspector Lisle of the Metropolitan Police and his lackey Sergeant Stovell were also there, all polished buttons and unearned authority. I wasn't sure if my loins could take much more girding.

"Mr Bigge," said Helena, "do join us. You've met the chief inspector."

"I have. Good evening."

"Good evening," he replied, although it was clear neither one of us wished the other anything of the sort. "I didn't have you down as a card-carrying member of the National Vigilance Association."

"I'm not. But after tonight's rousing speeches, I could be tempted to join."

"We must swell our numbers," said Helena. "The good fight will not win itself."

"May I commend you on your choice of words," I said.

"You may. I'm known for my oratorical skills."

"Especially your use of metaphor – the one about purging the body politic was most provoking."

"Thank you," she beamed.

"Did you have a purgative in mind?"

"Bourbon?" The offer came from Percy, materialising with a full plate of biscuits. We all helped ourselves, relieved to have something to line our insides. Percy left us with a sympathetic wink; Helena was his mother after all.

"My, what a question," she said, smiling. "We do have some rather big plans in the pipeline."

The chief inspector coughed in the manner of a ham actor cast as a bumbling policeman. "Mrs Fortescue, perhaps we should continue this conversation in private."

"Whatever for?" she said. "Miss Smythe is a family friend and Mr Bigge is fast becoming one."

A worse punishment currently eluded me.

"You see, the National Vigilance Association cannot take the law into its own hands but we can work hand in glove with the police."

"My dear, I was just thinking how nice your gloves are," said Theodora. "Are you and the chief inspector working together, then?

Lisle coughed again and Helena looked from him back to Theodora. It was clear she wanted to divulge their exciting little plan but he didn't want her to.

"All I will say on the matter is that it involves a dam."

"A dam?" replied T, baffled.

"And the betterment of London and the whole of England."

"How intriguing," I replied, my mind rushing through a number of possibilities, none of them good.

"Tell me, Inspector," said Theodora, "have you made any progress regarding poor Lancelot's murder? A more specific time of death, perhaps?"

"No."

"An explanation for the empty suitcase?"

"No."

"The whereabouts of the murder weapon?"

"No."

"Your lack of progress concerns me," said Helena and, for once, we were of accord.

"We have found those footprints," piped up the sergeant.

Lisle huffed loudly.

"Footprints?" Me this time.

"My sergeant is referring to a number of muddy footprints found not far from the Albert Memorial statue."

"I say, a clue!" said Theodora, slightly over-egging it.

"Whose are they?" asked Helena.

"We're yet to ascertain that," Lisle said gruffly.

"Surely there are lots of footprints there?" I asked.

"These happen to be in a flowerbed."

"How intriguing."

"It could be nothing," he said gruffly.

"Did you also find the weapon in this flowerbed?"

"Not exactly, but we have found plenty of stones large enough for the job. Our priority remains the search for Reginald Rolt."

"You don't think it was a chancing thief after all?" said Theodora.

"I'm considering all the possibilities."

Including the one we suggested but a few days ago!

"Reginald can't have hurt Lance," pleaded Helena. "He was such a kind soul."

"Even the most innocuous of people are capable of doing harm."

"So, your working theory is that Reginald killed Lance?" said T.

"It's one of our working theories, yes. Peculiar men do all sorts of damage."

"What makes you think Reginald was peculiar?" asked T.

"We have our sources," he said enigmatically. "Ones we do not share."

"That's absurd," protested Helena. "Your sources are misinformed. Reginald was as straight as an arrow."

The chief inspector had nothing to say to that. An unfriendly angel flew overhead, leaving the four of us silent. Oh, to have the resources of the Metropolitan Police at our disposal – we'd find Reginald in an instant and Lance's killer shortly thereafter. It was Helena who broke the silence.

"Perhaps we can retire to the small prayer room near the stairs, Chief Inspector, if you require privacy." Her stern face turned to Theodora and I. "It was so wonderful of you both to come. I do hope you'll consider joining. We accept donations."

"I shall give it much thought," said Theodora as we bade good evening.

The chief inspector gave me the once over as he went. Nasty brute. He was dying for an excuse to put me in prison.

"And, Chief Inspector," said Helena, striding alongside him, "I would also like to talk with you on the matter of female police officers."

I hoped he wouldn't be able to get a word in edgeways. Then along trotted the sergeant. As he walked past, I regarded his profile and noticed a reddening of the skin on his cheek. There was also a small trace of a white, paste-like substance.

"Sergeant," I whispered, "I think you missed a spot shaving."

I tapped the side of my head to indicate where the paste was. He looked both annoyed and worried as he wiped the white stuff away with the sleeve of his jacket.

"It would appear to be another queer case," I said to him.

"You'd know all about that," he hissed.

"Come along, Sergeant," beckoned the chief inspector, "we have a dam to build."

"Are you thinking what I'm thinking?" asked Theodora, as we watched them leave the Hall, my resting heart rate decreasing from panic to mild alarm.

"Cream finger?" offered Percy, appearing with yet more biscuits.

"Don't mind if I do," I said, taking two.

Off he went to serve the vigilant many.

"What are you thinking?" I asked. "That a cup of tea and a Jaffa Cake won't cut it?"

"That none of us are safe."

CHAPTER 16

I briefly dated a chap back in January. We met exactly three times, and on the third, I went back to his studio flat in Bayswater. He was middle class like myself, pale-skinned and a fellow escapee of a decidedly judgemental family. London's underworld had presented a freedom to the both of us that we'd never imagined possible. There we were, two men desiring of the bodies of other men, and finding that a most desirable thing. Like the emerging heterosexual, we made good on our erotic desires, regardless of their lack of a procreative impulse. Unlike the emerging heterosexual, we didn't let a lack of wedlock deter us. Nevertheless, the path to shared passion did not run smooth once we reached his bed, conveniently situated next to the sink and stove.

We started with a tight embrace and moved quickly to kissing. We then paused to remove our clothes – ties, braces, shirts, vests, trousers, garters, socks, and finally, underwear. His erection curved slightly to the left. Under the covers, we resumed our embrace. His hands slipped down my body and he squeezed my buttocks. I returned the favour. I then gently moved a finger between his cheeks and lightly caressed the rim of his arsehole. He batted my hand away immediately.

"I'm not a poof," he said.

So it was there were those who buggered and those who got buggered. For the Bayswater man he was firmly in the first camp, keen to demonstrate his masculinity, despite his musical temperament. To penetrate was a manly act after all, if not *the* manly act. Meanwhile, the poofs, fairies, queens and sissies were the ones who were penetrated. They took on the submissive role, thereby becoming the woman. This distinction of sex, so vital to the overworld, was thus reflected in the murky waters of the Styx. It wasn't manly for a man to enjoy the excitation of the nerves of the pelvis, confirmed by the various scientists who'd purported to have found similarities between the pervert's arsehole and the woman's vagina. So, I played submissive that night, partly for my own pleasure but also to dispel the Bayswater chap's discomfort.

He promised he'd write to me at Miss Wickler's but he never did, vanishing into the ether like one of Octavia Stubbs' ghosts, a habit he shared with far too many other fellows I'd bedded. In only three evenings I saw how haunted he'd been by the spectre of the man he was taught to be – the upstanding, stoic husband-in-waiting sort. He believed two men should be able to share the equivalent of the marriage bed, so long as he wasn't the wife. He believed his peculiarity should be granted entry into that great chalk circle of normality, so long as he behaved respectably and didn't associate with perverts. Some ghosts he sought to dispel, others he entertained. As for me, I refused to live in a haunted house. I would air every attic room and illumine every cellar. I was committed to a full exorcism. Saving my soul was paramount after all, despite the many demons I met along the way.

"We have more comings and goings than a night on the Dilly," said Theodora.

We had absconded to the River Styx and found it surprisingly quiet for a Friday evening. She'd been kind enough to pay my entry fee and for a bottle of champagne. The lamps were dim and a few candles had been placed on some of the tables. The effect was all rather romantic (or seductive, depending on one's ambitions). After an evening surrounded by those who would see us cured, it felt reassuring to be amongst the wilfully ill. No medicine for me, just men.

"And enough suspects," she continued, "to fill a bus."

"Not forgetting," I added, "that the true culprit might not even be on our list."

"Thank you for that reminder, Selby," she said sardonically. "How much simpler if the murder had taken place in a snowbound hotel in the highlands."

"Chance would be a fine thing," I quipped. "Now, to business. Let's be methodical."

Theodora's eyes briefly absconded their sockets for the back of her skull.

"I'm leagues ahead of you, Mr B," she said, reaching into a pocket in her dress – one that I'd never even realised was there. From within she produced a small piece of paper. She unfolded it and laid it on the table.

"My, my, method becomes you," I said.

10pm – S & I arrive at RAH; Lady S says hello. Helena already abed!

10.20 – S bumps into Lance and Reggie at the bar.

10.30 – Hector to bed, Percy dozes in drawing room.

10.45 – Cyril arrives at Pendragon Rise, wakes Percy.

10.50ish – Lance leaves dancefloor, waves to us. Lady S overhears Lance having an argument.

11ish – Lance returns, followed by plague doctor.

11.15 – I bump into Jackie, Selby joins soon.

11.40 – I get Jackie into a taxi.

11.45ish – plague doctor departs, then Grace, then Lance.

11.50 – I join S in the main Hall, Lady S bids us goodnight.

poor Lance coshed

Midnight – S & I watch the fireworks.

Grace back? Max corroborates?

12.10 – Grace back? Cyril sees her with caped figure. Who?

2 – bed!

"I say, Theodora, this is rather good!"

"That's why I made it, my dear," she replied. "There are a few too many 'ishes' and question marks for my liking, but it's something. Which is more than Chief Inspector Reviled has got because he still can't place the time of death."

"He's left us with a very large opening."

"Let's not talk of those," she teased. "But we can close the gap because we saw Lance leave the auditorium just before midnight. Giving us our next question – who had opportunity?"

"Possibly Grace," I said, tapping the bottom of the page, "or possibly not."

"Exactly. If Max is telling the truth, she may have had just enough time to kill Lance before making a very quick escape."

We both paused to imagine Grace haring through the streets of South Kensington dressed in her mistress' gown with blood on her hands.

"Or if Max is lying," I continued, "and Cyril's telling the truth, then she had ten minutes more to escape the scene of the crime in those heels."

"Furthermore, Grace confirms she saw Cyril at the house after midnight."

"So, it's one point against the chauffeur and one in favour of the secretary," I said.

"Which begs the question – why did Max lie?" She raised her glass and took a hefty glug.

"And who was the caped figure Cyril saw Grace with?" I said.

"Perhaps the plague doctor with his mask off?" she suggested.

"My thoughts exactly. It's a shame the shifty secretary didn't see his face."

"Personal prejudices aside," said T, "let's not forget the master and mistress of the house. No one can confirm they were in the land of nod at midnight."

"There's also Jackie," I said, "who may have asked the taxi driver to stop so she could nip off to murder her Lancelot. I wonder if he kept the meter going?"

Theodora laughed as I took a sip of Dom Perignon – utter ambrosia as the bubbles burst along my tongue. Like one of Wilde's witticisms, it was just the right side of dry. Often alcohol and a sense of humour were the only way to cope.

"There's someone else we haven't considered," I said.

"Who?"

"The as-yet-unknown suspect who'll appear in the penultimate chapter and surprise us all."

"Aunt Oscar did that in *A Funeral to Die For* and the critics did not approve."

"My regards to any critic unwise enough to insult your aunt."

"They usually end up dead in the next novel. Now, as well as most of our suspects lacking midnight alibis, we do have a further clue: Lady Splendid's overheard argument."

"While she was busy with the Scotsman," I said, trying to erase any trace of envy, "sometime before eleven, if I recall."

"Very curious," said T, tapping the end of her nose. "Remind me, what exactly did she hear?"

"*How could you betray him?*" I paused to let the words sink in. "Then Lance came back to the main hall for eleven."

"A very efficient argument," she observed. "Mine usually last much longer."

"I dread to think," I replied. "He didn't bother waving on his way back. There was a plague doctor hot on his heels, after all."

"So, it's possible," interjected Theodora, "that the row Lady S overheard was between Lance and the plague doctor."

"Many things are possible but I would say that one's probable because I saw them at it later on. Grace had to break up the altercation between the bird and the clown while you were hailing a taxi for Jackie."

Theodora poured the remains of the champagne into our glasses as we took pause for breath.

"How my aunt manages to write these things, I have no idea," she said. "The brain of a crime writer is an impressive thing."

"Mine's just warming up."

She glowered. I leant back in my chair and perused the room. Two youngish chaps were at a table in one of the corners. They'd pushed the candle to one side so they could lean across the table and take each other's hands – a most criminal act. They talked in hushed whispers, looking deeply into one another's eyes. Two love birds, I assumed, and just the sort of chaps the Vigilance Association would want to see arrested – or cured, if they were feeling generous.

"Given opportunity abounds," she said, "what about the means?"

"You think the chief inspector is right about the large stone?"

"If there's evidence one was removed, then yes. And those footprints in the flowerbed could be connected," she said. "Or else someone brought a weapon with them."

I tried not to picture Lance's look of terror as his life was most brutally ended.

"The latter suggests premeditation and the former a spur-of-the-moment crime," summed up Theodora. "What of motive?"

"I think we have two," I said.

"Go on."

"The first is hate: this past week has been full of it, not least from Lance's parents."

"But they loved their son."

"They loved the son they wanted him to be but hated who he truly was," I said. "In their eyes, he was a traitor."

"Hector may well attack the mind but I can't imagine him bludgeoning the body," she protested.

"Lance was his first patient. He built his reputation upon the curing of his son. And he lacks a midnight alibi," I reminded her, "as does Helena."

"I can't see her wielding a rock."

"But I can see someone wielding one on her behalf."

"Who?" she asked, surprised. "Cyril?"

"Perhaps. Being overly vigilant."

She shook her head. "You're biased. You've got it in for him."

"He's shifty *and* he'd happily see our world swept from the map."

"But Cyril has multiple witnesses for his midnight whereabouts, including Percy."

"The affable brother," I replied. "He reminds me of some of the bullies at boarding school – all charm until crossed."

"I hardly think that makes him the fratricidal type – and he has an alibi."

"I'm aware of that but we mustn't discount anyone. Including Jackie…"

"… who was at the ball precisely because she suspected Lance of lying."

We did have a habit of finishing one another's sentences. Great minds and all that (even if I liked to think mine a touch greater).

"Can you picture *her* wielding a rock?" I asked.

"Never underestimate what a woman scorned can wield."

She tipped her glass to me before draining it.

"Have you spoken with her maid regarding her midnight whereabouts?"

"I've tried, but she's keeping mum."

"Even your charm has limitations," I said. "Let's not forget Max. He had that set-to with Lance and may well have slashed the portrait in retaliation. He's up to something and I'd bet good money Grace knows what it is. What about blackmail?"

"Golly," said T. "Max seduces his master then extorts him."

"Happens all too often," I replied glumly.

"And if Grace caught wind of the plan, she might have wanted to profit from it."

"Grace, a blackmailer," I mused. "Do you think she hated Lance?"

"She didn't need to, nor even disapprove of his nature. She simply needed a desire to make money."

"One most of us possess," I said, "save the children of baronets."

"Now, now, what did I say about green not being your colour."

I scowled into my glass but enjoyed its contents nevertheless.

"What about Reginald?" I said. "Where the hell is he?"

My eyes wandered again but this time to another corner of the room – the one in which that man had been sitting a few nights ago. I hadn't recognised him, with his bushy beard, moustache and glasses, but he'd been watching me. It gave me the willies just thinking about it. There were often spies in our ranks. It proved a profitable enterprise.

"Our first answer to that question," said Theodora, cutting into my thoughts, "is that Reginald saw who killed Lance and subsequently fled, detouring via the house to steal Lance's car. Our second is he saw who killed Lance and was killed for it. Or number three, his disappearance has nothing to do with the murder or the car whatsoever and is just one big coincidence."

"I don't like those."

"Not forgetting number four," she said. "That he's our murderer."

"Which brings me to my second motive," I said. "If not hate, then love."

"A crime of passion?"

"Lance was lying to almost everyone he knew, apart from Reginald. When I saw them at the ball, I saw the affection they had for one another and I believe it was genuine."

"They were in love?"

"I think it's possible and Lady S did overhear that row. What if it was Reginald accusing Lance of cheating on him? One thing led to another, and in an explosion of anger, Reginald lashed out."

"But if Reginald left the ball much earlier why did he wait so long before he struck?"

"I don't know," I replied. "Unless in that time something happened which revealed the truth to him."

"Or revealed the truth to someone else. What's to say it wasn't the other lover who lashed out – murdering both Lance and Reginald for their affair."

"Hector said that us queers are doomed to unhappy, miserable affairs."

"Helena said much the same," she added. "That pair certainly did their damnedest to make Lance miserable."

"Either way, things don't look good for Reginald," I said, "especially now he's Lisle's prime suspect."

"Anything that policeman suggests, I assume the opposite is true. Poor Reginald, either he's utterly terrified or he's..." Theodora shook her head.

"If he's not dead," I said, "where would he hide?"

"His home?"

"That's the Fortescues' house."

"Or with his mother in Shepherd's Bush?" she suggested.

"Surely even the chief inspector in all his incompetence would have checked there."

"Then where would you go in a time of great panic?" she asked.

"Here!"

We looked about ourselves – the cramped tables, rickety piano and smoky atmosphere – it wasn't much but it was a haven of sorts.

"I think you're on to something, Selby. If Reginald was part of this world, then he may well have been a patron of the Styx."

"We should ask the mole," I said, referencing the chap who tended the cloakroom.

"He has a name, you know," reprimanded Theodora. "It's Martin."

"Martin the Mole!"

She tutted and raised her glass, only to discover it was empty, along with the bottle. Upping sticks, she strode for the hole in the wall. I followed suit.

"Hallo, Martin, how are you?"

"Oh, you know," he said, readjusting the pince-nez on the end of his nose. "It's a quiet night. But can't complain, I'm in good company."

He looked down at his reading matter and I followed his gaze – just the sort of stuff the National Vigilance Association would ban.

"Jolly good. I've a question for you."

He squinted at her.

"You've heard of that ghastly murder at Lady Malcolm's Ball?"

"I have indeed, that poor sod, and the one who's gone missing."

"Exactly. Do you recall if either of them ever came here?"

"Dear oh dear," he said, scratching his head, "that is a test for my old noggin. I've a good memory for faces mind, especially the pretty ones." He looked at me and winked. "A while ago, maybe, the doctor's son was here."

"Did he have company?" I asked.

"That's too much of a stretch for me, I'm afraid."

"Theodora, whatever's the matter?"

She had closed her eyes and put her fingertips to her temples – she either had a frightful headache or was receiving a message from the great beyond.

"I've had a thought," she said.

"Congratulations."

"Martin, what was the name of that club that closed down last year?"

"Do you mean Frank's Goldmine?"

"No, the one named after an animal or a bird."

"The Parakeet?"

"Bingo!"

"Plenty of strapping lads there," he said. "Pity to see it go."

"Where was it?"

"Inkerton Street."

"Thank you, Martin, you're a star."

"Orion's belt is my favourite," he said, tapping the page at which his magazine was opened – one which revealed a man distinctly lacking in a belt and any other apparel for that matter. Theodora ordered our coats and ordered me back into mine forthwith.

"Whatever's the rush?" I asked. "We could order another bottle."

"We have work to do." I hurried after her to the top of the stairs. "We're going to Inkerton Street."

"Why?"

"I was trying to remember a conversation we had when Bile and Shovel first arrived at Pendragon Rise. They'd been discussing Lance's old haunts with the Fortescues. The Parakeet was named."

"Didn't Martin just say it had closed down?"

"Selby, please, are you telling me you've never returned to the sight of a stolen kiss or a warm embrace?"

"I… Well, once or twice."

"Then perhaps the Parakeet was where Lancelot fell in love with Reginald or whoever his mystery lover might have been. Somewhere far from the prying eyes of his family and their staff."

"And you really expect to find Reginald camped out on the street?"

"Of course not, but it's another stroke of the brush."

"Another what of the what?"

"I'm likening the case to the painting of a picture."

"I thought it was a crossword."

"Can I not be allowed to indulge in my metaphors?"

"Ever your aunt's niece."

"Literary flourishes aside, the more we can learn of Lance's favoured acquaintances and old haunts, the more likely we are to learn the reason why he was killed."

"It's a thought, I suppose."

"A very good one," she said, starting her descent of the stairs. "Don't dawdle!"

CHAPTER 17

As we walked the slick evening streets of Soho, Theodora's recent comments played on my mind. Who was Lancelot Fortescue? I'd barely met him, but in a very short space of time, I'd learned how many sides he possessed. At dinner he'd appeared a confident, genial chap with a doting fiancée and a loving family. He was the dutiful son who'd done good, accurately captured in his portrait hanging on the wall – until someone had taken a knife to it. A few hours later I'd confirmed he was also a first-class liar. At the ball he'd been an entirely different person – scared, defeated and running from the pressures of not being the man everyone thought him to be. Sentiments I knew well. He also had a fruity sense of humour and had clearly encountered one or two men in his time. Then I'd seen him touch Reginald on the cheek, and in that simple intimate gesture, I saw love. I saw the hope that can endure the slings of Doctor Fortescue's outrageous treatments and the arrows of Helena's vigilance.

Looking back, I realised I'd seen a man living the last moments of his life. At least he'd gone out with a bang – dancing and drinking and dressed head to toe as Harlequin! I pictured his mask – four diamonds of different colours on a grinning face, made in Venice, as he'd said. That was not the only mask Lance had worn.

"Almost there," said Theodora as we hunkered down through the drizzle.

"I'll need a bath after this."

"Have one at mine."

"Really?"

"I can't imagine Miss Wickler would appreciate your bathing late on a Friday evening."

"The less imagined of Miss Wickler the better."

We took a left, passing down another poorly lit street. Laughter emitted from one of the pubs, its windows glowing orange and inviting. With Christmas not too far away it would soon be time for mulled wine and spiced beer, something to look forward to after all this was over.

"Evening, love," crowed a man as he stumbled out of the pub door. "Aren't you pretty?"

"He wouldn't have said that to Theo," she muttered under her breath.

On we went, soon to discover how many wild geese we were chasing. But Lance had liked the Parakeet, so there might be something in it. It was another letter on the grid and another stroke to his portrait. As for Reginald, I knew him even less, save for that charged encounter outside the Fortescues' WC. I could have fallen for his charms with ease. We passed a figure sleeping in a doorstep. He was wrapped in many shabby layers and was incredibly dirty. I smelt alcohol and misery. Poverty was rife in London, the great crash having resulted in a great slump, and much unemployment to boot. Men travelled from all corners of the country to find work in the capital, only to find themselves on the streets.

"Here we are," announced Theodora.

Inkerton Street was drear and uninviting. Tucked deep within the warrens of Soho it looked like it had seen better days. It was a narrow street for passing through, or better still, avoiding – the perfect place for one of our clubs.

"I went to the Parakeet once," she said.

"With Susan, was it?"

"Alone and not for very long. They booted me out."

"Whatever for?"

"Theo wasn't man enough for them."

We stopped halfway down the street, navigating the contents of an overturned dustbin and a number of wooden crates left to rot. One of the nearby gas lamps was long broken and another flickered unhappily. As for the building, it was as grey and unhappy as its surrounds, not a house but some sort of old warehouse. Next to the front door of peeling brown paint was a wooden garage entrance.

"It was a repair shop up front," explained Theodora. "Textiles upstairs as well as rentable rooms, if you catch my drift. Everything else happened in the cellar, which can only be accessed from the back."

"A top spot for secret love affairs."

She approached the front door, treading carefully over the

slippery paving slabs, and gave it a try. It didn't budge. She bent down and peered through the letterbox. "Looks uninhabited to me," she said.

"A good hiding place," I suggested.

"Perhaps there's another way in."

We approached the garage – it was two sizeable doors covered in chipped black paint with two rows of small square windows running along the top. I tried to peer through the glass but it was covered in grime. Taking my handkerchief from my inside jacket pocket, I wiped at the dirt, managing to smear it in a circular motion rather than remove it.

"Try the door," said Theodora.

There were no handles nor knobs, just the hole where a Yale lock had once been.

"Looks broken," I said, inspecting the damage. I noted the splinters of the wood weren't covered in grime. "I'd say this was removed fairly recently."

"Stolen?"

"For scrap, maybe," I suggested, not knowing how much an old lock would fetch. I inserted a gloved finger into the hole and gave the door a tug. It didn't move.

"Try harder."

"I can hardly open this thing with a finger."

"Then let me."

She bent down, placing her gloved hands under the door-frame. She gave the door a hefty yank – one had to admire her gumption – then she pulled again, and this time, the door groaned. I lowered myself to help, and after a few more heaves, the door finally creaked open, its hinges shrieking angrily. We stood up and pulled the door harder, giving us just enough room to squeeze through.

"Are you sure this is a good idea?" I asked.

"That's beside the point."

She produced one of her fancy pocket lighters and lit the flame. In she went. I'd left mine at home but did have a box of matches to hand. I struck one and followed her into the gloom. Inside was dank, dark and smelly.

"Careful where you tread," she said, as something scuttled away from us.

"The thought had crossed my mind."

She held the lighter aloft but the darkness was persistent. As my flame approached my fingertips, I threw it to the ground and took out another match. Theodora had taken a few steps forward.

"Selby, there's a car here."

"What type?" I said.

"A Bentley."

My stomach dropped. "Oh dear."

Her silence was answer enough as she slowly approached the back of the motor vehicle. More creatures scurried away from her tread and I was glad I couldn't see them.

"Come on," she said. "Don't make me do this alone."

In the flickering glow of the lighter flame, my hand found hers as we advanced towards the driver's seat. From the moment we'd learned Reginald was missing, a part of me had suspected he'd never be found alive – and now was the moment of truth. The window was too dark to see through. Theodora reached out to grip the handle.

"No fingerprints," I said.

We took a deep breath and held it as she opened the door. The smell was predictably awful, hitting me right in the back of the throat. I tried not to gag. Our eyes were drawn to the coated figure slumped in the passenger seat, his body resting against the far window. Mercifully, his face was turned away from us but there was no chance he was sleeping. He wore a hat, but underneath was a patch of dark hair and a slither of pale neck. There was the distinct odour of vomit. Something bright drew my eye and there on the driver's seat was the mask – an elegant thing painted with four colourful diamonds of white, gold, red and black. But it was dented. The red right eye had been crushed. And there, next to the mask, was a large grey stone with a dark stain.

"I'm going to be sick," I said, stepping back from the car. My insides roiled, my abdomen tensed and I retched. Nothing came up. I heaved again but still nothing.

"Selby, I must check who it is."

She leant carefully inside the car, her flame extending towards the body. My stomach churned. I looked away, trying not to imagine the state of the person's face. It was deathly cold inside the garage, which would have slowed the natural rate of decay, but certainly wouldn't have stopped it.

"Quick," said Theodora, slamming the door shut and taking me by the arm. "Off we go."

The flame wavered as we left the garage and she let go of me to give the door a good shove back into place.

"Was… Was it him?" I asked.

She nodded sombrely. I turned my face upwards as the

drizzle wet my skin, hoping it would wash away the stench of death.

"You're white as a sheet, Selby. We'll get you back to Wilkington Mews straightaway. But first I must make a telephone call."

"Theodora—" I began to protest but she cut me off.

"I don't like the police, but a dead man's body in an abandoned autocar is their business, not ours. There's a telephone box not far from here and I think it best they receive a call from a concerned yet anonymous member of the public."

One hour later, I lay immersed in warm water in Theodora's upstairs bathroom. A pleasant smell of lavender bath milk filled the air and the little window was covered in condensation. An empty mug sat in the sink – black tea with plenty of sugar for the shock. The water came up to my chin and I rested there a while, glad my stomach had settled. Over in Pimlico Miss Wickler would be wondering what I was doing, and given the circumstances, I'd happily have opted for pre-marital heterosexual intercourse with the daughter of a baronet. The images of moments before were still fresh in my mind, despite my best efforts to remove them. One thing that struck me above all else was how sad it all was – that poor man left in that car for six days, presumably never to be found. What a lonely place to die.

After telephoning through to the police we'd come straight back to Theodora's, not waiting for their arrival. Our lives were criminal enough as it was; we hardly wanted to be involved in the discovery of a dead body. The nearest station was located on Vine Street, just off Regent Street, which wasn't too far away.

There was a chance they'd ignore her call, but she'd mentioned Reginald and the information the newspapers had provided on his disappearance. Surely one had to have a certain amount of faith in the Metropolitan Police, however meagre.

Despite my desire to rest – and partly due to the multiple teaspoons of sugar – my mind raced through the possibilities. Rather worryingly, there was an obvious assumption to make, one the chief inspector had already jumped to – that Reginald and Lance were having an illicit and tumultuous love affair that had ended in disaster. Perhaps jealousy or anger or the threat of rejection drove Reginald to kill Lance. But then, on realising what he'd done, he couldn't live with the consequences. So, he drove off to an abandoned garage to do away with himself. This was a story the tabloids would relish – our suffering was always more newsworthy than our survival.

It was a familiar story, suicide far too common amongst people like us. Queer men, for example, whose secret love affairs were threatened by blackmailers or exposed by the vigilant type, all too often took their own lives. Ruined by scandal, racked by shame, rejected by those around them – sometimes taking one's life seemed like the only possible option. Earlier in the year, a taxi driver had driven himself off a bridge after his affair with one of his male passengers was exposed. The press had sensationalised the death without a shred of sympathy. As for Reginald – killing the man he loved, perhaps the only man he might ever meet who could reciprocate his feelings, and left facing a life on the run or the hangman's noose – there was only one way out. Theodora had also spotted mud on his shoes, which could have come from the Kensington Gardens flowerbed. The story almost wrote itself, which is exactly why I suspected it.

How considerate of Reginald to take the murder weapon with him. He could have left it behind or thrown it into the Thames en route to Soho. Instead, he'd decided to neatly display it on the driver's seat, along with the mask of the lover whose life he'd just ended – a veritable surfeit of evidence. At the ball, the colourful mask had been a gay thing to look upon, its smile one of joy, but now it was a rictus, like the grin of a skull. My mind hopped between that sordid little garage and the bar at the Royal Albert Hall – the former Reginald's resting place, the latter the last time I'd seen him alive. Had he really been plotting Lancelot's murder? It was by no means an impossible act. I'd known more than one person capable of concealing murderous intent behind smiles and good humour. Did Lancelot have any idea what was coming? That smiling man, hiding his face under that beautiful mask…

"My gosh!" I cried, emerging from the waters like Lazarus from the tomb. "Theodora, come quick!"

I heard her bedsprings groan and the floorboards creak as she rushed from her bedroom. A moment later, she burst through the door.

"Are you drowning?"

Fortunately, the bathwater was milky enough not to permit her a view of what lay underneath, although I think she'd seen me naked on a number of occasions – her sense of privacy alarmingly more lax than mine.

"It's been staring us in the face all along," I said. "Literally staring us in the face!"

"What are you talking about?"

"The mask! Lance showed it to me and I remember it distinctly – there was a red diamond painted over the left eye and a black one over the right."

"What of it?"

"The mask in the car had a dented right eye, which was painted red."

"Are you sure?"

"I am. It was such a glamorous thing, it made a strong impression. You do know what this means?"

"Absolutely," she replied, taking a seat on the lavatory.

"What?" I asked with a roguish grin.

"Don't patronise me, Selby. What this means is that there's more than one mask."

Suddenly another thought clicked into place and I wished to jump from the bath shouting "Eureka", like a twentieth-century Archimedes. But I saved Theodora the view. The figures at the ball danced through my mind again – Grace in Helena's dress, the bird-like plague doctor and then Lance – his face covered by the harlequin mask.

"I've been an unutterable fool," I said.

"Wouldn't be the first time."

"Lady Splendid said she overheard Lance's outdoor altercation sometime around eleven, but she couldn't be sure exactly when. I assumed it was before because that tallies with when we saw Lance return to the Hall at eleven."

"Where's the foolishness in all this?"

"We assumed he returned!"

"What are you driving at?" Theodora sounded a dash

irritated, which would usually have thrilled me if I weren't busy trying to tie it all together.

"If there was another mask, what's to say it was Lance wearing it?"

"I don't quite..." She stopped. She engaged her brain a moment. She gasped.

"Have you got it?" I asked.

"It could have been anyone under that mask!"

CHAPTER 18

Freud, or even Jung for that matter, would have profited greatly from my dreams. Masks of shifting colours danced before me as peacocks offered their plaintive wails, then champagne corks popped as I was drawn to a dank and derelict garage. Within was a car, the door already open, and inside someone was waiting. He turned to me with a smile – it was Harlequin. But the mask fell away to reveal a grinning skull. I woke in a sweat, hot despite the temperature of my attic room. I shifted position and then shifted again. The bedsprings protested as I tossed and turned. There was no use, I wasn't getting back to sleep any time soon. Slipping out from beneath the covers, I placed my feet into the slippers. My dressing gown was near to hand and I wrapped it around myself as I crossed to the attic window. I drew the curtain and wiped at the condensation on the window. There was ice in the corners.

The sky was cloudless. The half-moon was bright and there

were many stars. Frost glistened on the rooftops and a number of chimneys puffed, despite the late hour. London's skyline was one of smokestacks, spires and the occasional monument. Fortunately, that God-awful creature – the skyscraper – was yet to cross the Atlantic. I liked to gaze upon the city from a height, it helped me put things in perspective, and right now, that was something I desperately needed.

Inevitably, my mind returned to the Royal Albert Hall, except it wasn't Lance I thought of but someone else. A sinister figure, dressed in a harlequin costume, hiding in the shadows of the park, stalking their prey like a fox stalks a rabbit. Then, when the moment had arisen, they'd pounced. Lance must have been surprised to see his own reflection and then the argument ensued, a snatch of it overheard, resulting in a lethal blow. Now should have been the moment for the killer to melt into the night and vanish, but instead they had done something truly ghoulish – they'd returned to the Hall and danced as if they were their victim. Here was a personage most devious, capable of a crime most macabre. From the off, I'd done my best to understand Lance and the sort of person he truly was. But now I realised it wasn't just him I needed to understand, it was also his killer. Despite my racing mind, I yawned. I took myself back to bed, ready for more nightmares.

"What we're saying is that someone dressed in a near-identical harlequin outfit killed Lance before eleven and then returned to the ball?"

Theodora honked the horn of her Crossley as she overtook a

dithering Daimler. It was approaching midday on the following day, Saturday, and as predicted, Theodora and I had been summoned to 42 Pendragon Rise. The discovery of Reginald's body was yet to reach the newspapers, but the Fortescue household had been informed. For some the world was as it was before, for others it tilted askance.

"Not forgetting that this all may have been witnessed by the mysterious plague doctor who later confronted the second Harlequin on the dancefloor."

"An argument intercepted by Grace," I added.

"Meaning it's likely she knows who was under that mask."

We paused to ponder this turn of events. Grace had disliked my numerous incursions below stairs and now I might know why.

"What I want to understand first," I said, "is the purpose of the double masks."

"I'd have thought that was obvious," replied T breezily. "They cosh Lance and then prance around the auditorium for an hour pretending to be him. They leave around midnight, making sure to be seen, so it appears Lance was killed later than he was."

"Which is exactly what *we* thought," I said, emphasising the collective pronoun. "We've been looking for midnight alibis, when really the killer blow may have been struck before eleven."

"I've already thought about all of this, my dear, and it raises a number of significant questions."

"A whole number, I'm sure."

"One, who knew Lance would be at the ball? Two, who knew what costume he'd be wearing? And three, how did they lure him away from the dancefloor?"

"There's a simple answer to all these questions," I replied. "Someone who knew him well."

"Obviously. Which tallies with our thoughts from the very beginning."

An angry bus honked at us and T honked merrily back. I focused on keeping my breakfast in my stomach – toast with marmalade, as it happened, not a flake of corn in sight.

"Not only was it a wicked plan," she said, "but also a significant feat of logistical planning."

"Which suggests premeditation over a crime of passion," I said. "And did they know Lance owned two near-identical masks or did they have a second one made?"

"Perhaps we should make a trip to Venice."

"That would be nice." Oh, to have my friend's budget! "Not to mention the rest of the outfit. That would need to have been purchased in advance – or made."

"A killer and a tailor," she remarked.

"I can't help but think of the will."

"And testament?"

"No, the other sort."

"Honestly, is your mind ever out the gutter?"

"No! The sort of will it takes to execute a crime like this."

"Oh, I see," she said, finally cottoning on. "A damnably sinister one."

"The sort that might belong to a criminal mastermind," I said, fear and excitement mixing in my voice.

"Now, now, let's not get carried away," chided T. "Although, if the second Harlequin was Lance's killer, it crosses off most of our suspects…"

She paused mid conversation to take a sharp left turn, much to the amusement of three grubby children playing conkers on the edge of the pavement.

"Because we saw them in between eleven and twelve – making it impossible for them to also be waltzing around the Albert Hall dressed in the other costume."

This was a good point (not that I told her). Then it struck me. "There's one thing that would have made all of this much easier."

"What?"

"Someone else."

"An accomplice?" said T, tearing her eyes from the road to look at me.

"It's worth considering – someone to lure Lance from the Hall and kill him, someone else to take his place afterwards so no one would suspect he was dead."

"A couple in cahoots," she mused. "That makes it all far more complex."

"Where's Miss Marple when we need her?"

We drove on in silence as my head crowded with thoughts. Lancelot's portrait came to mind – he looked handsome but severe, just the sort of first-born son to carry on his family's lineage. I imagined the paint slowly peeling away from his face – first his forehead, then his cheeks and chin – and underneath, a brightly coloured mask. Perhaps the killer had been the one to slash the painting, which tallied with our talk of premeditation. I imagined a second frame, hanging on the wall next to Lance, except the canvas was blank – as was the identity of the murderer.

"Our next task is clear," said Theodora as we pulled up on

Pendragon Rise. "Establish where everyone was around eleven o'clock."

We soon arrived outside the house and T pushed the bell. I removed my gloves and placed them inside my jacket pockets. My fingers brushed against something. It was my poppy, looking rather worse for wear with drooping petals and a bent stem. It was the 15th today, a week since I'd bought it, and to think on all that had happened since then. Peacetime had claimed another victim. The door opened and Grace let us in – her face revealing nothing of her thoughts. I was told to continue along to Hector's study while Theodora was led upstairs to Helena's parlour. Barely moments after our arrival, we were being split up, but I knew my friend would remain as alert as me. Down the corridor I went until I reached the study door. I gave it a gentle tap and a voice from within bade me enter.

"Ah, Mr Bigge, you're here."

"Good afternoon, Doctor."

"I found that pamphlet we were talking about."

"You did?" I asked, completely forgetting he'd ever mentioned one.

"John Kellogg's defence of selective sterilisation," he said, holding out the offending material. "He makes a terribly compelling case."

Or compellingly terrible. I took the folded booklet from him, hoping it wouldn't burn my fingertips, and pretended to skim-read the cover. I would make a point of avoiding that man's breakfast cereals for the rest of my life.

"I'm with Malthus, you see. There are simply too many of us on this good Earth and some of us have got to go."

You first?

"Talking of death, Doctor," I said, desperately veering the conversation away from another treatise on degeneracy, "Miss Smythe told me of the discovery of Reginald's body."

"Found in an abandoned garage in Soho, of all places."

"What… What happened?" I asked, trying not to picture too vividly said locale.

"Suicide," replied the doctor. "The police think he ingested some sort of poison. They found a hip flask on his person, you see, and are testing it. Given the state of his body and presence of vomit, the current wager is cyanide."

"Oh my," I said, "that's awful."

"No, it's good. It means we can finally put this ghastly ordeal behind us."

"We can?"

"We've found the guilty party – the murder weapon was right next to him."

How suspiciously convenient!

"And his footprints match the ones found in the flowerbed."

"So, Reginald hid amongst the shrubbery, killed your son and then took his own life in a fit of remorse."

"Precisely."

"Why?" I asked, trying to sound sympathetic rather than accusatory. "I thought he was loyal to Lance."

"I thought so too but I see now his loyalty disguised ulterior motives. They're very patient, you see."

"They?"

"Degenerates. He wheedled his way into our household, earned our trust, all the while attempting to lure my son back to a life of depravity. But Lancelot was strong, like his namesake, and I know how he would have resisted. And when Reginald didn't get what he wanted, he struck."

For a moment the doctor broke, his voice cracking and head falling.

"Doctor, I'm so dreadfully sorry," I said, stepping around the desk and patting him gently on the back. It was an intimate gesture, us Englishmen so used to a lack of physical touch, but despite all his awful beliefs, a part of me still pitied the man.

"I always told Lancelot that he needn't fear his heterosexual passions. They were perfectly normal. He and Jacqueline would have been so happy together, providing she performed her wifely duty." He wetted his lips again and I wondered how successfully he restrained his own passions. Helena supported him in his work but that didn't mean she was as ardently heterosexual as he. "It was his homosexual perversions that needed repressing. Reginald was the snake in Eden. A damned incurable."

"Some men simply will not change," I said, speaking for us all.

"There are some truly hopeless cases," he agreed.

"Are you thinking of anyone in particular?"

"There was this one man who refused to wear trousers."

"What do you think made him so resistant to change?"

"For starters he didn't even want to use the correct pronouns. He was convinced his body housed both the spirit of a man and woman."

"I've heard talk of such people." I knew many.

"He even gave himself a most ridiculous name."

"Which was?"

"Lady Splendid!"

His answer surprised me. The murderer's portrait was quickly filled with the face of the beautiful peacock. Theodora had never mentioned any of this, so presumably she didn't know of her friend's brush with family Fortescue.

"Now, Mr Bigge, I have work to do but tea will be served in the drawing room shortly. Do have a read of that pamphlet."

"I will," I said as I withdrew from the study, with every intention of throwing the damned thing on the fire.

The ground floor of the house was eerily vacant as I considered taking myself below stairs to do some snooping. Perhaps I could blame hunger this time and say I'd got lost en route to the pantry. But as I approached the drawing room door, I noticed it was slightly ajar and from within came the sound of hushed voices.

"You've got to be careful." That was Grace's voice.

"What are you talking about?" And that was Max's.

"I found this."

I wanted to peek through the gap to see what she was referring to but my hiding place was too good to risk.

"What are you doing going through my belongings?" Max again.

"I found it outside!"

"I hardly meant to leave it there, did I?"

"I thought you burnt it all," she said.

"Burnt what?"

"If they find this—"

"It won't mean anything."

"It will mean enough to put you there," she warned.

"Who cares, it's over now."

"You really think so?"

Whatever response he gave was non-verbal – assent or dissent, I wasn't to know. All of a sudden, the door burst open and there he was, as displeased to see me as ever.

"Good afternoon, Max," I said, my voice quavering at a higher octave.

He didn't bother to respond and barged straight past me, pushing against my shoulder. He was storming down the stairs before I could even muster a complaint. How bloody rude! Flustered, I entered the drawing room just in time to see Grace slipping her hands between the cushions of the far settee.

"Mr Bigge," she said, turning quickly, "would you care for a cup of tea?"

"That would be delightful."

She moved to the tea and cake tray on the mahogany side table by the wall, and for a while, her back was to me. I took myself to the far sofa and sat myself down just where she wouldn't want me. I saw the flash of shock she wasn't quick enough to hide as she turned around. The cup contemplated divorcing the saucer.

"Thank you," I said, reaching out. "Earl Grey, is it?"

"Assam."

"That will do. Terrible news about Reginald."

"Yes, sir."

Not even a flicker this time. She was good!

"It's come to my attention that he was seen at the ball around eleven o'clock," I said, lightly flavouring the truth. "Perhaps you saw him then too?"

"I cannot remember, sir."

"Perhaps you were with others?"

"I met with some friends from other households, yes."

"And you spoke with Lance, of course."

That stopped her in her tracks.

"As I said to you yesterday, I saw you talking with Harlequin more than once."

"If you say so."

"I do, but what I'd also like to ask is whether you can be sure it was him."

This time her eyes widened and she let out the smallest of gasps.

"Not every mask covers the same face," I said, hammering home my advantage, "and if you know any of the truth, I will prove it."

"How can you think I'd hurt Lance, or Reggie?"

Lance – a surprisingly informal name for her employer's son.

"Time will tell, Grace."

She turned on the spot and headed for the door.

"You wouldn't care to cut me a slice of that cake?"

She left the drawing room without a backwards glance. I wasn't one for bullying staff but I had to rattle a few cages. If she knew it wasn't Lance under that second mask, then she may well know who killed him.

Currently, the excitement was beating the fear as I very carefully placed my cup and saucer on a side table lest I spill its contents. Then came my next task. I slowly inserted my hand into the gap between the cushions and fished around until I found something. Much to my disgust, it was damp. Bringing it up, I discovered a long black glove – just the sort of thing to be worn with a costume. Why it was wet I had no idea.

Given the snippet of conversation I'd overheard between Grace and Max it sounded as though he was meant to have burnt the costume. As far as I could remember, Lance hadn't been wearing gloves with his harlequin costume but that's not to say the second Harlequin hadn't – especially if they'd just coshed clown number one over the head. The door handle turned and I shoved the glove back between the cushions.

"Ah, back again." It was Percy.

"I am indeed. I hope not to your disappointment."

"No, indeed not," he replied, chuckling. "I heard there was cake."

This time it was a fruitcake, to which Percy helped himself to a large slice. It looked alluringly moist and packed with fruit, just the sort of thing I'd have liked to sink my teeth into.

"You've heard then?" he said, taking a big bite.

"Most distressing."

He nodded, chewing thoughtfully.

"Your poor brother," I said.

"At least it's over."

"Are you sure of that?"

"Of course! Has anyone suggested otherwise?"

"They haven't," I assured him, "but I have encountered Chief Inspector Lisle before and know him to be a most thorough man. No stone unturned and all that."

An utter lie but it served a larger purpose.

"As far as I can see, he's found the incriminating stone. Has he said anything to you?"

"Not directly but I am aware, as I'm sure you are too, that there's another angle to this."

The slice of cake hovered in front of his mouth.

"That someone else killed Lancelot and Reginald."

The cake was returned to the plate, unbitten. "Surely not?"

"It's a possibility and I think it might have occurred around eleven o'clock."

"And now you'll want me to confirm my whereabouts," he said with an unexpected amount of good humour, which was better than him hurling the plate in my general direction.

"If you wouldn't mind."

"I was here with Cyril Blanford, as I've already told you," he said patiently.

"What time did—"

He held up a hand to silence me. "As I said, *he* told me it was a quarter to eleven."

"Did you not check the grandfather clock in the hall?"

"No, I didn't," he replied, his tone approaching annoyance, "but nor do I have Cyril pegged down as the sort for chicanery with the clocks."

Behind my questions lay an ulterior motive regarding cats and pigeons. I assumed Percy would talk to his parents upon our departure and it wouldn't take long for the news to percolate below stairs. He might have an alibi for eleven, but if the murderer resided in this house, I wanted them to know they hadn't gotten away with it just yet. Panic might prove an ally. Percy leaned back into the cushion and looked to the ceiling.

"This must be very hard for you," I said earnestly. "Were you two close?"

A faint smile traced his lips. "He was the Lancelot to my Percival, you know. When we were boys, my brother and I used to play with wooden swords, trying our best to live up to our mythological namesakes. In lieu of a damsel, sometimes I'd have to be kidnapped by the dragon. He would come riding to the rescue on his trusty steed."

It was easy to picture this sibling bond. Sometimes my sister and I had put on amateur theatrical productions in the drawing room for my mother and grandparents. I'd played Hamlet once. Not very well, I might add.

"But this time it was my turn to save him," he said, staring me dead in the eye. "And I failed."

"Please don't blame yourself, Percy."

"He had such a flair for the dramatic. He'd make costumes for us and spend an age practising his chivalric voice. I suppose he was used to playing many parts."

"Did you ever suspect he was different?"

"No. But he did confide in me once. Told me how miserable he was – what with Father's treatment and Mother's crusade."

"Do you share their beliefs?"

"I don't know if that matters any more." His voice had softened; gone was the rugger player so sure of himself. "I always tried to support him. He was my brother. I just wish he'd found some peace."

He smiled wearily and my heart went out to the chap. Perhaps he wasn't like those bullies at school, after all. His grief seemed genuine, attesting to the strength of the fraternal bond. My heart went out to me as well – to have a sibling sympathetic to one's struggles was not something I'd ever experienced. Despite our close childhood, time had distanced my sister and I, especially as she'd married a man as disapproving of my lifestyle as my father. No one in my family could ever know.

The doorbell rang and soon voices were heard in the hallway. Shortly thereafter the drawing room door opened and in walked Helena, dressed in black and looking as poised as ever. Jacqueline followed, her poise diminished and her face tired from heartache. Lastly came Theodora. She maintained her composure and I hoped the parlour conversations hadn't been too taxing. Every visit to this house was a veritable assault course (emphasis on the word assault). Percy and I rose to our feet.

"Mr Bigge, I was just saying to Theodora that you must stay for luncheon."

My heart sank.

"And I was just saying," said Theodora quickly, "that Selby has a prior engagement."

"Alas, I do," I lied quite brazenly, "but thank you for the kind invitation."

"Surely one cup of tea couldn't hurt?" asked Helena, sitting next to Percy and bidding Jackie to sit on her other side.

"Selby's the punctual sort," said T before I could get a word in edgewise, "but I'd love some Earl Grey."

It was oddly generous of her to take this bullet, not that I was sure why. Jackie looked thoroughly repulsed by all the talk of drink and food. She took a small lace handkerchief from her sleeve and dabbed at the end of her nose.

"Miss Bosanquet," I said, "I trust you are keeping well."

"As well as can be expected," she replied.

"Darling, that cake is for teatime!" interrupted Mrs Fortescue. "We haven't even lunched."

"I couldn't resist," said Percy.

"Ever my naughty boy. You must save room for the roast venison."

"I do hope it won't be burnt," I said.

Theodora shot me a quizzical look.

"Why would it be burnt?" asked Mrs Fortescue.

"I was merely referencing your cook's recent trouble with the oven."

"Fortunately, Cook has recovered."

"And those ashes found all over the kitchen floor – was that ever cleared up?"

"With a dustpan and brush the moment they were discovered."

I almost laughed. Had that been a purposeful evasion of the question on behalf of the mistress of the house or an accidental pun?

"Although she was complaining of someone rifling through the pantry."

"A stolen feather duster?" I asked.

"Disordered bottles."

Unlike Hector's pamphlet, I filed that one away for later perusal.

"Will Cyril be joining you for lunch?" asked Theodora.

"Not today, he's been taken ill. The stress of recent events has proven a strain on him."

"All that dam-building," I quipped.

"Precisely!"

"Mother, what are you and Mr Bigge talking about?" asked Percy.

"Let's just say," she said, sounding as excited as a schoolgirl before an exeat, "that it won't be long until the river is drained."

Her elation only augmented my creeping dread. As bad luck would have it, I was probably intimately acquainted with the river she wished to dry.

"It's about time," said Jackie. "Those sewers of corruption need to be washed clean away."

Again, that undercurrent of ire surfaced as her placid looks broke into a sneer. How much passionate hate lay repressed in that heart of hers? And what might happen when the dam burst?

"Selby, you should probably be heading off soon," said Theodora. "Your aunt will be expecting you."

"Of course, my aunt! I owe her a luncheon."

"What a lovely nephew you are," said Helena. "Where does she live?"

"She's the one out beyond St John's Wood," said T.

"Yes," I replied, still decidedly at sea.

"She's a dear," said Theodora. "I'd offer to motor you myself but I've rather said yes to a cup of tea here. And all that London traffic."

"I've just the ticket," said Helena. "I'll have Max drop you off."

"No, no," I said, "You mustn't go to the—"

"Selby, don't be rude," butted in Theodora. "It's very kind of Helena to offer Max's services."

"As it turns out, he'll be heading in that direction shortly," she said. "He's taking flowers and oranges to Margaret."

"Margaret?" I asked, now very much drowning in the sea.

"Margaret Rolt, Reginald's mother."

Finally, the waves parted and I was back on dry land – Theodora wanted me to meet Reginald's mother!

"The poor woman," said Helena. "Reginald was her only son and now he's dead."

"And a murderer," said Jackie coldly. "Why waste the flowers?"

"Come, Jackie," said Helena, "she can hardly be blamed. She is a mother."

"It's a shame none of us saw him at the Albert Hall that night," I said. "Miss Bosanquet, remind me what time you arrived?"

"I don't recall," was her frosty response. Having lacked a midnight alibi, she also lacked one for eleven.

"Or perhaps Reginald was seen sneaking about the house?" I asked.

Both Helena and Percy shook their heads. We silenced ourselves for a moment, thinking on the second dead body discovered in the space of a week.

"Do say hello to your aunt from me," piped up Theodora.

"I will," I replied. "Do have an extra slice of cake for me."

"I'll inform Max," said Helena. "He'll be heading off soon."

I gave T the quickest of winks as Mrs F led me from the room.

"Good afternoon, Miss Bosanquet, Mr Fortescue," I said. "I'm sorry the news has been so distressing."

"At least this ordeal has ended," said Jackie firmly.

"Amen," said Percy.

I closed the door behind me, silently wishing Theodora good luck in running that emotional steeplechase.

"You wait here, Mr Bigge," said Helena. "I'll fetch him."

"Before you do, may I commend you on your calm, given the circumstances."

"You may," she said. "I am shocked nonetheless. I can hardly believe it of Reginald."

"That he murdered your son?"

"That he kept his true nature hidden."

"People wear so many masks," I said. "Even those closest to us."

Her look of stern composure slipped, if only for a moment.

"HMS *Fortescue* does not sail itself," she said, squaring her shoulders. "My husband needs me at his side."

"He must so depend upon you."

"There's nothing I wouldn't do for my Hector."

She spoke with all the might of the reincarnated Cleopatra. I didn't doubt her for a moment.

"I do hope Max has remembered the oranges."

"Oranges?" I asked.

"It's so important to consume citrus fruit," said the doctor's wife. "Marie Stopes is adamant on the matter."

"I imagine John Kellogg would concur."

CHAPTER 19

Unsurprisingly, Max was far from pleased to have to chauffeur me through London. He also wasn't aware that the aunt to which he was driving me was a very recent fabrication of Theodora's making. Nevertheless, if I played my cards right, I might just meet Reginald's mother. The rain persisted and our drive through South Kensington was predictably slow. I noted he wasn't taking the most direct route to Shepherd's Bush.

"I quite understand," I said out loud.

"I beg your pardon."

"I said I understand. You're avoiding the Royal Albert Hall."

"Yes, sir."

I was sitting behind him, giving me a good view of the back of his head.

"It was meant to be such a gay night."

The car slowed almost to a standstill as a man on a bicycle cut out in front. Not looking where they were going was a common pleasure for cyclists, along with busy roads and inclement weather. I thought now as good a moment as any to take my shot.

"Before you take me to my aunt, I'd like to offer Mrs Rolt my sympathies."

"You would?"

I'd caught him off guard. He sounded both surprised and peeved.

"Why?"

"She's a mother who's lost her son," I replied. "That should speak for itself."

"Her son the murderous lunatic."

"You really think so?"

Our eyes met in the mirror. Hopefully I was proving full of surprises.

"Surely it's what you think," he said.

"Why do you presume to know what I think? I often find the good people of this country far too quick to believe what they read in the papers."

"Good people, ha," he muttered under his breath. "What makes them so good?"

"Well, they… I think you'll have to get back to me on that one."

That was met with a grunt that could have been interpreted as a laugh.

"Max, we didn't get off on the right foot but please know that I do care about discovering what happened to Lancelot and Reginald. The *good people* of this country readily believe whatever rubbish they're told."

"Why do you care?" he asked.

"Because the truth matters."

"At what cost?"

"Two men are dead! The cost is already too high."

"And that's why you've been sneaking below stairs, trying to get me and Grace in trouble?"

"Yes, because you two are so obviously hiding something."

"That makes us murderers, does it?"

"In all truth, Max," I said, "it quite possibly does."

I should have lied, told him I didn't suspect him, but what difference would it have made? He already knew I had my doubts. I had little to lose in his eyes, but as we stared at one another in the mirror, I saw his were watering. He wiped the tears away before they could fall. He was wearing his pristine white chauffeur gloves.

"If you want to meet Maggie," he said, "then tell me one thing."

"What?"

"Anything. Something about you that's genuine."

"You already know," I replied without hesitation. "That's why I was at the River Styx, if it wasn't obvious already. I'm peculiar."

Sometimes the truth demanded a calculated sacrifice.

"And perhaps," I continued, "we have that peculiarity in common."

"You already think me criminal enough, Mr Bigge. You don't need more ammunition."

Even association with the Stygian lot was dangerous, regardless of whether or not one indulged in a dip. We drove on in silence; the rain eased but refused to stop. With each week the temperature dropped and it wouldn't be long before the rain turned to snow.

"Reggie mentioned you," he said, "after that dinner. Said you had a pretty face."

"That was nice of him."

"He was very nice, Mr Bigge."

"Please, call me Selby."

Having achieved some sort of entente cordiale, we drove on through the dreary streets and eventually reached Shepherd's Bush. Once upon a time it would have been a bushy place inhabited solely by frolicsome shepherds and their flocks, but in the last few decades, it had undergone swift development. Various trains, trams and underground lines had scared the sheep away. Now the fields were houses – red-brick and art deco sat alongside Victorian townhouses and rows of terraces.

It was a bustling place that attracted all sorts of culture. Films were made at Lime Grove Studios and the Pavilion cinema was a huge temple of the silver screen. I'd watched one of the lesser Chaplins there, with a bag of toffees and my signature buttery ham sandwiches with extra mustard. Other stunning buildings had been built to house the various Empire exhibitions of yore, yet all the glamour and all the glamorous facades couldn't hide the relentless poverty.

People begging on the streets were a common sight, including the injured and maimed servicemen who'd been left desolate after the Great War. A few of the grubby children I saw from the car window clearly hadn't eaten a decent meal for weeks and some had been left in charge of their grubby infant siblings. England was a country of disparities and a city like London placed them one on top of the other. And then there was someone like Max – whose skin set him apart from the most of us. That will have made his life even harder.

The car slowed alongside a row of shops that included a bicycle repair shop and a butcher's lined with the plucked carcasses of dead chickens. Max parked the car outside a laundry and it transpired that Margaret Rolt lived above it. He rapped the knocker loudly and some time later a woman appeared. She was short and neatly dressed, with a very wrinkled face. I recognised Reginald's bright-blue eyes.

"Max," she said, with evident warmth, "come in, come in. Who's your friend?"

"This is Mr Selby Bigge," he said. "He'll have some questions for you."

"Will he now? Is he with the police?"

"He's a friend of the Fortescue family."

"Come in then," she said, giving me the once over. "Let's not let the cold in."

We bustled up a narrow flight of stairs into a gay if cramped living room that smelled strongly of soap and washing powder – better than dead chickens or axle grease. A sagging settee and an armchair with doilies to cover the threadbare arms took up much of the space. A polished cabinet housed a plethora of knick-knacks including a chipped porcelain shepherdess and a one-eyed teddy bear. I saw a photograph of Reginald as a young boy. He was smiling and had a football under his arm, blithe to the awful fate that awaited him. The Ancients had devoutly believed in the power of divination but I was often glad we didn't know what the future had in store.

"These are from the doctor and his wife," said Max, handing over the lilies and the oranges. I noted his accent had changed a fraction – fewer of the clipped vowels reserved for his employers and more of the Liverpool with a touch of India.

"That was kind." Margaret sniffed them both and smiled. "Tea?"

"Yes, please," he said.

"Plenty of sugar for you. And you, Mr Bigge?"

"The same, thank you."

Margaret disappeared into a back room, presumably the kitchen. It was chilly up here – the fire hadn't been lit and there was no sign of a radiator. Max and I waited in silence, but it wasn't as uncomfortable as before. The sounds of the street echoed through the rickety glass windows – children shouting, an autocar honking and the butcher advertising a cut of beef. There were more photographs on the wall showing unsmiling relatives of distant times. I saw one of a man in military uniform.

"Reggie's father," explained Max. "He died in the Somme."

"Does he have siblings?"

"Three sisters," said Margaret, returning to the room with a tray.

"Let me," said Max, getting up to help.

"You sit down, young man, I'm not old, you know!"

Formality silenced the conversation as the tea was poured and the sugar spooned. I was grateful for the heat against my fingers. Margaret took the seat next to Max. She opened her palm to him and he took it.

"I don't have the words," he said quietly.

"I know," she whispered.

I looked to the window as they shared this moment of quiet anguish. Theodora and I had only found Reginald's body last night – the news was painfully fresh. Margaret coughed for my attention.

"What do you want?" she asked.

"I wanted to say how dreadfully sorry I am," I replied but my words rang formal and hollow.

"Thank you," she replied without feeling.

"My associate Theodora Smythe and I have been asked by the Fortescues to enquire into the events surrounding these awful deaths."

"Why?"

A good question bluntly put.

"They were at the Servants' Ball," said Max.

"And?"

"And I saw Lancelot and Reginald at one of the bars. We spoke for a moment…" I paused. She was still staring at me, as was Max, I felt it right to tell the truth even if it might hurt. "They seemed very happy together."

Max bowed his head. Margaret nodded curtly. She didn't seem the sort for displays of emotion – certainly not while I was here.

"I want to help," I continued, "because I believe it won't be long before the newspapers accuse your son of murdering Lancelot and then taking his own life."

She didn't appear taken aback at my frankness, so on I went.

"But I don't think that's what happened. I believe, if I may be so bold, that your son was deeply fond of Lancelot, and that his fondness was reciprocated. I believe both men were murdered by someone who dressed everything to look a certain way – as if a brutal, spur-of-the-moment killing had led to a sudden suicide. But I believe none of this was left to chance and these deaths are the result of a cold and calculated act. I wish to find the culprit."

"What's to say there's only one?" asked Margaret.

Lord Peter Wimsey be damned!

"Nothing, there may well be more."

She nodded, seemingly satisfied by my deductions so far.

"You trust him?" she asked Max.

"I trust his intentions. He wants the truth."

"So do I," she said.

She stared into her drained tea mug, examining the leaves at the bottom. Whether or not she believed they foretold future events I thought better than to ask. People looked for all sorts of things at the bottom of drinking receptacles. What she said next took me quite unawares.

"Peach or plum?"

"I beg your pardon?"

"You're a fruit, aren't you?"

Now it was my turn to stare into my cup as Max burst out laughing. He had a pleasant laugh, and although it was at my expense, it was nice for the gloom to temporarily lift. I finally returned her stare, my cheeks the colour of a fresh peach.

"I have crossed the River Styx, if that's what you're asking."

"My dear," she said, "you were born in Hades!"

I glanced at Max, who surprised me with a wink. My cheeks were approaching plum.

"I always knew Reggie was never destined to be a ladies' man. When he was little, I'd tell him stories of knights in shining armour rescuing damsels in distress, but he never cared for those princesses. He'd ask me endless questions about the knights and I had to come up with elaborate origins for them all." She smiled at the memories, crinkling the many lines around her eyes. "As a boy, he was just like the others, naughty and smelly, but I saw the way he looked at his friends. He had a chum when he was twelve, thick as thieves they were, getting into as much trouble as they could. Any minute of the day they could spend together they did. It wasn't hard to spot young love."

"You could give Miss Marple a run for her money."

"Never heard of her. The lad moved to Brighton with his mother and Reggie fell apart. He moped as if the bloody world had ended and I put up with that for a weekend. Then I made him a cup of tea and a sandwich with extra jam, and I sat him down at the kitchen table. I asked him if his friend had broken his heart and he nodded. I told him life could be unfair when it came to affairs of the heart and he'd have to get used to it. He asked me if I expected him to take a wife one day. I told him that I expected him to live the life he wanted."

"You didn't mind?"

"Why would I?"

"He was different."

"No, he wasn't," she said. "He was himself and that's all I wanted for my child."

Her words caught me off guard and somewhere deep within my heart a chord was struck. It sent a melancholy note throughout my chest, filling me with the sorrow of hopes that had never come to pass. I thought on that other little boy – the Selby who grew up as Selby, free to live and love just as he wanted. Selby unbound. He'd never been born.

"I didn't care tuppence for what my Reggie liked to do," she continued. "It's much more common than you might think. Surely you've been to Hyde Park?"

I didn't think I was capable of blushing any further. Max was grinning from ear to ear – at least someone was having fun.

"It's just men being men," she said. "And then there're the ones who are women inside."

Fortunately, we did not discuss the intricacies of who gave and who received, and what that signified for giver and receiver alike. Instead, I steered the conversation back on track. "And Lancelot Fortescue," I said, "where does he come into all this?"

"Well, Reggie got into service, as you know, and one day this handsome well-to-do man turns up on my doorstep. It was the Brighton lad situation all over again. Lance was charming, well-spoken, polite, never patronising, and he treated my Reggie well enough. But I could see there was something else to him – he was askew."

"Askew?" I asked.

"On the inside. One time he spoke of his father's work and how the doctor tried to cure men of their homosexuality. I could have laughed. That's not a word we use around here. If men like men that's their own business, and plenty of them turn it into a business on the side as well."

This time it was my turn to laugh. Margaret Rolt was a well-informed woman! Many working-class chaps sold sex – the soldiers in Hyde Park, train workers under the bridges of Charing Cross and the painted queens on the Dilly.

"I tried to explain this to Lance," she said. "That it didn't make him different where it counted. A soul is a soul and God loves us all. But it was too late. His father's doctrine had done its work."

"So, Lance and Reginald were a couple?"

"For a while, yes, and Lance was very good to my son, took him to the Pavilion to watch the talkies. They even stayed at a hotel in Bournemouth once. In time they stopped being lovers and became friends instead. Good friends."

Finally, I had an answer to what I had seen at the ball – Lance and Reggie, a close friendship born of intimacy and kindred spirits. No longer a romantic love but more than a Platonic one. A love that had shone until it had been extinguished.

"Was Reginald upset when they parted?"

"Of course! I had to make another jam sandwich but he was quick to recover. Plenty of laundry in the basket as I like to say."

Max and I smiled. It was nice to be able to talk so frankly. I could remove my armour. This cramped living room wasn't a warzone. I wasn't under assault simply for being alive.

"When was this?" I asked.

"A year ago or thereabouts."

"Did your son explain why Lance and he parted ways?"

"He said Lance had been kind to him but he'd also been honest – his heart was for someone else."

"Lance had taken a new lover?"

"More than just a lover, I think. Perhaps the love of his life."

It truly was a fairy tale, with love in abundance. And hadn't I recently said to Theodora that love might lie at the heart of this mystery – a love that had inspired jealousy, then rage.

"Did Reginald find someone else after Lance?" I asked.

"Yes."

But it wasn't Margaret who'd answered, it was Max.

"You?" I blurted.

"Is that so surprising?"

"No, it's just…" How I liked to put my foot in things! "… I suppose this morning has been full of surprises."

"How about I refill the pot?" said Margaret, putting our cups back on the tray.

"Thank you, Maggie," said Max, as she shuffled from the room.

"I didn't mean to be rude," I said.

"You don't mean a lot of things, Selby, but you end up implying them all the same."

"A habit I'm trying to break, I assure you."

He tried to repress a smirk but didn't succeed. Was the frost finally starting to thaw?

"So, you and Reginald were lovers?"

"I'll only answer that question if you promise me something."

I nodded for him to go on.

"That you'll find who killed them."

"I have every intention to."

"And you'll get them hanged."

"If justice can be done, it will be."

"Then, yes," he said, "Reg working for the Fortescues was one of the best things to happen to me."

"Was this before or after he was with Lance?"

"After. I started working for the Fortescues last spring. I knew there was something between them, so I held back. I didn't will things between them to end, but when they did, a part of me was thrilled."

"I know the feeling."

"I let some time pass and then, this January, I made my feelings known to Reg."

"And they were reciprocated?"

Max nodded. His gaze turned to the photographs on the

wall, stopping at one of Reginald in his neat servant's attire – a dishy chap if ever there was one.

"Did anyone else know of your love affair?"

"Only Grace. We kept it as private as possible."

"Did Lance know?"

He shook his head, unable to look me in the eye, and it left me wondering. Loving Reginald and killing him were not necessarily mutually exclusive. People so often hurt the ones they loved and Max might be no exception. Nevertheless, having gained his trust, I didn't want to lose it. I would tread carefully.

"I'm sorry to ask, but did Reginald still have feelings for Lance?"

"I think so," said Max, "but he had feelings for a lot of chaps. Don't look so surprised!"

"Reginald played the field?"

"That's not a nice way of putting it," he said. "I didn't own him."

"Were you not jealous?"

"He didn't own me either. Love can be shared, you know."

"I have tried," I said, "but I struggle with all that."

"If we let go of possession, jealousy can go with it."

"Sounds almost Marxist," I said.

"Would that be so bad?"

As a clerk at a bank, I felt it better not to answer that.

"It's not as if Doctor Fortescue's damned heterosexuals are known for their stable relationships," he continued. "So why copy them? The Fortescues might punish us for our abnormality, but they're hypocrites and unhappy to boot."

I found this whole new side to him quite revealing and a

shade attractive. Here was a man so unlike the obedient servant he was forced to play at Pendragon Rise. Here was a man who loved and protested and resisted – here was a man to be reckoned with.

"Where were you at eleven the night of the ball?"

He looked surprised by the question but not necessarily annoyed. "I was in bed. You know I wasn't allowed to attend the ball."

"You'd argued with Lance."

"I had."

"Why?"

He shook his head. I could tell I wasn't going to get much more from him.

"Did Grace wake you when she got back?"

He nodded.

"At what time?"

"I've told you, midnight."

"Are you sure?"

"Yes."

But Cyril had seen Grace arrive at ten past twelve and why would Cyril lie for the sake of ten minutes – especially as Lance was most likely murdered over an hour earlier?

"And the burning," he said.

"I beg your pardon?"

"The smell of burning woke me as well."

"What time?"

"Later. Sometime in the early hours I'd say."

"You didn't think to investigate?"

"Cook has been known to have an Ovaltine before sunrise."

"You didn't get much sleep that night." I heard the clinking of crockery next door as Margaret refilled the pot. "One more question if I may – have you ever been to Venice?"

"Venice? No. The Fortescues didn't take me to Italy."

"Did they take Reginald?"

"They did, but I wish they hadn't."

"Why?"

No answer proved forthcoming as Margaret re-entered the room.

"Mr Bigge," she said, depositing the teapot, "I don't wish to be uncivil, but I'd like to be alone with Max now. From the moment Reggie went missing, I feared the worst and now those fears have proven true. I wish to attend to my grief."

She spoke with such dignity; I couldn't help but be devastated.

"You have been most kind, Mrs Rolt," I said, getting up. "I'll let myself out."

"Good day, Selby," said Max. "I trust these words will remain private."

"They will."

I looked again at the photograph of Reginald as I left. That was the name his employers had known him by, but he was Reggie to his mother and Reg to his lover. Like Lancelot, he too had worn many masks, but at least he'd had a home where he could take them all off and still be loved. And now he had nothing at all. Why was it that the happiness of so few could ignite the hatred of so many? They called our love peculiar but theirs was morbid.

CHAPTER 20

"If the heterosexual is redeemable, then surely the homosexual is as well."

Candlelight, gin, academic discussion and the reassuring musk of the River Styx – I was on a date! My date may well have been a cold, calculating murderess, but one had to play the cards one was dealt. After meeting Margaret Rolt, I'd supped alone in Soho – a nifty little French place that did a sublime onion soup – and then taken myself for a beer at one of the pubs. I was a stone's throw from Inkerton Street. The ghastly image of poor Reginald slumped in the passenger seat was still too fresh for my liking. The question was obvious – who had driven him to that garage and handed him the laced hipflask? And just as I'd suspected Lance's killer was someone who knew him well, so I was sure this applied to Reginald as well. Often the deadliest of crimes were close to home.

"It's the hypocrisy I can't stand," said Lady Splendid. "A man like Hector Fortescue wants licence to fondle his wife in their marital bed while someone like me should be jailed."

"I can't fondle anyone in a marital bed," I added. "Because I can't get married."

It was a gin and tonic for me and a white wine for the lady.

"Precisely! It's one rule for them and be damned the rest of us."

"Do you identify as a homosexual?" I asked.

"Perish the thought. I don't need a Hungarian journalist to tell me who I am."

I had no idea who she was talking about and the look on my face attested to that.

"Karl Maria Kertbeny," she explained, "he coined the term some sixty years ago – and 'heterosexual' for that matter."

"Surely to aid our cause, though."

"The cause of well-to-do European men, doubtlessly, but hardly the likes of me."

"Who is the likes of you?" I felt quite bold. It was a question I'd been yearning to ask.

"I identify as many things."

"Such as?"

"Wazhazhe."

"Bless you."

Her eyes narrowed. My joke hadn't proven a funny one.

"I'm sorry," I mumbled. "That was rude."

"Say that again, but louder," she commanded.

"I'm very sorry," I repeated.

"There are plenty of men who'd fill your seat, Mr Bigge. Don't be trying."

"It's the gin speaking."

"Then shut it up."

Suitably reprimanded (and just a mite aroused), I let Lady S continue.

"My mother is a Wazhazhe woman – she belongs to the Osage Nation of Turtle Island."

"I haven't heard of that one."

"Yes, you have. It's also known as North America. My father's one of you lot."

"A well-to-do European man?"

"One of those tiresome English adventurers who thinks fun is studying natives in their local habitat. Except he was rather surprised to discover the natives were even richer than him."

I cocked an eyebrow.

"Our Nation struck oil decades ago. Many of us made millions."

"I say, that sounds like rather good luck."

"It wasn't."

Her brow clouded. She placed a finger on the rim of the glass and slowly began to circle it. What she saw in that glass I didn't know, but perhaps, like many of us, she found escape.

"You know death," she said.

"A little."

"That oil brought death on a scale unimaginable. And it hasn't ended. White men will not share."

Every day I was made aware of the bent of my love but never the shade of my skin. Still, it was the injustice of the former that helped me better understand the injustice of the latter.

"I don't want to talk about it tonight," she said, her usual archness gone. "After marrying my father, my mother left for

England, taking some of the family with her – hoping to escape the curse. As of yet, our luck hasn't run out."

I knew enough of history to know those native to North America were the victims of the English, French and Dutch, to name but a few. Cowboys and Indians in the Wild West was a game I'd played as a child. Evidently for Lady Splendid and one side of her family it was no game at all.

"And all that," she said, "just to reveal one part of who I am."

"I imagine you contain multitudes."

"Are you quoting Whitman?"

I nodded.

"Please don't. Some of the things he wrote about the Indian ought never to be repeated."

"You must dislike Hector Fortescue's work as well," I said, swapping one racialist for another.

"Your white doctors don't invent new words to explain, they invent them to imprison, and anyone who tries to escape is punished. I will not be bound by their vocabulary."

"You must have hated being his patient."

"What makes you think I was?"

"He told me."

"Whatever happened to the Hippocratic Oath?"

"Hypocritical, more like it."

As far as dates went, I had no idea how I was doing. Was the attraction she'd felt for me at the ball waning? Or was she deciding between a stone to the head or a hipflask of cyanide?

"It was my father's idea to send me to him. My mother didn't approve. She knew I wasn't ill, but he had to be convinced I was incurable. Suffice it to say, I'm not close to my father."

"When was this, if you don't mind my asking?"

"Of course I mind, but I assume if we are to bed, you want reassurance that I'm not a murderer."

"You wish to bed me!?"

"Why else are we here?"

"I… I was starting to worry you were going off me."

"Not yet. Compared to many men with skin as pale as yours, you're mildly refreshing."

Mildly refreshing, cheers to that!

"I was sent for *treatment* in April of 1928. Hector tried to make a man of me. It didn't last a month."

"Did he get you eating flaked corn?"

"That was the least of my concerns. He told me not to cross my legs and never to place one ankle behind the other. I was to remove any trace of make-up and always wear a shirt and tie – the more starch the better. He even suggested I find a wife."

We laughed.

"And before you ask, that was when I first met Lancelot."

"He was very handsome," I said.

"He was."

We smiled. It was nice to have something in common.

"Could you tell?" I asked.

"Please! There was one afternoon when I turned up for my appointment but Hector wasn't there – held up on the Underground, as it transpired."

"The worst of fates."

"I can think of worse. I waited in his study. A few minutes became a few too many and eventually Lance appeared to apologise on behalf of his father. I told him it was to be my last appointment anyway. My case was terminal."

"You actually said those words?"

"I did. He was shocked. And as I left the room, I kissed him."

My mouth gaped.

"I told him to meet me at The Prancing Mare that night."

She referenced a pub near the Seven Dials. One I'd never frequented.

"It's hard enough for a woman to get a drink in this city, let alone one with darker skin."

"Did he come?"

"Not quite. He shilly-shallied on the street, lacking the courage to come inside. So, I took him down an alley and introduced him to a world of pleasure I knew he'd been longing to discover."

"Were you his first?"

"I was. I could tell he found me peculiar but my feminine appearance made it easier. More acceptable. He could trick himself into believing he wasn't straying too far from that straight-and-narrow path. And I aided him in that deception."

"That can't have been too pleasant for you."

She was a little taken aback by the sentiment and I was pleased to demonstrate I wasn't all insensitive jokes and saucy innuendo. There was a heart in my chest somewhere.

"The spring of 1928 was a difficult time for me." She sipped on her white wine. "I'd been arrested."

"I'm sorry to hear it."

"Fortunately, my mother has deep pockets, so my time in prison was brief. But this city is not safe for me when I express this part of who I am – a part that my mother's people accept."

"The Osage Nation accepts you as a woman?"

"It's not as simple as that. We inhabit a different cosmos to yours. Many of my ancestors have lived beyond the bifurcation your colonisers imposed and been honoured for it. We know that all life is sacred." She paused to think on a world I could barely imagine. "But here in London I am far from that world, and while I have my family, we are few. It makes me lonely."

"You must struggle to belong," I said, speaking for myself as well.

"I exist between many worlds, some of them at war with the others. But I still believe peace is possible."

I knew my journey was not like hers; there were whole mountainscapes I had not climbed, deserts I hadn't crossed, winds not endured, but I still knew conflict within, that fecund seed of conflict without. And I knew that desire to be more than the battles one fought.

"I was very lonely then," she continued. "I took what I could get and Lance was to hand. There was passion and a passing glimmer of something more, but it soon extinguished. Besides, seducing the doctor's son felt a fitting parting shot."

"I say, you're not one to be underestimated."

"You don't know the half of it!"

We clinked glasses.

"Did you meet Reginald when you were there?"

"Briefly."

I left a suggestive silence.

"But nothing happened, if you must know."

I took her word for it but filed it away under *possible lies* all the same.

"Now, there's something I've been meaning to tell you," she

said. "But you must promise you won't accuse me of murder."

"I'll try my best."

"I woke up very early this morning and simply couldn't get back to sleep. There were words ringing in my ears."

"Which ones?"

"The ones I heard outside the Albert Hall that night."

"You can remember more?"

She nodded and my heart somersaulted. Another clue – I felt like I'd won a hand of Blackjack. Theodora would be delighted.

"You've been lying to him, to all of us."

I said nothing for a moment as I let the words settle in. It had been so cold outside the Hall – all the fun happening within. Lady Splendid enjoying a moment of pleasure, and not yards away, Lance was breathing his last.

"Was it Lance who spoke?"

"I can't be sure. One pale educated voice sounds so like another."

"How could you betray him?" I said, repeating the first sentence she'd overheard. *"You've been lying to him, to all of us."*

My theory of the lovers' tiff was reaffirmed. A few tables away, three men burst into a peal of laughter and somewhere else a glass went falling to the floor, shattering against the old, pocked floorboards.

"This was just around eleven?"

She nodded.

"You didn't see who Lance was talking to?"

"I was too busy kissing the Scotsman's cheeks."

"Which ones?"

She dabbed at an invisible speck of dust on the side of her lip.

"It could have been a woman speaking," I mused.

"Of course! But I think it's important that when it comes to these murders, you know you are looking for man."

"I'm inclined to agree, but isn't that a little presumptive all the same."

"I didn't say *a* man, I said man – that straight-backed, white-skinned, seed-sowing progenitor of the race." She stopped for breath and glugged down more wine.

"Hector Fortescue's cure," I said.

"Exactly, the gospel of man according to your doctors and politicians. We threaten that. Whether we enjoy wearing dresses or opening our arseholes to penises, what we do is sacrilegious and we must be punished for it, just as Lancelot was. Whatever the sex of your killer, they are someone who is devoutly committed to the gospel of man."

She got up, to a round of silent applause.

"But does that gospel include heterosexuality?" I asked.

"That depends on the preacher and whether or not he considers it perverse. Now, if you'll excuse me, I must avail myself of the facilities."

I watched her cross the bar, admiring the sway of her hips and the curve of her buttocks under her silken dress. What a woman! My mind clouded. *You've been lying to him, to all of us.* Who had accosted Lance outside the Hall and accused him of treachery and deception? Or was it the other way around and Lance had accused someone else? Either way, the argument had escalated – one of them must have crossed the road and the other followed. Into Kensington Gardens, past the statue of Albert and then across the grass. Perhaps more words had been spoken – angry, bitter, hostile – until a single blow had felled Lancelot. And then a deception most scandalous had ensued as the murderer returned to the ball disguised as Harlequin. Or their accomplice had stepped in to play that part.

Once again, love struck me as the motive. Max had said Lance was no longer romantically involved with Reginald but heavily implied there was someone else. Who was this secret lover waiting in the wings? *How could you betray him?* Had Lance been having two affairs and one had been caught out? *You've been lying to him, to all of us.* It was clear Lance had lived a double life. Maybe he'd lived a triple life as well. After all those years of repression, perhaps one lover hadn't been enough to sate his passions. Then again, Max had spoken on behalf of a less-possessive way to love, although Lance might have struggled with that, given his upbringing.

My thoughts were distracted by a man sitting on the far side of the room – the one with the glasses and bushy beard. He'd been there the other night but Martin the Mole hadn't known who he was. What if he was following me? What if he was the unexpected criminal mastermind behind all this, waiting to strike again? He was seated at an angle, allowing me a good view of his profile, and despite the facial hair, a rather alarming bell rang in my mind.

"Buggery," I whispered.

Heart verging dangerously close to my mouth, I took myself across the room. Here was quite a different class of criminal. I pictured a great torrent of water running deep underground – a subterranean river wanting only to do what all rivers do, flow. And then I pictured a dam, blocking the path of the river and bleeding it dry.

"Good evening," I said, taking the seat next to the man, "I don't think we've met."

The look of abject horror that crossed his face proved his identity but at once.

"I'm Selby," I said, offering him my hand.

"Er… George," he replied, touching my hand briefly as if I might transmit a communicable disease.

"I saw you here the other night. I saw you looking at me."

He squirmed.

"I like your beard."

"Thanks," he mumbled.

"You thirsty?" I eyed him up and down suggestively, terrifying him yet more. "Perhaps a little sip?"

He shook his head.

"Selby! I leave you for one minute!" It was Lady Splendid. Her toilet complete, she towered over the both of us, wafting a rather appealing lavender scent.

"I want to introduce you to George," I said. "He's my new friend."

"Is he now?" she said, eyeing him sceptically. She held out her hand and the so-called George quickly shook it. But Lady S tutted and her hand remained aloft. I watched in delight as he leant gingerly forward and briefly kissed her fingertips.

"I've got bad news for you," she said, skewering him with her stare.

"You do?" the hapless George replied.

"I'm not performing tonight."

I had to suppress a giggle as George gawped, none the wiser.

"Perhaps you could offer him a private performance," I said.

"Now, now, Selby, only I trade my wares. I do like your beard."

She reached out to stroke it. He tried to duck away but wasn't quick enough as her fingers laced through the hairs.

"Are you that hairy all over?" she asked.

He pushed her hand roughly away and sprang to his feet.

"My, my, you are strong," she said, tittering.

"Good… good evening," George managed as he bolted from his corner table. Lady S took his place and we watched him retreat for the exit. He vanished down the stairs.

"That beard was as real as my pearls," she said critically. "A friend of yours?"

"Quite the opposite – an avowed enemy. One Detective Sergeant Stovell."

"Pray tell?"

"In a moment," I replied. "We need to tell Martin."

We got to our feet and made for Martin's hole in the wall. To my surprise, he wasn't perusing a magazine filled with male erotica but was in fact reading a dog-eared copy of *The Mysterious Affair at Styles* – a good read, even if the ending was a little too guessable and one aspect of the twist had rather irked Theo.

"You upsetting my customers?" he asked, giving me a disapproving look over his pince-nez.

"Just the ones who are undercover policemen."

"Shit. If you'll excuse my French, Lady Splendid."

"I'm not that much of a lady."

"It was Sergeant Stovell, by the way," I added. "He works for Chief Inspector Lisle."

"I've heard of him," said Martin disapprovingly. "He's got a reputation for queer-hunting. But this isn't his turf."

"Whose is it?" I asked.

"Someone who has a few secrets he wants kept."

He alluded to the bribes and backhanders that kept the underworld afloat in the face of all those who'd see it drained.

"Right," said Martin, clambering off his stool to reveal he really was very short. "We're closing early tonight and I need to make a few calls."

"Why do you think he's sniffing around?" asked Lady S.

"They wish to drain the river," I said solemnly. "And they've got help from Helena Fortescue and the National Vigilance Association."

"The witch!"

"It wouldn't be the first time they've stuck their nose into things," said Martin, "and if they're not careful I'll chop it off."

He straightened his back and arched his shoulders – and despite his diminished stature, he looked remarkably brave.

"Thank you," he said to me. "You get yourself home and stay safe."

"I will."

He gave us back our coats and off we went. As we descended the narrow staircase, we heard Martin clapping his hands and announcing early closure to the remaining customers. His words were met with a chorus of protestations but they'd soon shut up once they knew what was at stake. Back outside, Lady S and I huddled close together.

"I was at one of those awful Vigilance meetings last night," I explained, "and he was there. I noted a red rash on his cheek and a small quantity of paste near his ear."

"Glue?"

"Exactly. He's been scouting out this place."

"Martin will know what to do," said Lady S confidently. "This isn't the first time someone's threatened to close the Styx. We can't afford to lose it." She wrapped her arm in mine. "It's one of the few places where I am neither too dark nor too feminine. I've been barred from so many places, even the dances at Frank's Goldmine. Britain might lack the laws of North America but you find ways of excluding all the same."

"I… I'm dreadfully sorry. If there's anything I can do."

She laughed – a lovely sound – and I didn't mind it was at my expense. I doubtlessly deserved it.

"If you could undo the British Empire, that would be fantastic."

"That can be next week's task."

I pulled her a little closer to me, our bodies warm in the cold.

"Now, what were we speaking of earlier?" she asked. "Something to do with draining the river."

"I say! How very forthright."

"Suddenly so coy, Mr B," she said with a fruity chuckle.

"No," I replied earnestly, "I would very much like to bed you."

"Good. But I'm afraid I can't offer you a bed as I'm staying with Mother at the moment."

"As it happens," I said, "darling Theo said if all went well we could treat ourselves to his master bedroom."

"Providing I hadn't wrapped my hands around your throat and strangled the life from you?"

"Precisely. Although speaking of wrapping hands around—"

"Yes please!" she squealed, with a raucous laugh. "Let's get out of this cold at once."

And that we did, almost running back to Wilkington Mews.

Theo had left the door key under the mat – he too was on a date but hadn't specified with whom – and soon we were up in his bedroom. The reclining nude female watched us from above the bed. She was in for a treat!

"I was meaning to ask—" I began, but Lady S was quick to place a finger on my lips.

"You've had enough questions for the night," she said. "I didn't murder Lancelot and presumably neither did you."

I shook my head.

"Good." She began stroking my neck, her fingers delightfully cold, but then she paused. "Although, if I'm to be completely honest, I did speak with him."

"When?"

"Early on, before ten."

"What did he say?"

"*Sorry*. He apologised for not having treated me very well and for his father's awful treatment. Then he wished me farewell."

"That was all?"

She nodded, lost briefly in thought. "No more questions."

Despite my obedience, there were still so many things I wished to say and so many more I wanted to ask – none pertaining to murder but all to do with this most beautiful object of my affection. If Lady Splendid objected to the notion of containing multitudes then she was something else entirely – a lake, perhaps, with depths to be plumbed and mountains to reflect. Or a river, bursting its banks and washing that great chalk circle from the ground. She was the wind that rippled the waters and rushed through the city streets, whipping the homburgs from our heads. She seemed a force of nature. Or maybe she would have objected to that description as well – too reminiscent of the noble savage so beloved of those pale-faced enlightenment chaps. Maybe she was more than metaphor. Maybe she didn't contain multitudes because she was uncontainable.

As the night unfolded, I left all my questions unspoken as we communicated only with our bodies. Skin against skin under the big bed's blankets we warmed to one another's touch. We kissed slowly then fast then slow again. Her mouth was hot and wet, as was mine, and it was a thrill to meet so much more of her. Her hand was gentle heat against my nipples and my tummy as she ran her fingers through the hairs beneath my belly button and down to the thatch of pubic hair. Our members – like well-used thermometers – went up. Hers fitted neatly into my hand then my mouth. The favour was returned. And as the night wore on, we plumbed further depths to find new heat and, despite the city's relentless chill – of temperature and law – we stayed warm.

CHAPTER 21

I didn't look awful but I didn't look my best. My hair was tousled, my eyes bloodshot and the skin beneath them was light purple. The weak Sunday sunlight penetrated the undrawn curtains as I sat at Theodora's dressing table, entirely naked, save for a bright red kiss on my forehead. That was the proof the night before hadn't been a dream and hopefully the promise that Lady Splendid would return one day. I looked a little longer at myself – the stubble growing on my chin, the few hairs sprouting in the middle of my chest and those circling my nipples. The body before me was twenty-six years of age and regretting its current lack of clothing, my scrotum in particular. It was a body Lady S had seemed to like. I liked it too, sometimes, at least on my good days – and I hoped there would be more of those to come. For most of my life, I'd never thought about whether this body was queer or normal or homosexual. I hadn't considered whether my attractions were simply my attractions or the expression of an essence within – something concrete, able to be labelled and called an identity. It was enough to make the mind boggle.

I thought on Lancelot and his reflection. For so long he must have seen a pervert – a loathsome being secretly lusting after the bodies of other men. But to act on that lust would damn him. So he'd dammed those desires and repressed his peculiar nature. But repression wasn't enough when respectability was everything. He'd had to direct his attractions towards women instead. Yet even that ran the risk of perversion unless he found a singular woman to wed. With his father's blessing, then, and only then, would he be able to act on his desires. This was the respectable, if protracted, route to middle-class pleasure, verified by the new science – the recipe for turning a morbid sexual passion into a normal one.

But at some point, he'd learned a most valuable lesson: it wasn't passion that was morbid but passion's repression. Bottling up one's feelings for too long was a most dangerous thing, violent even. His peculiar nature had refused its suppression and sought release. When it came to Lady Splendid and Reginald, he certainly hadn't waited for wedlock. Lance had lived a whole life away from Pendragon Rise and what torment this must have caused – torn between normality and perversion. Then, on a cold November eve, someone else's bottled-up feelings had shattered the glass that contained them. Only a truly morbid passion could have resulted in such violence.

"Well, well, the plot thickens!"

This was Theo's take on good morning as I ambled into his kitchen – the smell of burnt toast surprisingly alluring despite the added charcoal.

"She didn't have the heart to wake you," said Theo. "Apparently you were sleeping like a baby."

"Will she be back?"

"Not today. Scrambled or fried?"

"Scrambled, please."

Theo was at the stove, a rare sight, and began cracking some eggs into a bowl. I plonked myself down on the rickety wooden chair at the equally rickety wooden table. Theo wasn't one for sensible furniture – none of the chairs matched, one wasn't even a chair but a stool, and the table looked as if it had been caught in the crossfire of no man's land. A bounteous array of preserved fruit spreads lay before me – strawberry and raspberry jam, marmalade with great chunks of shredded orange peel and something else orange that I hoped to be apricot.

"Hector Fortescue wouldn't approve of all this," I remarked.

I took one of the slices of toast and brushed some of the charcoal off with the knife. Theo whisked the eggs with a fork.

"Don't you have a cook for that?"

"Aren't you droll this morning," he replied. "Lady S said you interrogated her last night."

"It was the least I could do. I think she enjoyed it."

"And she told me what else she'd overheard."

"*You've been lying to him*," I quoted, as I smothered the toast with a generous layer of butter. "*To all of us*."

He nodded. "Sounds like Lance was spreading his wild oats."

"He hardly seemed the type," I said, dipping my knife into the marmalade jar.

"Excuse me," chided Theo, "there's a teaspoon for that."

I quickly changed condiment-spreading implement.

"If Lance was romantically involved with someone," he said, "then who?"

"Well, Lady Splendid told me she was his first lover of the queer variety. And Max said Lance and Reginald were once lovers."

"Not forgetting Jackie," said Theo, pouring milk into the whisked eggs.

"But there must be someone else – the mystery lover."

"Any ideas?"

"No names," I said, "but a few people have mentioned the Fortescues' trip to Italy. Apparently, Lance came back a changed man."

"For better or worse?"

"His father seems to think it helped cure him, but given what we know, he may well have fallen in love."

"It's a shame there aren't any convenient Italians to hand," said Theo, chopping off a scandalously thick slab of butter and dropping it into the pan.

"*How could you betray him?*" I said, quoting Lady Splendid's initial overhearing. "If the argument had been between Lance and one of his lovers then the phrase would surely have been: *how could you betray* me?"

Theo lit the stove with his fancy lighter and the flames sprung to life. My tummy growled.

"That suggests," he said, "that someone else was speaking on behalf of the wronged party."

"Clearly someone close to them."

"Dangerously close."

Silence lingered as the butter melted in the saucepan and

Theo poured in the milky egg concoction. The heat was on low as Theo stirred the eggs with a wooden spoon. Had Lance and his mystery lover shared a domestic moment such as this? Perhaps Lance held a feather duster as the lover polished their shoes. Had Lance thought he'd finally found someone able to cherish his lonely heart? But maybe whispered promises and gentle caresses had turned to jealousy and control, then a lethal violence. I shook my head. I was getting ahead of myself. I couldn't know the mystery man and his motives until we found him.

"There's someone else we should consider," he said. "Shovel."

"Lance and Sergeant Stovell having an illicit affair! How much were you drinking last night?"

"No, no," he said, waving the spoon, "but think of what Lady S heard – *You've been lying to him, to all of us.* That final part suggests a group."

I mumbled assent through my mouthful of toast and was relieved to see the wooden spoon return to the eggs.

"Well done for spotting him last night."

"Why, thank you." I beamed at this rare compliment. "I knew the bearded stranger looked familiar but it was only when I recalled the paste you use for your moustache that I finally painted all the letters."

"You did what?"

"Sorry, mixing my metaphors – that the crossword was complete."

"It's far from complete but I'd say we've inked in another line." A look of alarm suddenly crossed his face. "Selby, why's the toast for our eggs not buttered? Chip chop!"

I swiftly did as commanded while Theo finished scrambling

the eggs, and moments later, we tucked in to our hearty breakfast. I was generous with the brown sauce and Theo opted not to pass judgement. Yesterday had been an eventful one that had ended in a most memorable night. After a few bites, we returned to murder.

"What if," said Theo, "Lance was privy to Helena and Chief Inspector Lisle's plan to drain the river?"

"And he gave the game away."

"Maybe he'd had a change of heart and his betrayal was of Lisle and the Vigilance lot. *You've been lying to him, to all of us.*"

"And someone wanted to silence him," I said, picking up the thread. "His mother perhaps? It's not very vigilant having a queer son. There's her ever-faithful secretary as well, who turned up at the house that night uninvited."

We mused a moment as we munched.

"We've almost forgotten the plague doctor," said Theo. "We still don't know who it was under that costume."

"Or who was wearing the second harlequin costume."

"And why an empty suitcase was found not far from Lance's body."

"And if those ashes in the kitchen and disordered bottles in the cupboard are connected."

"Oh dear," said Theo solemnly, "you're not thinking what I'm thinking?"

"That the Fortescues' cook brutally murdered her employer's son and one of her colleagues?"

We smiled, despite ourselves.

"What we need," said Theo, once he'd polished off his plate, "is to return to the scene of the crime."

"Not that awful garage, please," I protested.

"The other one – the Royal Albert Hall. All those costumes, and comings and goings, it baffles the mind. But if we can see where it happened, then we might get some more words on the grid."

"As far as ideas go," I said, "that one is approaching rather good."

CHAPTER 22

I enjoyed Hyde Park as any Londoner might – for Sunday afternoon strolls and listening to the orators at Speakers' Corner. I also enjoyed it as a subset of Londoners did – for sex. My first time had been in my early, rather naïve, days in the city. I'd got lost on a Thursday evening and approached a young guardsman for directions, who then promptly led me up the garden path. At the end of said path, he took my hand and placed it to his crotch. He asked me if I'd like to suck it and I almost choked. When he requested a fee, I was even more surprised, but paid it to avoid a fuss. Apparently, this was a profitable place for renters, especially the military sort. Perhaps Lance had been heading off to the park for a secret assignation with his mystery lover.

Theo was now Theodora and we were sitting on the same bench at the edge of Kensington Gardens. At least the weather, if not the temperature, was on side today as a weak sun lit the scene. The autumnal colours were making way for winter's darker palette and a few men pottered about the park with rakes, sweeping the fallen leaves from the grass and dormant flowerbeds. It was most morbid to think Lance's body had been found nearby, but the truth demanded our discomfort. Theodora produced her timetable once again, with a few additions:

10pm – S & I arrive at RAH; Lady S says hello (she also talked with Lance).
Helena already abed! allegedly!
10.20 – S bumps into Lance and Reggie at the bar – where did R go?
10.30 – Hector to bed (no alibi), Percy dozes in drawing room (Cyril confirms).
10.45 – Cyril arrives at Pendragon Rise, wakes Percy.
10.50ish – Lance leaves dancefloor, waves to us.
Lady S overhears Lance having an argument.
LANCE MURDERED!?
11ish – phoney Lance returns (can't be Grace or Jackie in disguise, we saw them), followed by plague doctor (who? where's costume? burnt!?)
11.15 – I bump into Jackie, Selby joins soon.
11.40 – I get Jackie into a taxi (does she stay in it?)
11.45ish – plague doctor departs, then Grace, then phoney Lance.

11.50 – I join S in the main Hall, Lady S bids us goodnight.

~~**poor Lance coshed**~~ no! coshed earlier.

Midnight – S & I watch the fireworks.

Grace back? Max corroborates?

12.10 – Grace back?

Cyril sees her with caped figure. Who?

2 – bed!

"I don't know if this is a help or a hindrance," she said.

"Suspects abound, unfortunately."

"Let's put them to one side and address the logistics of this rather elaborate plan. It would have taken some planning."

"Worthy of our criminal mastermind," I added.

"Or mistressmind," said Theodora. "First things first, Lance leaves the ball at ten minutes to eleven, giving us a merry wave as he goes. All very gay, but we'll never know what look his mask was concealing."

"*It doesn't matter any more,*" I quoted. "That's what he said to me in the bar. Perhaps he knew he was going to his death."

Theodora shivered. "He heads outside whereupon he meets someone. They immediately start arguing, overheard by Lady Splendid. *How could you betray him? You've been lying to him, to all of us.*"

"You say *immediately*," I added, "but, if we're to be precise, we don't know exactly *when* Lady S overheard the argument – a few minutes here or there could make all the difference."

"They could," Theodora concurred without so much as a

sarcastic rejoinder. "Presumably, the argument escalates as Lance crosses the road and enters the gardens."

"An odd place to go, especially if he was worried for his life. Why rush off into the dark when he could have remained somewhere more populous?

"Another good point," she said. "Well done."

I sensed a trap.

"Then our killer raises the stone," she continued, "which they must have taken from one of these flowerbeds in advance."

"Unless they'd brought another weapon with them but changed their mind at the last minute."

"Or they'd chosen the stone precisely because it made the murder look unplanned."

"Any which way," I continued, "poor Lance dies a cold and lonely death."

We looked out across Kensington Gardens – so stately and commanding in the bright wintry sun. A few people strolled, dressed heavily in coats and furs and scarves. I was glad to have remembered my gloves. I couldn't count the number of pairs I'd left behind in various places. Gilded Prince Albert shone resplendently under the pagoda. To think what those ageless eyes of his had seen. We left the bench and headed back for the Hall.

"Two possible paths followed," said T. "One, the killer had arrived dressed as Harlequin with the second mask to hand."

"That would have given Lance a shock."

"Or perhaps the killer brought the costume in the suitcase and changed quickly."

"Miraculously so, given they'd have to sprint back to the

Hall, making it appear Lance had only been absent for a matter of moments."

"Ten minutes, to be precise," corrected T.

"An awfully narrow timeframe within which to complete all the aforementioned tasks."

"Which suggests path number two – an accomplice. As the killer vanishes into the night, so someone else, already dressed as Harlequin, slips into the Hall to dance the eve away."

We had our backs to Kensington Gardens now, and crossed the road to the Hall. As splendid as ever, the great brick bosom commanded the gaze of any passer-by, indifferent to the murderous affairs of man. The nearest entrance was the one we'd all used – Lady S for her liaison, Theo and I for our trip to the fireworks and Lance for the last time in his life.

"In a mask that was very subtly different to the one Lance was wearing," I added.

"Was it a mistake, do you think?"

"I don't think our killer makes many of those."

"Like me," said Theodora before I could beat her to it.

"What if it was a test set by the killer," I said.

"To see who could spot the difference?"

"A dastardly game of some sort. Perhaps we have our very own Moriarty?"

"Let's not get carried away. We're not successful enough to warrant an arch-nemesis."

"One thing we've forgotten," I said, "is the original mask. It wasn't found near Lance's body and it wasn't the one that ended up in the car with Reginald's body. I wonder where it got to?"

A nearby pigeon ruffled its feathers at us, fed up of having to share the pavement. Pigeons didn't have to worry about labelling their attractions normal or perverse, they just got to peck dirt and harry pedestrians.

"Now, this whole plan could have been executed fairly smoothly," said T, "if it weren't for our other mystery figure. I assume the second Harlequin intended simply to dance for a while before vanishing into the ether. Little did they know that the plague doctor had arrived. Perhaps the clown did their best to avoid the bird, but things eventually came to a head and Grace was forced to intervene."

"Which implies that both Grace and the plague doctor know who was under that mask," I said.

"And are covering for them?"

"Perhaps inadvertently. They might not have connected the second Harlequin to Lance's murder."

We mused in silence for a while as we circumnavigated the Hall, bringing ourselves back to the entrance we'd used on that fatal night. What fun we'd assumed was ahead of us – a night of artfully enjoyed decadence and debauchery. Nearby was the other grand statue of Prince Albert and at its base stood a man I recognised – Max. I tapped Theodora's arm and pointed. He wore his own suit, not his uniform, and a trilby, cocked at an angle. He looked very dapper. We slowly approached. The weak sun shone on his face, his head was tilted upwards. I followed his gaze and realised he wasn't admiring Victoria's late husband but the figures beneath him.

"That's Europe," he said, not bothering to say hello. He pointed up at one of the statues. "Nice dress, isn't it? She even gets a crown."

He spoke of an elegant woman of indeterminate age carved in black stone. She was splendidly apparelled.

"America doesn't look too bad," he continued, indicating the next one. "But a little more violent with her axe and bow."

Slightly odd additions, I thought, but so be it. Max walked further around the base and we went with him. He pointed to the third.

"That's Africa, looking the most savage of the lot."

Unlike the others, her dress covered only her lower half, leaving both her breasts on display. He took a few more steps and stared at the fourth statue.

"Finally, there's Asia," he said. "In case you're wondering, that's a banana leaf she's got there. I don't like bananas."

I had barely given these statues a second glance but now I learned they had a significance all of their own.

"As for old Albert, he won't have to worry about catching a chill – that big robe reaches all the way to his thick boots."

Completely unaware of the four women beneath him was the Prince, standing atop the pillar and surveying the Empire upon which the sun never set.

"All those white people at the ball dressed as tribesmen and savages, it makes me wonder," said Max bitterly. "If the racialist shoe were on the other foot, you lot wouldn't find the joke funny at all."

"I assure you," said Theodora, "we're not laughing."

I thought back to my school days and some of the jokes we boys made. We used to laugh so loudly. I couldn't look Max in the eye and tell him I wasn't a part of all that. But truth was acquainted with change and sometimes one followed the other.

"How did you know men were dressed like that when you didn't go to the ball?" I asked, thinking I had him.

"I went last year," he replied calmly, "and I hardly credit your lot for originality."

Touché.

"Costumes are proving rather troubling for Miss Smythe and I."

He stared at me, a mite uncomfortably this time.

"We think whoever murdered Lance was dressed as Harlequin."

"Then tell the police," he said.

"We don't trust them," replied Theodora.

"To get to the bottom of that mystery we need to solve another," I said. "One that has been puzzling me from the very start – the mystery of the four tickets. Why did Reginald buy so many and who were they for?"

He shrugged, as if he didn't care, but he wasn't the best of actors.

"One for him and one for Grace – those two had been granted permission to attend after all. Number three went to Lance – despite what he'd told his parents. What about the fourth?"

I hated to take a leaf from the chief inspector's book but I left a pregnant pause – they worked wonders on the guilty (and served only to irritate the innocent).

"I think he gave it to his chum," I said, answering my own question. "The one who'd been forbidden from going."

"Me?"

"I assume you attended to your evening tasks and went to bed. Then, when the appropriate hour arrived, you took yourself to the ball dressed head to toe in a costume."

"Look, I wasn't there and I certainly wasn't wearing that damned clown costume."

"I never said your costume was of a clown."

"You bloody implied it when you said Lance's killer was dressed up as another harlequin."

"I didn't say *another* harlequin, I simply said *as* Harlequin. They could have been wearing Lance's original costume."

"What, covered in blood?" said Max.

"What makes you think Lance was dead by then?"

"I... I don't know. You're confusing me."

"All along the assumption has been Lance died around midnight."

"Then he did," he said, his tone nearing anger.

"But perhaps you think otherwise."

"Stop it!"

"But you do know there was a second Harlequin because you met them."

Finally, I'd got him! Of course, he'd always known more than he was letting on, despite what he'd told me at Margaret Rolt's. In my heart of hearts, I struggled to believe him a murderer, but hadn't so many people killed the ones they cared for?

"I can't stop, Max. Not when I'm so near the truth. You know there was a second Harlequin that night because you met them. You went up to them on the dancefloor, expecting Lance, only to discover someone else was wearing the costume.

"And that explains the mystery of the fourth ticket – it was for you. There was no way you'd let Doctor Fortescue rob you of your night of fun. Reginald got you the ticket and you went to the ball dressed as a plague doctor."

"So what if I did?"

"Are you acknowledging it?" asked Theodora.

"I didn't hurt anyone."

"But we think you know someone who did."

The anger left his face, replaced by unhappy comprehension. His shoulders slumped, and in that moment, I saw the man who'd lost one of his best friends and lovers. My heart went out to him.

"We think whoever was wearing that second costume was involved in Lance's murder," said T.

"No… no, that can't be true."

"Why not?"

"You're barking up the wrong tree," he said.

"Who was under that mask, Max?" she implored.

He could no longer look at us. He stared at Asia but she was unable to speak, merely the object of other men's creation. He cast his gaze away from the Hall and its statues to look out at the grand houses of South Kensington. They stared back, caring nothing for the affairs of his troubled heart. He took a deep breath and exhaled, a plume of mist surrounding his face.

"It was Reg."

"Oh dear," said Theodora quietly, "oh dear."

"Are you sure?" I asked.

Max nodded solemnly.

"Then the tabloids are right," I said, and it truly pained me to say it. "A quarrel that ended in murder and suicide."

"They're wrong," said Max defensively. "Reg loved Lance. He'd never have hurt him."

"Then why was he in that costume? Why were his footprints found in that flowerbed?"

"That's what I want to know," he said urgently. "I was worried about him. There was something going on between him and Lance but I couldn't work out what."

"When was this?"

"Over the past few weeks, I think. There was something he wasn't telling me."

"Was he afraid?" I asked.

"Not afraid, but nervous, on edge."

He rubbed at the back of his neck putting on his own demonstration of being on edge.

"It's all right," said T. "You can tell us. If the information is sensitive, it stays with us."

Unless it pertains to murder, I might have added.

"Reg wasn't troubled like Lance," he said. "He liked what he liked and that was that. And he was a romantic with a soft spot for well-spoken gents."

Our eyes met and I didn't need to blush – my cheeks were pink enough from the cold.

"He fell for Lance hard and it was all roses until it wasn't. I remember when Lance called it off. Reg spent weeks sobbing himself to sleep, forced to work in the same house as the man who'd broken his heart. They straightened things out eventually but Reg always lived in hope."

I thought on my own love affairs and the many that had lingered far longer than they should have.

"More recently I spotted the signs – Reg was getting excited about someone and I worried it was Lance."

"Did he confirm that?" I asked.

"No, he swore they weren't lovers. I wouldn't have minded, I just wanted to hear him tell me the truth."

"You believed him?"

"I think so. But I did confront Lance. I wanted to hear it from the horse's mouth."

"That's what your argument was about?" said T.

"I told him he shouldn't lead Reg on and he told me to back off – although with words more forceful than that. I called him a brute, and one thing led to another, then he ended up on his rump on the floor."

I laughed despite myself. "Lance said you bumped into each other."

"He was lying," said Max and even he had a slight smile.

"Did you later slash his portrait?" I asked.

He shook his head. "That wasn't me."

"But you did argue with Reginald at the ball."

"I hadn't expected to find him under that costume," he acknowledged. "I asked him what the bleeding hell was going on and he said if I knew what was best for myself I'd go home. I didn't like that one bit, and I admit, I got quite upset."

I remembered – the grand plague doctor with his fearsome beak and round dead eyes, gesticulating expressively at the colourful harlequin. It was like a scene from Shakespeare – one of his tragedies, mind, not a comedy.

"If I'd known that was the last time I'd ever see him I… I'd have told him…"

He couldn't finish his sentence, pinching the exposed skin of his wrist so as not to cry. Theodora stepped towards him and placed an arm around his shoulders.

"You would have told him you loved him," she said.

He didn't correct her. His silence was his assent. Two deaths had broken so many hearts. And somewhere out there the murderer was laughing.

"Where did you go after that?" I asked.

"Back to Pendragon Rise."

"With Grace?"

"She caught up with me."

"And you arrived at the house at ten minutes past midnight."

He nodded. "I might have paused en route a few times to vent my anger."

"We understand why you lied about going to the ball," said T. "But when you told us Grace woke you upon her return, why did you plump for midnight?"

"I was nervous, wasn't I? It was bad enough with you two poking your noses in and you'd already told Grace the murder might have been around midnight. We needed alibis."

"We now believe Lance was murdered closer to eleven," I said.

"Then my lie was pointless."

He rubbed his gloved hands together and blew onto them. All this standing around was getting mighty chilly. We should have absconded to a café.

"Once you were back," I said, "how long did you wait before burning your costume?"

"What are you talking about?"

"But you were in a rush and got ashes all over the kitchen floor."

"That's got nothing to do with me," he said, sounding angry again.

"And you didn't quite finish the job. Grace found one of your gloves. She tried to hide it down the sofa but I saw her."

"Look, Selby," intervened T, "you must listen to Max – he didn't burn his costume."

"I didn't," Max affirmed, "and I've already told you – I woke in the early hours of the morning and that's when I smelt burning."

"Do you remember what time?" I asked.

"No. I fell straight back to sleep."

"Where's your costume now?"

"If you must know," he said, "it's packed away in a suitcase under my bed, not that I'll ever wear it again."

"Would you mind showing us?" I asked, opting for politeness rather than insistence.

He looked at us again, half-appealing, half-suspecting. "I want to find who did this as much as you do. It's why I came back, to see if anything came to mind."

"And has it?"

He shook his head forlornly. "Only how much I miss him."

CHAPTER 23

"Wherever I went, there you bleeding were, sticking your nose in."

Theodora was driving us from the Albert Hall, Max up front, me behind. Currently, he was critiquing my sleuthing skills.

"Selby can be a bit heavy-footed," added T.

"Heavy?" said Max. "More like an elephant."

They laughed at my expense. Delightful.

"You can't blame me for being wary," he continued.

"We don't," said T.

"I'm used to men like him treating me badly. I wasn't born into a comfortable house in south London after all."

"I was born in Horsham," I corrected. "And Theodora was born in a mansion, if we're making notes."

"Now, now, my dear!"

"Bet you went to a boarding school as well," said Max.

"I worked very hard for it," I replied.

"And a good university?"

"Oxford," I muttered.

"I think I've heard of that one," he quipped. "And I bet at every turn no one ever looked at the colour of your skin and thought you lesser for it."

"No," I replied quietly.

"My father moved here from Bombay to work the Liverpool docks. Set up his own business fixing equipment on the ships. The whites hated an Indian in business and they hated it even more when he married one of their own."

"Your parents must have been very brave," said Theodora.

"They didn't have a choice. My father fought in the Great War and do you know what he got when he came back?"

"A medal?" I hazarded.

"He got accused of stealing Englishmen's jobs. I was eleven in 1919, when the riots came. My father's offices were looted and he was attacked on the streets. One man was lynched. We had to move to a bridewell."

"Max, I am—"

"Keep your sympathy, Mr Bigge."

Theodora parked the car on Pendragon Rise but we didn't make to get out. It was clear he had more to say and it was only right that we listened, not least because I'd spent the last week suspecting him of murder.

"After the riots came the deportations. Whole families were sent packing. Mother fought tooth and nail to keep her children here while Father was paid three thousand pounds to leave. He sent her back the money."

"I never knew," said Theodora.

"Why would you? Your skin's just skin. I came down to London with my mother and siblings, and was put to work in my uncle's factory. Service seemed better than factory work and I couldn't believe my luck when the doctor took me on – him and his wife were so considerate – and Grace was friendly enough. I thought perhaps not every Englishman hates the likes of me." He let out a bitter laugh. "But I soon learned what that pair was really like."

I thought of the pamphlet the doctor had placed in my hand – the one for the betterment of our race.

"They wanted to civilise me, crush the savage within and make me a gentleman. This house is cursed. Grace, Reg and I should have fled when we had the chance."

This time we did not use the front door but followed Max down the narrow flight of steps that led one storey below. Fortunately, the ice and frost had been scraped from the steps, and grit had been added. Trying to navigate these at night, especially a cold one, would have proven very difficult. The patio was equally hazardous as Max unlocked the servants' door and led us in.

"Where does Cook keep her bottles?" I asked, as we crossed the threshold.

Max took us to the pantry and opened the door quietly. Cook could be heard next door, amongst a clatter of pans and curses. Sunday lunch was clearly proving an arduous task. A plethora of bottles, jars, tins and boxes lined the many shelves. There was enough flour for a hundred cakes, sugar for endless cups of tea, pickled vegetables, fruit preserves, and on a separate shelf, an array of poisons. With my gloves still on, I inspected them – there were the usual household standards from Brasso to arsenic (good for killing wasps). In and amongst these was a brown bottle, long opened, rather dusty and as inconspicuous as the rest. Cyanide. I wondered if the police had even bothered to dust it for fingerprints. The case was closed as far as they were concerned, but for those of us gathered, it presented a possibility – one slowly gaining in probability.

"Maybe they were wearing gloves," I muttered under my breath.

Max took us to his room next. It was small and square. There was a narrow, single bed on either side of the door, and on the far side, a tarnished mahogany wardrobe took up most of the space with a small wash basin next to it. He must have shared this room with Reginald. It would have been perfect for nightly shenanigans but difficult given the late servant's fondness for his master's late son. A threadbare rug covered the worn floorboards and a small window permitted a view of a portion of the back of the house. While the room was sparsely furnished it was not an unhappy one. There was a small painting of some colourful flowers on one of the walls and postcards above the sink.

"Lance wasn't as bad as his parents but he wasn't much better. He used to tease Reg, calling him his bit of rough trade. I didn't like that." His resentment was clear – what a minefield it must be working here. "I think Lance wanted a posh chap like himself. I know it made Reg sad but I was glad when it ended."

Max's bed was the one on the right and he knelt down and removed an old suitcase from underneath, so old in fact that the leather handle was almost worn through. From his bedside table he produced a bible, within which was the key.

"God's good at keeping secrets," he said.

He unlocked each latch. Inside were the remains of the plague doctor – the billowing black cape, the hood to cover the back of the head, the hat and that dreadful mask.

"I wore it for the drama," said Max, "and because it hides my skin. They used to stuff flowers down the beak, to ward off the stink of plague."

The unseeing eyes stared at the three of us. It was the stuff of nightmares. Just like the doctor upstairs, so this one knew the efficacy of fear. We all got the fright of our lives when someone knocked at the door. Like naughty children, we'd been caught in the act.

"Who is it?" asked Max.

"It's me." The voice belonged to Grace. "What's going on in there?"

"Nothing to worry about, we'll be out shortly."

"We?"

She opened the door and any words she was about to say died on her lips when she saw Theodora and I. She looked startled and so did we.

"Good afternoon, Grace," said Theodora, quickly taking charge. "We're just tying up a loose end."

"Which one might that be?" she said.

"The one that concerns you hiding a glove."

The two women, both alike in dignity yet desperately unequal in status, stared at one another. I was glad not to be caught in between. As unfair as it was, Theodora had rank over Grace, but both had secrets.

"It's okay," said Max calmly. "Miss Smythe and Mr Bigge are here to help."

"Are you sure about that?" she said.

"They want to know who killed Reg and Lance just as much as we do."

We waited a moment as Grace mulled this over. Prior to this I'd done a very good job at irritating her, but I tended to win people over eventually. The clattering of pans echoed down the corridor – Cook was in a mood.

"I found the glove in the flowerpot outside our front door," she said.

"I dropped it there the night of the ball," explained Max, "when I'd taken out my key."

"That's why it was damp," said Grace, looking at me. "Stuffing it between the cushions was a silly thing to do but I don't have pockets."

"I overheard some of your conversation with Max," I said.

"I know," she replied sternly.

"You told him he should have burned all the costume."

"To get rid of any evidence he was ever at that ball."

"Which he didn't do," I added.

"More fool him."

"This cost me a lot of money," protested Max.

"And could get you in prison if you're not careful."

"But why did you think any costume had been burnt at all?" asked Theodora.

Grace looked to each one of us in turn, presumably weighing up just how much she could trust us.

"Cook found a button in the oven," she said. "It was only partially melted."

"I knew it," I said, before I could stop myself. "I always said clothes were burnt in that fire."

"No, you didn't, Selby," said Theodora. "You were all for ignoring those ashes at first."

Max laughed and even Grace smiled. I would endure this mild humiliation if it curried us a little favour.

"That button might belong to a different costume," said T.

"It might," replied Grace evasively.

"Perhaps it was Reginald burning the second harlequin costume."

Grace tried not to gasp but the surprise was obvious.

"They know," said Max gravely. "They know about Reg."

"And they're going to try and pin Lance's murder on him too?"

"Only if he did it," I said, "and the evidence doesn't look good."

"He's innocent," she protested.

"Then what was the argument about in the Hall?" asked T.

Grace stood before us dressed in her maid's garb, when a week ago she had held sway on the dancefloor in ball gown and jewels. The faint morning sun lit the lines of worry on her face and revealed something else – sadness.

"I didn't even realise it was him at first," she said. "I assumed it was Lance under that mask. We even danced together at one point. It was Max who finally worked it out."

"The hair," said Max, "Reg's was chestnut, Lance's walnut."

"Reggie refused to explain himself and that incensed Max."

"I asked him if he was seeing Lance again," said Max, "and he told me to bugger off."

"Max!" chastised Grace. "There's a lady present."

"Don't mind me," said T. "Selby's the sensitive one."

"It looked like things might escalate to fisticuffs," continued Grace, "so I separated them."

"Do you have any idea why Reginald was wearing that costume?" asked Theodora.

"I thought it was some silly joke at first," said Grace, shaking her head. "Him and Lance playing a game on all of us. But now I think it was worse."

"Much worse," said Max. "These two have been investigating, you see, and there was another clown costume. It seems like some horrible plan was at play."

"And it's possible," said T, "even though you won't want to hear it, that Reginald was a part of that plan."

"To kill Lance?" she asked.

Theodora nodded gravely.

"Reggie wouldn't hurt a fly."

"It's also possible he had an accomplice."

"Please, this isn't one of those daft novels," said Grace.

"Lance was overheard having an argument outside the Hall," I said. "Someone accused him of betraying a man and we think that man might have wanted vengeance."

"Reggie wasn't a fool," said Grace. "He knew where he stood with Lance and he took what he could get."

"That's what I said," piped up Max.

"Then it's likely there's someone else Lance was involved with," I said.

"A mystery lover," added Theodora, rather needlessly, if I might add.

Grace rolled her eyes. "I said this wasn't one of those novels."

"Nevertheless, please consider this," said T. "That Lance had a lover who initially knew nothing of his previous relationship with Reginald. Then, at some point, this lover learns the truth and becomes bitterly jealous."

"Why assume that?" asked Max. "Not every relationship has to involve envy. I was happy to share Reg with others."

He made a good point. Were Theodora and I wrong to presume that Lance's affair was such an awful one? Perhaps any morbid passions should be left with the heterosexuals.

"You are more generous than many," T conceded. "But let's assume the lover didn't want to share and concocted a plan, which would see Lance punished for his betrayal."

"And you expect me to believe Reggie jumped at the chance to join in?" said Grace.

"Not necessarily," I replied. "As you say, you first thought it was a silly joke. What if that's what the mystery lover told Reginald and that's why he took part. An unwitting accomplice in Lance's death."

"That's horrible," said Grace.

I nodded. That was all I could do. This whole thing was horrible.

"Then who's this bleeding mystery man?" asked Max.

"We were hoping you might know," said T.

"I don't," he said, sitting down on his bed. The rusty hinges creaked. "I wasn't close to Lance. I didn't like the way he strung poor Reg along."

"Grace, any ideas?"

"I'm too busy down here," she said. "Unlike some, I don't have time to go snooping."

"What about cleaning? Have you found anything in Lance's bedroom?"

She shook her head. "If he was conducting an affair, he was doing it far away from here."

I would have tutted and sighed, maybe even kicked the old suitcase for good measure. Just when the crossword looked complete, we were nine across, another word for baffled, seven letters, starts with an "s" – stumped. I stepped away from the others, it was all starting to feel rather oppressive.

"Any idea who took that small suitcase from the attic?" asked Theodora.

They both shook their heads.

"Or rifled through Cook's bottle supply?"

"You think the cyanide was taken from the house?" asked Grace, cottoning on very quickly.

"It's good for killing lice," added Max.

"Or slashed Lance's portrait?"

I approached the small window but my eyes were drawn to the postcards above the basin. One was a sunny scene from Clacton-on-Sea, another the Guinness pelican and a third showed the Bridge of Sighs in Venice.

"Who was that from?" I asked, pointing at the third postcard.

"Reg, to me," said Max.

This tallied with what I'd already been told – that Reggie had been out there in Italy. I remembered, too, how people had confirmed that trip had changed Lance. It may well have been the time he met the mystery lover.

"Do you know who else was there?"

"Just the family, I think."

I pictured the Fortescues abroad – Hector doing his best impression of Freud, learning about the ins and outs of chemical therapy; Percy turning red in the sun; and Helena, most likely with a dainty parasol and another tract on moral vigilance. Then it hit me. There would have been someone else!

"I think I know who it was," I said.

"Who?" said Theodora.

"Think about that second costume for a moment," I said. "What does it achieve?"

"To bloody baffle us." That was Max.

"It made it look like Lance was still alive long after eleven and that he left the ball at midnight. Someone wants us to think Lance was killed later than he was. Which means we need to find someone above suspicion. Someone who gave themselves a very obvious alibi at midnight."

"Someone who turned up here out of the blue," said Grace, the spark of deduction aflame in her eyes.

"Exactly! Someone who made a point of telling me he saw you returning at ten minutes past twelve."

"Of course," said Max. "*He* would have been in Italy."

"Exactly! Because Helena Fortescue can't go anywhere without him."

CHAPTER 24

Theodora never needed an excuse to drive fast. Soon we were speeding through West Kensington for Cyril's flat in Hammersmith. Grace had given us his address and stayed behind with Max. The Fortescues would be back from church soon, hungry for their Sunday lunch. I tried not to think of food as my stomach grumbled. All this detecting was hungry work.

"What's our line of attack?" asked Theodora.

"We need him to confess."

"To a most ingenious plan and a double murder?" she replied sceptically. "Then we can be back in time for roast beef."

"Now, now, we want proof he was Lance's secret lover."

"He'll hardly give that to us."

"I know, but if he was, the poor chap has just lost his partner."

"Who he may have murdered," she added.

"Either way, he'll be on edge and we must exploit that. It's damned rum, mind."

"What is?"

The Crossley hit a bump in the road and we were temporarily lifted from our seats. There was no point in complaining, T seldom spared the horses.

"He's Helena's secretary and a card-carrying member of the National Vigilance Association," I said. "He's the last person I'd expect to find in the fruit bowl."

"It's a good hiding place."

"How can he live with himself?" I asked. "Hatred in one hand, desire in the other."

"We're about to find out."

We came to an abrupt stop at the top of a street not too far from the station. Theodora wanted the element of surprise and suggested not parking too near Cyril's flat. Off we went, the weather holding for now, the sun still shining despite the interminable cold.

"Quick," she commanded, "this way."

We hotfooted it down the road, passing under a wide tunnel. A train rumbled overhead, shaking dust from the tunnel roof and filling our ears with noise. Pigeons flapped angrily about us and I felt the rush of their wings.

"Rats of the sky, I call them," I said.

"Lovely. Onwards."

We emerged relatively unscathed from the tunnel and carried on down the road. The buildings were predominantly low red-brick warehouses but they soon gave way to some terraced houses. Cyril's flat was…

"Number 103," said Theodora, reading my mind.

The street was empty, eerily so, but it was a Sunday. People were most likely at church or preparing for luncheon. It wasn't a bad street by any means, not like the slums of the East End, but it had evidently seen better days. Refuse still hadn't been cleared from outside some of the houses and the paving slabs were uneven – lethal in the frost. Sagging net curtains hung in many of the front rooms and the paint around the windows was often chipped. We finally reached 102 and realised we were on the wrong side of the road. We turned to face the other way as a rickety old van ambled past. Number 103 was tall and painted in white that, over time, had turned to grey. A leafless tree was all the front garden could boast, as well as some dented dustbins and a flowerless flowerpot. It wasn't the sort of place I imagined the fastidious Cyril Blanford living, but in a city such as London, appearance was often everything.

"He's flat 2b, probably on the second floor."

We looked up, counting the windows, and when my gaze reached the appropriate height, I swore. Theodora did exactly the same, reaching out to grip my arm and steady herself. For there, standing in the window looking down at us, was someone – or something – I'd never expected to see again. Harlequin. The gold, black, white and red diamonds seemed to glow with a preternatural light (or possibly the reflected sunlight from the opposite window).

"Oh my God," I blasphemed.

All of a sudden, the figure stepped back and the empty staring eyes vanished.

"What… what now?"

"Quick," said Theodora, still holding my arm and pulling me forward. "This isn't right."

Knowing that to be true, I followed her across the road to the house. The cold brought tears to my eyes as we jumped onto the pavement, through the gate and up the steps to the front door. Theodora went to knock but as her gloved knuckle collided with the wood, the door retreated an inch.

"It's been forced," I said, noting the dents in the wood.

"Come on."

"Are you sure?" I said, hovering at the threshold.

"Cyril might be in trouble."

She entered the house. I stared up and down the empty street, wondering if there were any neighbours peeping through their net curtains, then followed. A few envelopes and a crumpled newspaper were on the floor near the door. It was a narrow hallway and it wasn't long until we reached the stairs. Theodora took two at a time, bounding up to the first-floor landing and then continuing up to the next.

"Be careful, Theo," I said, saving on syllables.

"I know," she whispered.

We slowed our pace as we crossed the second-floor landing and reached 2b. It was very cold and dim up here. Cautiously Theodora reached out and took hold of the doorknob. She raised her other hand and held aloft three fingers. One went down to leave two, then the next, and when the final one was gone, she pushed. The door swung open and my first sensation was of a cold blast of air.

We rushed into the flat. It was one large room – dining room, kitchen, study and lounge all in one. The predominant colour scheme was beige and brown but that didn't matter as we searched the place. I turned right and went to the window that overlooked the road. The one at which Harlequin had just been standing. There was no trace of the masked figure, and for just a glimmer of a moment, I entertained the notion that we'd imagined the whole thing. Ghosts were so often cropping up in Octavia Stubbs' crime fiction.

"Oh my," said Theodora, who had turned left and entered the other room. "Selby, quick."

Steeling myself, I crossed the room and approached the open door. Horrible images flashed before my mind and the only thing I felt was dread. Cyril might well have been Lance's lover, but given what had happened to Reginald, who knew what fate had befallen the unassuming secretary?

"Quick, I need your help."

Inside was the bedroom and there on the bed – amongst crumpled sheets and rumpled eiderdown – lay Cyril. He was fully clothed in shirt, tie, suit trousers and socks but his shirtsleeves had been rolled back and resting near him on the mattress was a shaving razor.

"Mr Blanford," cried Theodora, sitting on the edge of the bed and placing her fingers at his neck. "Cyril, are you all right?"

The only relief this horrible scene afforded was the razor blade being closed. Cyril's wrists were pale and traced with thin veins but there was no blood.

"There's a pulse. Cyril, can you hear me?" She shook him gently by the shoulder. His head threatened to loll sideways but she held it back. "Cyril, it's Theodora Smythe. I've come to help."

Finally, he emitted a sound, just a muffled groan, but it was enough.

"Should I call for an ambulance?" I asked.

"I'm not sure. Let's stay with him for a while."

"What about the harlequin?" I looked around the room, spotting a writing table next to the bed. A small clock read midday and next to it was a single, blank piece of paper and a fountain pen. I also spotted a pair of circular glasses – the ones Helena Fortescue wouldn't let him wear. The desk overlooked an open window, through which gusted a cold breeze. I went to close it, but before I did, I threw caution to the wind and stuck my head outside.

"What are you doing?"

"Looking for demented clowns," I replied.

Directly beneath the window was the roof of whatever first-floor room was below. It slanted and I noted a few of the tiles had been damaged. This must have been how the harlequin had vanished – scrambling over the roof and dropping down into the scraggly garden beyond. The fences leading into the adjoining gardens weren't particularly high and would have been easy enough to scale. There was no point in pursuit – the masked assailant would be long gone by now. I closed the window. Theodora had spread the eiderdown over Cyril and placed the razor blade far out of reach. He looked almost peaceful, as if he'd decided to take a nap.

"Will he be all right?" I asked.

"I think so. He came to for a moment. There's a hint of pear about him."

"Pear?" I said, not sure I'd heard her correctly.

"Chloral hydrate, perhaps poured onto a handkerchief."

"Do you think the harlequin barged in and attacked him?"

"Something like that," she concurred. "Any trace?"

"No, they've got clean away. But who?"

Theodora shook her head, equally dumbfounded. The clock ticked as we waited for Cyril to recover. I perused the artwork on the walls and found a small painting of a Venetian gondola – the water was crystal-blue and the gondolier stood proudly with his stick. It reminded me of punting on the Cherwell when I'd been a student at Oxford. I too associated that time with love, and sadly, also with death. How gay it must have been to fall in love in Venice. I'd heard all about those beautiful churches reaching for the heavens and city streets made of water. Then I thought on what had happened after they'd fallen in love and all the misery that followed.

"How do you feel?" she asked.

Cyril was coming to. "Awful," he mumbled. He spotted me nearby. "Who's that?"

"It's Mr Bigge," she said.

"Why… why…" He was struggling to get the words out, still under the influence of the chloral hydrate.

"Why are we here?" completed Theodora. "To find out who murdered Lancelot and Reginald."

"Oh, Lancelot," he sighed.

"Did you love him?" I asked.

"Oh yes," he replied, with a woozy smile on his face. It was rot to capitalise on a chap so out of sorts, but at least he was being honest for once.

"And you fell in love in Venice?" said T.

"I fell in a canal!" He laughed. His short-sighted eyes were glazed over and clearly whatever he saw was a happy memory from his past. "Lancelot pulled me out."

I smiled. It was the stuff of an E. M. Forster romance – if he were ever allowed to write about men loving men.

"Did you go to the ball that night?" asked T.

"The ball?" he slurred.

"At the Royal Albert Hall. Did you argue with Lance that night?"

"Lance, oh Lance." He sighed again.

"Did you hurt Lance?"

"Never!" His eyes opened wide for a moment. "I would never hurt him."

"Did you row with Reginald?"

"Poor chap," he said. "He's dead."

"We know," replied T gravely. "Were you jealous that Reginald loved Lance?"

"*I* loved Lance."

"We know."

"I waited for him."

That sentence could be interpreted in a number of ways but I took a punt. "Where did you wait for him?"

"At the corner."

"Which corner? Were you outside the Hall?"

"No, no," he said, a dopey smile on his face. "Hyde Park."

"You were at Hyde Park Corner?"

His smile only widened.

"Did you have a suitcase with you?"

"Oh yes, just like he told me."

"Who?" I asked.

"He wanted one final night to remember."

"Who?"

Cyril didn't reply, shifting to get more comfortable on the bed.

"Did Lancelot tell you to meet him there?" Theodora this time.

Again, nothing.

"Did you wear one of the costumes?" she asked.

"What costumes?" he asked, bewildered as well as drugged.

"The two harlequin costumes with the masks. Like the one worn by your assailant."

"I hate clowns," he moaned.

Theodora turned to me and whispered. "This is useless."

"Not completely," I replied. "Cyril, why were you a part of the National Vigilance Association?"

"Silly me," he said.

"Was it a front?"

"I liked her. Very bossy, like my mother."

"Did you really believe all those things?"

"I did," he said, "then I didn't. He changed my mind."

He dropped his head and a few tears fell from his eyes. I wondered if a part of him was pleased to be able to get this off his chest, despite the peculiarity of his confessors. After Lance, he may well have had no one to talk to. How one soul could contain so much contradiction was a perennial question for the Englishman.

"I'm tired."

"Perhaps best to stay awake awhile."

"Just a little nap."

He closed his eyes.

"Can we really leave him like this?" I asked.

"I'm not sure."

Suddenly Cyril grunted and his head darted back up.

"What was that?" he said.

"Nothing, Cyril, we're still here. Do you want some tea?" offered T.

"You shouldn't be here," he said, his voice sharper now.

"We want to help."

"Thank you," he replied coldly. "I can take care of myself."

Theodora rose from the edge of the bed, her knees clicked as she went.

"You're not safe," she said.

"I know. I will dress and head to a neighbour's."

"You should call the police."

"I don't want them here."

I looked about the place, wondering what evidence there might be hidden away – love letters, maybe even photographs. We left the bedroom and waited for him to don a dressing gown. I sniffed, wondering if I could detect a hint of smoke on the air. Cyril ushered us to the door and opened it.

"There's one more thing," I said, blocking the doorway. "Something doesn't quite tally. You say you arrived at the Fortescues' house at a quarter to eleven that night. Then, at ten minutes past twelve, you say you saw Grace arriving with a man through the servants' door."

"That's correct."

"How?"

"I beg your pardon?"

"I want to know how you saw them. Because, from my understanding, you must have been standing outside the front door and looking down at the below-stairs patio."

"That must be it then," he replied dismissively.

"So, you were outside the house?"

"I presume."

"Why?"

This time he paused and I knew I'd got him.

"You could just tell me the truth. Whoever tried to kill you will try again."

His face was a compound of misery, fear and loathing.

"I… I'm not sure I deserve to live."

Completely reflexively, I reached out and held his arm. "You mustn't say that, you mustn't. Too many are dead already."

"I know." He lowered his head, the tears returning. "And to think the part I played in all that. I once believed so strongly in all Helena proselytised. I regret every minute."

"Why not tell us the truth? Who are you protecting?"

"Myself. I'm no murderer but I am a criminal. I wish you didn't know. I wish no one knew." He placed his hand on mine and removed it from his arm.

"Ours is no crime," I tried to reassure him. "Who told you to meet them at Hyde Park Corner at eleven?"

He put his fingers to his temple, a wounded look upon his face.

"Were you near the Albert Hall at eleven?"

"I did it all for him." He started to close the door.

"Who? The killer? Lance?"

On that final word, he looked at me and I had the answer.

"Good day, Mr Bigge, Miss Smythe. Thank you for saving my life."

It was with heavy spirits we left the flat. Clouds had appeared to dim the sun's light and the street was even more forlorn. A single dead leaf clung to the tree outside number 103 as I clung on to my dwindling hope.

"Why won't he trust us?" I said.

"Why should he? We're not his friends."

I shook my head, angry. "But we have learned a few things."

"Is this to do with all that business about him seeing Grace?"

"It is."

We walked the road back under the tunnel to the car and clambered inside. Theodora was just about to fire up the engine when a car passed us.

"I say," said Theodora. "Look."

The car was driving slowly enough to afford me a good view of the driver and passenger, namely one Chief Inspector Lisle and Sergeant Stovell.

"You think Cyril had a change of heart?"

"Even if he had," I said, "they can't have driven that fast."

"Then why else are they here?"

"I don't know," I said. "Should we go back?"

"I don't think Cyril would appreciate it," she said. "He made clear he doesn't want our help. And we hardly want to have to explain ourselves to those two."

"What I want is to find the final letters to fill the grid."

"Are they starting to spell something?"

"A name, to be precise, just not the one I expected."

"Whose?" she asked.

"Someone who's been pulling more strings than I ever thought possible. The same person who told Cyril to pack a suitcase. The man he loved."

"But he's dead," she exclaimed.

CHAPTER 25

"I suppose *suspect everyone* is our motto," said Theodora, as we sped back the way we'd come. "I wonder what it is in Latin."

"*Suspicari omnes*," I replied. "Although my Latin is rustier than my Greek these days.

"Aren't you clever?" she jibed. "Now, are you really suggesting we've been looking at all this the wrong way around?"

"I am," I said. "Other than a number of comings and goings, a few overheard snippets of argument and two masks, we can't actually be certain Lance was killed before Reginald."

"So, Lance convinces Reginald to dress up as Harlequin and dance for an hour. Then what?"

"Lance picks him up in his car and does away with him in a derelict garage. He then walks home via Kensington Gardens, only to be coshed."

"It's certainly enough letters," she said, "but I'm still not convinced it's the right word."

"It ties to our notion that whoever killed Reginald was someone he trusted."

"The chief inspector will be delighted – two deranged inverts for the price of one. Although, I still can't see Lance as the cold, calculating murderer type."

"You're right," I replied.

"I usually am."

"But there's something Percy said about his brother – that he was one for theatrics. And all along this whole case has felt very theatrical."

"That I agree with," she said, "but it doesn't answer our next most pressing question – who just tried to do away with Cyril?"

"That mask gave me the fright of my life," I said.

"I'm too young to die of a heart attack."

"Don't worry, it's your driving that will kill you."

We hit a bump in the road.

"Do you think there's another criminal mastermind behind all this?" I said.

"That's the most obvious answer. Think about it, after Lance and Reginald, Cyril was the third – and only surviving – corner of the love triangle."

"And if there's another lover involved, we might be dealing with a love square."

"All these jilted lovers," she said. "I've lost count."

"What are the other options?"

"That the person who drugged Cyril was trying to frame him for the murders of Lance and Reginald, hence the razor blade."

"It wouldn't be the first suicide they've staged."

Theodora nodded sternly and I admired her profile for a

moment – sufficiently haughty given the baronetcy's inheritance offset by a smudge of kindness.

"Or Cyril is our murderer," she said, "and that person was avenging the deaths of Lance and Reggie."

"Perhaps they'd found Lance's original mask and put the pieces together as we did?"

"Which implies the murderer must have taken Lance's mask after killing him."

"And then left it lying about the place," I added.

"For a criminal mastermind, they would appear to have made many mistakes."

It was a good point and it got me thinking. We'd reached West Kensington by now, the sun long having fulfilled its winter quota for the day and gone to hide behind a cloud. Pedestrians hurried to and fro, buses ferried passengers (well, bussed them, to be precise), carts carried goods. All around us London ticked on as ever. The facades presented us were just as expected, but peel back one layer and this city was anything but the postcards tourists sent home.

"Our murderer has behaved unexpectedly in a number of ways," I said.

"Go on."

"If the killer or killers wanted us to think the murder took place at midnight, then why use two different masks? Why offer us a way of unravelling the plan?"

"Although you're the only one who spotted the difference," she said.

"That we know of," I added. "Why burn the second costume but not the second mask? Why leave the second mask with

Reggie's body when they should have left the one Lance was wearing? Why plan this elaborate scheme with the two costumes only to make such a mess of it?"

"Which brings us back to Cyril," she said, "because he said he didn't know about the second costume. Unless that was the chloral hydrate speaking."

"I almost think he's been the most honest with us, albeit thanks to the influence of that rather nasty drug and a near-brush with death."

"Do you think he could have been involved in the plan without knowing about the costumes at all?" she asked.

"Yes, and if he says he was waiting at Hyde Park Corner that night, then all he'd have had to do was walk through the park to get to the Albert Hall. He could have arrived before eleven, coshed Lance, taxied to the Fortescues', lied to Percy about his time of arrival and then killed Reginald later that night."

"So, he didn't know about the costumes but he did know that Lance and Reginald had been lovers?"

I nodded.

"Then how did he persuade Reggie to get into the car – Lance's car, mind – and get him to drink from a poisoned chalice? What hold did he have over Reginald?" Theodora shrugged her shoulders, looking as puzzled as I.

"Love," I suggested, "blackmail, threat, I really don't know."

"If Cyril had meticulously planned all this," said T, "why did he leave so much to chance and end up making so many mistakes?"

"I agree, it doesn't hang together, and he certainly doesn't seem the mastermind sort."

"Few do."

"If anything, the events around the ball feel ad hoc, as if the murderer was putting the pieces together that very night."

"That's a good point," she said. "Keep going."

"Well, if..." I took a moment to think. "If Cyril wasn't behind all this, but it was someone else there that night, then logically, they're the same person we just saw trying to bump off Cyril."

"Logically, yes."

"Indicating our earlier theory – that in killing Cyril they wanted to frame him. Or he knew too much and had to be silenced."

"Which brings us back to the same question we've had all along – who?"

"The puppet mistress or master. Someone connected to Lance and Reginald, who knew about the ball all along, and was emotionally involved enough that they turned to murder."

Silence remained our companion for the rest of the journey as Theodora doubtlessly attempted to fill in her mental crossword grid and I continued to paint the culprit's imaginary portrait. Once T had parked the car, we set off on foot. I was getting fed up of Pendragon Rise and hoped our last visit was imminent. We walked slowly, both lost in our thoughts, when Theodora finally spoke.

"Ravioli!"

"I was hoping for a roast."

"No, no, spaghetti."

"The Italian pasta dish, I'm aware of it."

"Shush, don't you remember – she said she'd eaten it. In Palermo, with her mother, when they'd met with the Fortescues."

"Oh, you're right! I'd forgotten that she was in Italy then."

"Meaning she might know about everything – the blossoming love between Cyril and Lance, the historical one between Lance and Reginald, possibly even the masks."

"She could be the fourth corner of our love square," I said.

"And with all that knowledge, imagine how betrayed she'd have felt."

"Beyond reason," I said.

"Jacqueline!" she shouted.

"Theodora, you don't need to sh—"

She gave my arm an unpleasantly sharp pinch to keep me from talking. Up ahead, not far from number 42, stood Jacqueline Bosanquet.

"Jackie, how lovely to see you," she said, at a less-offensive volume.

"Theodora, Mr Bigge," she said, "what a surprise. Are you here to lunch?"

My stomach sang at the possibility of food but now wasn't the time.

"If you must know," said T conspiratorially, "we've been asking questions."

"About Lancelot?" asked Jackie. "Are you any closer to the truth?"

"We are," she said, "and I have a question for you."

"For me?"

There was adequate surprise in her tone and her eyes widened to match. She looked just the part, dressed darkly with little make-up and a face that hadn't seen a smile in weeks. But was it all an act? The trouble with this blasted murder business was that it made me second-guess everything. Was this a recently bereaved fiancée standing before me or Moriarty's equally damnable niece?

"When we met you at the Royal Albert Hall that night," said Theodora, not wasting a second, "why were you there?"

"I told you," replied Jackie, her tone hardening, "I was worried about Lance."

"But why that night of all nights?"

Jackie hesitated, and by Jove, Theodora must have hit on something.

"Was it the tickets?" she asked. "At dinner, we all learned that Reginald had bought four tickets. Did that arouse your suspicions?"

Again, Jackie said nothing. Hell hath no fury like a woman scorned, but then again, that applied to men just as much.

"It was something he said after dinner."

"Lance?"

"When he took me to the door to say goodbye." She looked up the steps to the front door; perhaps the last place she'd ever seen him alive. "He said sorry."

"He apologised to you?" I said.

"He said he was dreadfully sorry for getting me caught up in everything. And then he said..." Her words caught in the back of her throat as she stifled a sob. "He said it would all be over soon."

Lance had said those exact words to me, just before I'd left him with Reginald. If Lance had also apologised to Jackie, he must have felt guilt for what he was about to do. What's more, he'd apologised to Lady Splendid that night as well. These acts of atonement hardly seemed like the behaviour of someone engaged in a murderous love affair but nor was I convinced they tallied with the words of someone about to take their own life.

Theodora and I followed Jackie as we walked the path to the steps that led to the front door. To our left was the railing. I peered over it, down at the servants' patio. I pictured Grace returning in the dead of night, accompanied by Max, only the tops of their heads visible. I spied the plant pot in which Max must have dropped one of the plague doctor's gloves.

"That's it," I said.

"What?" asked Theodora.

"He wasn't leaving!"

"Who?"

"Cyril," I said. "He said he saw them from up here at ten past midnight, which they've confirmed was their arrival time. But what if it was something else he was lying about?

I waited for Theodora to ask the relevant question but she'd given up humouring me.

"What if he saw them from up here because that wasn't when he was leaving the house? He was arriving."

The front door opened and there was Grace, quiet and subservient. Standing a few yards deeper in the hall were Hector and Helena.

"Good news," said the patriarch. "They've arrested the man who killed our son."

"Oh," exclaimed Jackie, almost tripping over the doormat. "Who?"

"I'm afraid to say," said Helena, "that it was my secretary."

CHAPTER 26

"He seduced our son in a most despicable manner," said Hector.

"He was lying to me," said Helena, "feigning his vigilance when all he wanted was access to Lancelot."

Once again, I was seated at the dining table of the Fortescue household, except this time, the table was laid for six, not seven. I was on Helena's left and Percival her right. Next to him was Theodora then Hector, at his head of the table. Jacqueline was seated on his other side. Lancelot's seat – formerly occupying the space between his fiancée and I – had been removed.

"I feel almost guilty," she said. "I never should have trusted him."

"You mustn't say that, Helena," commanded her husband. "He fooled us all."

The pair wanted us all sitting down to hear the news. Aperitifs had been skipped and food would not be served until after (and, for now, even I could ignore the smell of roast potatoes). I'd played my usual trick and headed for the water closet before joining everyone, giving me a moment alone in the corridor with Grace. We'd spoken briefly and I'd tasked her with finding Max. Now she was standing quietly near the door, just as she'd done on the night of the ball. I flashed her a quick glance and she nodded her head ever so slightly.

"When did you learn of this?" asked Jackie.

"Mere moments before you arrived," he said. "The chief inspector has just arrested him. They found an incriminating letter half-burnt in the grate."

How convenient, I didn't say.

"I always knew there was a heartless, calculating agency behind all this," said Helena.

"There, there, Mother," said Percy, trying his best to comfort her.

"And a queer one at that," said Hector.

"How did the chief inspector arrive at such a conclusion?" asked Theodora.

"He received a call."

"A tip-off?" she said. "From who?"

"The person who rang didn't give his identity," said Hector, "but we owe him a debt of gratitude all the same."

"Amen," said Helena.

I coughed in a manner to garner attention, and one by one, the heads at the table turned to regard me. Most appeared sceptical, save Theodora, who signalled for me to go on. We'd had a split second to converse before taking our seats – just enough time to tell her I'd filled the grid.

"If I may, I have something to add."

"Not now, old chap," said Percy. "We want our luncheon."

"It won't take a moment."

"If you're quick," said Helena. "Perhaps you too suspected my secretary?"

"I did suspect him," I said, "but that's because I suspected everyone."

"Heavens, even me?"

"Even you, Mrs Fortescue. That is the job of a detective."

"I thought you were a clerk at a bank," said Jackie.

"I juggle professions."

The scepticism remained. I envied Cnut his far simpler task of turning back the tide.

"I do believe Cyril loved your son but I don't believe he killed him."

"It wasn't love," said Hector. "It was perversion."

"Call it what you will," I said, "I still do not think him a murderer."

"How could you possibly know that?"

"Because the investigation I've pursued with Miss Smythe has revealed something quite different."

"Is this true, Theodora?" asked Helena.

"Selby and I followed your instruction, Helena, and we have reached an alternative conclusion. However, I believe only Selby can finish the crossword."

"Crossword?" asked Percy, baffled.

"From the start, the case was presented as a simple one. At first, it was suggested Lancelot was killed by an opportunistic thief while Reginald had made off with the car. However, once

Reginald's body was found, the next solution was given – he had killed his master and then himself. Queers behaving madly is a story readily believed by the press and the public."

"Because they are mad," said Helena.

"But Miss Smythe and I long suspected things might not be so simple," I said. "We developed an alternative hypothesis – that there was a cunning villainy behind all this, a criminal mastermind even, staging the murders in the way I have just described. And the more we investigated, the more our hypothesis was corroborated. That someone had concocted the most baffling of plans, which they executed on the night of the ball."

"Executed?" echoed Jackie with a gasp.

"Sorry, a poor choice of word. Off Miss Smythe and I went, in search of this source of cunning. The one who had planned it all, down to the very last detail. And much to my surprise, the mastermind was someone I'd never even thought to suspect."

I cast my gaze around the table. I had their attention.

"The plan I talk of began in Italy – in Venice, to be precise."

"Venice?" said Helena quietly, her hand going to her heart.

"It was there your son fell in love with your secretary."

"No! Cyril manipulated him," she protested.

"Mother, let Mr Bigge speak," said Percy. "The quicker this is over, the sooner we can eat."

"Call it manipulation or peculiarity or romance, the result was just the same – love. And that was the catalyst that led to all this."

Jackie choked but she did not interrupt.

"It was at a shop not far from the Piazetta di San Marco where Lancelot commissioned not one but two harlequin masks. They were almost identical, apart from the positions of the red and black diamonds over the eyes. He also purchased matching costumes to go with them. The summer passed into autumn and soon arrives November, time for Lady Malcolm's Servants' Ball and the next part of the plan. For that, Lancelot needs an accomplice. So, he calls upon the services of his ever-loyal valet, Reginald."

Hector spluttered in disbelief, reaching for his pocket square.

"He provides Reginald with the money to buy four tickets – one for Reginald, Grace and Lance."

"Who was the fourth ticket for?" asked Helena.

"That I do not know." Even though I knew it was for Max, I had no desire to have him punished for his innocent part in all this. Dressing as a plague doctor and sneaking to the ball was no crime.

"We all sit around this very table and eat our early dinner," I continued. "I remember a tension between Lancelot and Reginald – I see now they were both decidedly nervous. Miss Smythe and I depart at around eight o'clock and Lance tells you he's off to his club. He lies. He goes to the Royal Albert Hall dressed as Harlequin and Reginald accompanies him. It is for one final night of gaiety: he will dance across the ballroom floor, listening to the band and the merriment of the other ball-goers, sipping champagne and meeting with old acquaintances."

"Lance knew none of that lot," said Hector.

"There's much you didn't know about your son and his acquaintances," I said. "Meanwhile, Cyril Blanford is preparing himself for an eleven o'clock rendezvous at Hyde Park Corner, as instructed by your son. This was the most crucial part of the plan. However, I must stress, Cyril knew nothing about the two masks."

"This is most confusing," said Helena.

"What's all this nonsense about masks?" That was Hector.

"Sounds like fiction to me." Percy this time.

"Why go to all that trouble?" said Jackie. "Was Lancelot truly planning to do something so awful?"

"I will come to that very soon," I said, "but first I need to relay what happened next. At around twenty minutes past ten, Lancelot sends Reginald back to the house. He does this for two reasons. The first is so Reginald can collect the second costume, packed in a small valise. The second is to have Reginald seen to be leaving the Hall, so he won't be associated with what happens next. It was a kindness on Lancelot's behalf."

"A kindness," said Percy, disbelieving, "but they turned on one another."

"Let's not rush ahead," I replied. "I must introduce the final player in this tragedy, and they are in this very room."

I was aware of my theatrics, which I felt in keeping with this whole affair.

"The clue that set this whole tragedy in motion was one we all overheard because we were sitting at this very table on the night of the ball. We all learned of Doctor Fortescue's disciplining of Reginald for having bought four rather than two tickets. We all wondered who those extra tickets were for. And for someone, their suspicions were sufficiently raised that they would head to the Royal Albert Hall."

I sensed Jackie bristling.

"Later that evening, at just gone half past ten, that same

person overhears Reginald quietly letting himself back into the house via the servants' door. He creeps through the house, retrieves the valise and promptly leaves again – distinctly odd behaviour. Suspicions raised, our final player goes in pursuit, lacking the time to retrieve their gloves."

"Gloves?" said Helena.

"Reginald does not know he has a shadow as he's followed all the way back to the Albert Hall. Upon arriving, he hides in the bushes and extracts the costume. He places it over his suit. This explains the footprints. Then, at around ten minutes to eleven, dressed as Harlequin, he heads for one of the entrances to the Hall, at which point another Harlequin appears. Lancelot. The two converse, Reginald hands Lancelot the empty valise, perhaps they embrace as well. They might even have kissed."

Displeasure spread around the table like a Freudian disease of the mind.

"Our final player sees all this happen and they are outraged. Reginald has entered the Hall by now, so they confront Lancelot. An argument ensues. And it is at this point, at the eleventh hour, Lancelot is forced to reveal the truth of the plan he has masterminded. The masks, the costumes, the ball – none of it is to do with murder, but all to do with life. His one desire."

I paused for breath. My heart rate was high, but it was nothing compared to Lance's on that fatal night. Thousands of joyous servants behind him, interspersed with all manner of queers, and before him the great dark of the night. Only a few paces more and he could finally do what he'd been planning for so long.

"To run."

"Run?" spluttered Hector. "Where?"

"I do not know where he was running to but I do know where he was running from." I slowly gestured around myself, taking in those gathered and the room itself. "He was running away from all this.

"Despite all his best efforts and all your treatments, Doctor, he hadn't changed. Out there in Italy, you'd spoken of chemical methods to suppress his deviant behaviour and I think that must have been the final straw. He'd had enough. He finally understood that there was no cure.

"Outside the Albert Hall, the argument escalates. Lancelot storms off into Kensington Gardens. Our final player pursues, snatching the mask from his grasp and demanding to know what it's all about. And then hatred boils into violence as a stone is retrieved from one of the flowerbeds, raised high and brought crashing down on the back of Lancelot's head."

Everyone was stunned, save one.

"All along, Miss Smythe and I had been looking for a criminal mastermind because we knew something so elaborate had been planned. We assumed the point of the plan was to result in a double murder, but actually the plan was quite innocent and its architect intent only on one thing."

I recalled Lancelot sitting next to me at the dining table. His straight back, his formal tone, his appropriate comments, but underneath it all was a man on the verge of getting that which he desired the most.

"Escape. That's what he meant by those words he said to you, Miss Bosanquet – *it will all be over soon*. He was running away, whether to America, Venice or even just Yorkshire, as long as it was far from here."

I didn't tell them what he'd said to me – *it doesn't matter any more* – because they still didn't know I'd met Lance and Reginald at the ball, and they never needed to as far as I was concerned.

"But it all went horribly wrong."

"What happened?" whispered Jackie. She sounded genuinely concerned – torn between her fiancé's betrayal and her love for him.

"It's obvious," said Helena, "Cyril turned on him. You said it yourself, Mr Bigge. He was waiting for Lancelot in the park. I told you he manipulated my son, all part of some wicked plan to kill him."

"Yes, Cyril does form a vital part of this story," I said, "and he was indeed waiting for Lancelot at Hyde Park Corner, with his own suitcases packed. But at eleven o'clock Lancelot does not appear. More time passes and Cyril begins to worry. Worry turns to panic and he gives up waiting. He heads here and arrives at ten past midnight, moments after Grace's return – who he sees entering via the servants' door." There was no point in mentioning Max's arrival with Grace – he'd been through enough. "Desperate, Cyril quietly taps at the door, hoping against hope Lancelot will open it or at least someone sympathetic to his plight. Unfortunately for him, the door is opened by the very person who has just killed the man he loves."

Having walked through the door of 42 Pendragon Rise so many times I could picture that moment all too clearly. I could feel Cyril's fear and hope, even his cluelessness, as he stepped across the threshold.

"It was you, wasn't it?"

I'd addressed the man sitting opposite me – the one who so resembled his older brother save for his squarer jaw and broader shoulders – Percival Fortescue.

"You devil," he protested. "I loved my brother."

"You did and that made his betrayal all the worse," I replied. "*How could you betray him. You've been lying to him, to all of us.* Those were words overheard from your argument. At first, I thought *him* might be a lover, but you were referring to your father. And *us* was the family."

"How dare you," he said.

"I will dare – for the truth must out."

"I didn't invite you to lunch," said Hector, "so you could accuse my son of murder."

I expected Helena to add her own protestation but she was surprisingly quiet. Instead, Theodora spoke: "As God is my witness and my father the Seventh Baronet of Etherley, I implore you to let Mr Bigge speak."

"Miss Smythe—" began Percy, but he was interrupted by Jackie.

"Let him speak," she said. "This hell must end."

"I do not believe you went in pursuit of Reginald with murder on your mind, but when you accosted Lancelot and learned of his plan, you were incensed. How dare he run away? You follow him into the park. How dare he turn his back on the family that has given him everything? You take a stone from the flowerbed. How dare he reject you – his own brother? You raise the stone high. If he refuses to be normal, he will be nothing at all. And bring it crashing down against his skull. And all of a sudden, you are a murderer and now your most urgent priority is to get away with it. So, you must concoct your own plan.

"Knowing your fingerprints to be on the mask and the stone, you take them with you as you flee the scene. You arrive back at the house some time after eleven and I can only imagine the turmoil you felt – you are Cain, your brother Abel. You stow away the mask and stone, and wash any trace of blood and dirt from your hands. No one saw you go to the Hall and no one saw you come back. Perhaps luck is on your side? Too tense for sleep, you pace the drawing room and then, at ten past midnight, there comes a quiet tapping at the door – Cyril.

"He's distraught and this worries you. What might he know? You console him, offer him a whisky, maybe a second, and slowly coax the truth from him. He tells you of his plan to meet your brother in the park and run away, thinking he can trust you. To your relief, he knows nothing of Lancelot's death. Your mind is racing, wondering if there's a way you can turn this situation to your advantage. There is, one you stow away for later use.

"Cyril departs shortly after your chat, his presence noted by Grace, leaving you to brood and worry. Then you smell the burning. Investigating, you head below stairs whereupon you find Reginald burning the second harlequin costume in the kitchen. You confront him, ask him what the devil he's doing. You apply pressure, perhaps threatening his job. And he confesses. He tells you of his part in your brother's plan – that he was pretending to be Lancelot to give him sufficient time to walk away through the park and make his escape. By this point, Reginald has burnt most of the costume save the mask, which he shows to you. It is then you see how you can use their plan to your advantage.

"You tell him of Cyril's hysterics and how the plan has gone awry. You convince him that Lancelot might be in danger and tell him to get into the Bentley. This time you do put on your gloves. Thinking on your feet, you take the mask from the kitchen and collect the stone from wherever you've hidden it. You may well have wiped your fingerprints off the first mask, but Reginald's one will be covered in his, which suits your plan all the better. You enter the pantry to retrieve the bottle of cyanide. Then off you go.

"The ensuing search for Lancelot proves fruitless – as you knew it would – and you suggest visiting some of his old haunts, including the Parakeet. It is there Reginald passes you his hip flask and you lace it with the poison. Moments later, you give it back to him and watch as he dies. You break the lock on the garage and park the car inside. You leave the stone and the mask, to implicate Reginald as Lancelot's killer. You return home and then, I assume, you go to bed."

Surprisingly Percy did not protest, nor did he grab one of the forks and try to jab it into my throat. On I went.

"Your plan almost worked – many did believe the servant had killed his master – but there was one thing you missed, which unravelled it all."

I pictured the colourful face – a white diamond over the mouth, a gold one on the forehead, red for the left eye and black for the right. Harlequin smiled at me.

"The masks. You never saw it and Reginald never told you of the one difference between them. This was always a sticking point for me – if the masks had been part of some wicked plan, then they should have been identical. Not to mention all the other mistakes that had been made. No matter how I tried to look at that night, there were too many inconsistencies for me to piece together a masterplan. It was almost as if Machiavelli wanted to be caught. But the truth is, he never existed.

"This wasn't the plan of a criminal mastermind but the innocent, theatrical flourish of a man hoping to vanish into thin air. It didn't even matter if the whole thing unravelled. Lancelot wanted to go out with a bang and those different coloured diamonds were a little clue he left behind. And they have proven your undoing."

"I will stop you there, Bigge," said Percy. "This is madness. Sheer lunacy. I don't know anything about these damned masks and I've never been to the Parakeet in my life."

"That's not true," said Helena, of all people. "We all went, that night Lancelot had one of his nervous attacks."

"That was last summer," he said. "I'd forgotten."

"But it was you who mentioned the place," I said.

"No, it wasn't."

"Yes, the morning after the murder. We were all in the drawing room with the chief inspector. You were the one who steered the conversation towards Lancelot's old haunts. You mentioned a place called the Parrot, knowing full well someone would correct you. You wanted the police to find Reginald's body, so they would come across the clues you'd left behind."

"Poppycock," he said, "this is poppycock. I was here all night and Cyril's my proof. He arrived much earlier than you said he did – at quarter to eleven."

"That's what you told me he said, but you were lying. And I was the one that prompted the lie. A few days ago, I told you I was investigating the crime and that I knew Cyril came to the house on the night of the ball. I wanted to rattle your cage and it worked. That's when you said Cyril arrived earlier than he had. You were giving yourself an alibi for the time of the murder – the exact time of which only you knew.

"That's also why you ended up going to Regus Hall, so you could talk with Cyril and convince him to go along with your lie. You probably said you were doing him a favour, given he'd never want the police finding out he was near the Albert Hall that night. Meanwhile, Miss Smythe and I were proving more dogged in our investigation than you'd anticipated and even the police were considering a different murderer. So you gave them one.

"You went to Cyril's flat this morning, planning to stage his murder as a suicide. You must share your brother's flare for the dramatic because you wore the mask as you enacted your plan – you could clean it of fingerprints afterwards. Fortunately, Miss Smythe and I arrived just in time, but you still rang the police – even if Cyril confessed to his side of the story that would still leave him as the prime suspect."

"Where were you after church?" asked Helena.

"Mother, what do you mean?"

"Your father and I went for tea with Lady Prendergast. Where did you go?"

"I told you, I came here. I had a head."

"Is that true, Grace?" asked the mistress of the house.

"Don't ask her," said Percy. "I let myself in at midday."

"It was half past twelve, sir," corrected Grace.

I could have shouted for joy!

"How dare you!" he yelled.

"Keep your voice down," commanded Hector.

To Grace's credit, she maintained her composure quite brilliantly.

"This is all palpably absurd," said Percy. "You have concocted the most ridiculous of stories for reasons I cannot fathom. Reginald murdered Lancelot and hoped to make off with his car. As for Cyril trying to slash his wrists, I know nothing of that. He's hardly lacking in reasons to kill himself."

"I never said that's how he was planning his suicide," I said.

"Or a gas oven for all I care."

"Percy!" It was Helena. She sounded truly shocked.

"What proof do you have?" asked Jackie.

"Jackie!" protested Percy. "There's no proof because this story is entirely fictitious."

It was at this point the dining room door opened a fraction and Max silently entered the room. No one bothered to notice him, but I did. He nodded gravely at me, his hands behind his back. Thank Zeus!

"As for proof," I said, "Cyril will confess to lying about his time of arrival and that Percival was the one who told him to lie."

"That still doesn't make me guilty of murder," said Percy. "If anything, it incriminates Cyril. I was merely trying to help him."

"Then there's the mask."

"What!?" A number of people spoke that word all at once, Theodora included.

"You wore it when you attacked Cyril but you didn't leave it behind. Perhaps you were to give it one final polish. Fortunately, that mask has been found."

A stunned silence.

"Do you really have it?" asked Jackie.

"I don't, but I know who does."

Max stepped forward. He held his right hand aloft, encased in his chauffeur's glove, and in it was Lancelot's harlequin mask – the left eye red and the right one black. Percival rose from the table, his chair crashing to the floor, his face a portrait of fury. Max held his ground.

"I found this in your room, sir."

"Liar. You're trying to frame me."

"Under your bed."

"No, no, I never killed my brother," said Percy, a trace of desperation on his voice. "I loved him."

"You loved the man you thought he was," I said, rising far more calmly. "Not the one he yearned to be."

"He was that man."

"No, he wasn't the brother you'd looked up to," said Theodora. "He wasn't the knight in shining armour. He was a liar. For years, he'd been lying to you."

"I tried to cure him," said Hector. "I really did."

"Father, you can't believe me guilty of this."

But clearly my words had struck home. Doctor Fortescue shook his head, utterly crestfallen.

"Mother, I'm not guilty."

Helena looked down at the empty place in front of her. "I may be vigilant, but I am not violent."

"How can you say you loved him," said Jackie, "when you could do that to him?"

With his parents, his brother's fiancée, the maid, the chauffeur and two rather persistent, if unwanted, houseguests turning against him, the final string of Percy's resolve snapped.

"Because someone had to teach him a bloody lesson."

Jackie gasped.

"Percy!" exclaimed the doctor.

"Oh dear," said Helena.

"He lied to us, to all of us, and then he planned to vanish," he said. "And that oily snake Reginald was in on it too. And all those despicable men at the ball, the ones in dresses. I told him he was a selfish coward, leaving us without saying goodbye, after everything Father had done for him. He told me to back off, said he was done with this family. I told him a real man doesn't back down from the fight. He said the endless treatments had made him miserable. He no longer cared if he was incurable. I told him to buck up. Every man knows struggle and he just had to face it. I grabbed him by the shirt. He started to cry. He hit me. So, I shoved him to the ground and that's when I did it."

He glared around the room, spittle at the sides of his mouth, and his glower ended on me.

"I put him out of his misery."

CHAPTER 27

The following Saturday, 22 November, Theodora and I attended two funerals. The first was for Reginald Rolt – dead at the age of twenty-one, poisoned by the younger son of his employer. His body was buried in the graveyard of a small church out west beyond Shepherd's Bush. It was what his mother, Margaret, could afford. The pews were filled with folks in mourning apparel, predominantly family and friends. I quickly ascertained that I wasn't the only plum in the bowl – having caught an eye or two. I tried not to grin as Theodora rolled her eyes.

"Reginald would have approved," I whispered.

To that, she just rolled her eyes more. The vicar praised God and commended Reginald's soul unto eternal rest. I used to be a believer but five years at an all-boys' boarding school put paid to that. Now I wasn't sure what I believed, but if there was an afterlife, I knew which one I wanted. Begone the misery of the

Ancient Greek Hades accessed by Charon's ferry across the River Styx and lo the everlasting bliss of a house amongst God's many mansions. Why die into torment when one could inherit paradise? Lord knew, Reginald deserved it.

"I'm so sorry for your loss, Mrs Rolt," said Theodora as we filed our way out of the church. They held one another's gloved hands and I saw how tightly Margaret gripped.

"Thank you, Miss Smythe, for what you did. And you, Mister Bigge."

"It was the least we could do," replied T.

"Reginald deserved justice," I said, "and we all deserved the truth."

"Amen," she whispered.

With Percival's confession and subsequent arrest, the truth had indeed entered the public domain. The press had the expected field day, and finally, the double murder made front-page news. While Percy's acts of killing were condemned, his motives were granted a galling but entirely expected degree of sympathy. Reginald and Lancelot were both referred to as criminals, but the former was of the deviant, working-class sort and Lancelot a hapless, middle-class homosexual. Percy was the would-be knight in shining armour, trying to save his brother from the snake, except it all went horribly wrong. I was quite happy to commit *The Times* to the fireplace in Miss Wickler's living room.

"Will you come for a drink?" asked Margaret. "We're going to The Old Cock – one of Reggie's favourites."

"I'm afraid we have a prior engagement," said Theodora, "but I'm sure Reginald will receive the send-off he deserves."

"That he will," she said. "God bless."

In defiance of the fierce cold the sun shone and the sky was almost perfectly blue. I had my scarf and gloves and an extra vest to keep myself warm but even that wasn't enough against the coming English winter. Gravestones vied for ever-diminishing space in the churchyard, all watched over by the large cross built to commemorate those who'd died during the Great War. Rotten flowers lay at its base. So many dead. And how many more? Despite the Armistice, we were still at war and poor Reginald was one of its victims.

"Hullo," came a voice.

"Hello, Max," I said, shaking his hand.

"Good morning, Miss Smythe," he said, tipping his cap.

She smiled and offered her welcome.

"It was a good send-off for Reg," he said.

"Truly. He was a well-loved chap."

"That he was." He smiled. "I've quit, by the way. I'm not working for those Fortescues any more. This savage doesn't need civilising."

"Hear, hear," said Grace, joining us by the gravestones. "The doctor and his wife don't need as many staff now."

"They didn't fire you?" asked Theodora.

"I didn't give them the chance," she replied. "I also quit."

"Quite right! Have you both found new employment?"

"I'm off to Lady Asher's," said Grace.

My expression was blank.

"Lady Splendid's mother!" she said.

"I say, that should be quite an experience," said T. "And you, Max?"

"Nothing yet, but Maggie's putting me up. Says she likes having me around. She's even teaching me to sew."

I pictured the small living room above the laundry shop – the family photographs, well-used armchair and tarnished tea service – there was love in that place.

"I, um..." I began, "I, well... I owe you both an apology."

Max and Grace turned their glances at me.

"I'm sorry for the pain I caused you. I know I was rootling around below stairs rather often."

The pair continued to stare, their faces giving nothing away.

"My friend has a habit of thinking people guilty of murder," said T.

Finally, Max's face broke into a very handsome smile. "Bleeding annoying, is what you were," he said.

"I'll second that," said Grace.

"It's never fun having a white-skinned gent thinking me guilty of crimes I didn't commit. The police do that enough already," continued Max. "But, to your credit, you did work it out in the end."

"Reggie and Lance would be grateful," added Grace.

"I do hope so," I replied. "In a different life I'd have liked to have known them. Perhaps we all could have danced at the ball?"

"Now there's an idea," said Grace.

They left us to join Margaret and her daughters – welcome in a family that cared nothing for the colour of skin and the tilt of attraction. There was still love out there, despite the world's best efforts. Theodora and I returned to the Crossley in sombre silence, lost in our reflections. We set off for our next destination.

"I was wrong, you know," I said, as T drove us to South Kensington.

"It's a regular occupation of yours."

"At least one of us has an occupation, my dear."

We chuckled, despite the solemnity of the day.

"For too long I thought a botched love triangle, even a square, was at the heart of this. Max told me that love doesn't have to be possessive, but I still assumed trysts, treachery and the usual trappings of affairs."

"Of course you did, as did I," replied T, "because that's what most people believe of our love – that it's perverse. When really all they're doing is projecting their own experiences onto ours."

"And adding a good dose of bigotry."

"Far be it for them to imagine Lance and Reginald becoming friends after romance," she said. "And such a deep friendship. Reginald even helped Lance plan his escape. That's love. Nothing like the repressed marriages of dysfunctional heterosexuals."

"To think they want to cure us!"

Lancelot's funeral was held at a far grander church not too far from the Royal Albert Hall. Far be it for a doctor to afford such an expense, it would have been paid for by Helena's family money. The pews were still filled with men and women in funeral attire, except the suits were of a sharper cut than those worn by the men at Reginald's funeral and the lace on the women's dresses was more expensive. Lance's portrait from Pendragon Rise had been placed near the altar. It had been mended – the slash completely invisible.

"We never worked out who did it," whispered Theodora. "Do you think it was Percy?"

"No," I replied, "because that would imply premeditation

when his killing of Lance was a crime of passion. But I have a feeling I know who did it."

"Who?"

"Lance – I think it was his final disavowal of the man he'd been forced to be. He was leaving him behind, off to a new life, to become someone else entirely."

His stern face watched us all and I hoped, wherever he was now, he'd found more peace than he'd known here. Another victim of this endless war. The vicar climbed a high pulpit and preached from behind a gleaming gold lectern. He spoke of fire and brimstone, but also of forgiveness.

The event was underscored by a note of scandal. The newspapers had printed the truth and Lancelot's affair with Cyril had been made public. While the short-sighted secretary might not have been found guilty of murder, he had been found guilty of gross indecency – despite Percy's faked letter left in the grate, the fool had also kept an incriminating postcard from Venice. He was awaiting trial. Theodora had sent him the best lawyer she knew and even offered to pay some of his expenses. Cyril had resolutely rejected the offer of financial support but there was every chance he would receive a significantly reduced sentence. He'd implied it was his penance, for all the damage he'd caused with the National Vigilance Association.

"I loved my son dearly," said Doctor Fortescue, addressing us all for the eulogy, "despite the turmoil in his breast and the confusion in his mind. He was a good man."

The press had asked the doctor for his medical opinions and he'd even been interviewed by the *Daily Telegraph.* I knew all too well his theories and they remained entirely unchanged. A haggard of pale old men – Cambridge dons, yet more doctors of the mind, even a bishop – had also been asked for their views, which they'd poured forth onto the page with gusto. The consensus varied but they all agreed that perverts and nancy boys were irredeemable. However, some felt that the homosexual was salvageable – if that upstanding, middle-class man could turn himself away from base lusts so typical of the working classes then he too might find happiness in marriage. Heterosexuality was debated and there was an emerging consensus that one day it might be considered normal. Still, what all agreed upon was that the most important thing, after wedlock, was the raising of children. For that was the duty of any civilised Englishman – to keep his passions in check and perpetuate our splendid race. Needless to say, my copy of the *Daily Telegraph* went the way of *The Times*.

"I'm so sorry for your loss, Helena," said Theodora, but this time the women did not hold hands.

"As am I, Mrs Fortescue," I added.

"Thank you," she said tersely.

"Lance had such a shining spirit," said T.

"He did." She paused, as if she might choke, but quickly checked herself. She would not cry. "If only he'd been more honest. Then perhaps things would have been different."

"Now, now Helena," said Hector, approaching us, "we cannot undo what has been done."

"If only we'd worked harder to help him," she implored. "If only I'd closed down more of those detestable drinking houses and dancing halls."

"One day medicine will have advanced and men like Lance will finally be free," he assured her.

"Free?" I asked, easily predicting what his response would be.

"Free from illness. Perhaps there might even be a pill for it."

We left them standing in the porch of the church, receiving condolences from the grieving gathered. This churchyard was much bigger, the well-tended grass was emerald-green and the gravestones all a respectable distance from one another. Chief Inspector Lisle and Sergeant Stovell were conspicuously absent from the funeral. They had failed Helena, after all.

For now, the River Styx continued to flow, ferrying the likes of me from overworld to underworld. Theodora and I had checked in with Martin the Mole, and much to our delight, word on the street was that Lisle had been ticked off by one of his superiors. His private investigation in Soho had been entirely unofficial. He and Stovell had trodden on a number of toes. His plan to drain the river had been dammed and the National Vigilance Association had subsequently cut ties with him. That Theodora and I were the ones to solve the double murder added only to his list of frustrations.

I watched as Jacqueline left the church and made her way towards us. I bowed my head in greeting.

"This is not the life I'd envisioned," she said, her eyes red from crying, "but I'm glad Lancelot can finally rest in peace."

"As are we," said Theodora.

"A part of me thinks him wicked for all the lies he told, but another part pities him." She was not as unrelenting as his parents. "Perhaps it would have been better for us all if he'd simply moved to Berlin."

"Berlin?" I asked.

"I hear they let inverts walk hand in hand in the streets."

I didn't know where she'd heard that, as much as I wished it to be true.

"The world is often an unkind place," she said. "Good day."

She returned to the porch to stand next to Helena. Her head was bowed while Helena's was held high – her family might have fallen into scandal, but by Jove, she wouldn't let them see her bleed. I couldn't imagine it would be long before she found a new secretary and resumed her vigilant battle.

"Come, Selby," said Theodora, putting her arm in mine. "I've had enough of death for one day."

So it was we returned to 14 Wilkington Mews. The central heating was turned on and the fire in the drawing room lit. We passed a very agreeable afternoon reading books and eating cheese on crackers. I must confess to feeling a little nervous as the evening drew in, for we were entertaining a third guest. Lady Splendid arrived dressed in the colours of a peacock but lacking the tail.

"This way," she said, as my friends led me upstairs to the bedroom. A transformation began as I removed my trousers and shirt, and they were replaced with one of Theodora's dresses – a rather tight-fitting crimson number that just about did the job. I hardly had the shoulders of a loosehead prop but they were broad enough. I took the seat at the dressing table and watched as my cheeks were generously daubed in rouge, my lips painted and my eyelashes darkened with mascara. The shame of the years bubbled in my breast – Horsham, church, Bledwood – and I did my best to acknowledge it without feeding it. I had once believed in those things so fervently. Now they were unravelling and I could believe new things. But the truth is more than a belief, it is a feeling, and though the intellect sometimes works quicker than the heart, the latter is so much deeper. A feather was placed in my hair.

"Don't you look divine," said Lady Splendid.

"Selbina Bigge?" suggested Theo, who'd undergone his transformation as well.

"Or Sally," I said.

We went back downstairs and Theo brought a bottle of champagne into the drawing room. The cork nearly toppled a lamp.

"To the tragically taken," he said.

"To justice," I added.

"To life," said Lady S. "And to living it."

The bubbles were exquisite. Theo placed a record on the gramophone and *The Bigger the Better* began to play, one of the songs Lady S had sung at the Styx. We danced around the living room awhile, the light of the fire flickering merrily across our faces, until breathless, we plonked ourselves down on the various pieces of available furniture – nothing approaching a sofa in sight.

"I never knew Asher was your family name," I said to Lady Splendid.

"My father's, mind," she said pointedly.

"What's your first name, if you don't mine my asking?"

"My father had me christened Albert, so legally that's my name. I prefer to go by Albertine. My mother and my tribe have given me other names in dialects you do not speak. I hold them very close to my heart and maybe one day I'll share them."

Theo topped up our glasses and we watched the flames dwindle into embers.

"I'm rather tired," said T, yawning loudly. "Solving murders really does take it out of one."

"Rather," I agreed.

"I might add," said Lady S, "that being accused of murder is also rather tiresome."

"I'm afraid that comes with the territory," said T. "Accusing people of murder is one of Selby's favourite pastimes."

"*Suspicari omnes,*" I said. "If your aunt's books have taught us anything, it's to suspect everyone."

Theo laughed. "Goodnight, gentlefolk. I shall be exceedingly generous and take the spare room."

I didn't need to worry about blushing as my cheeks were already rouged.

"Goodnight darling," said Lady S.

"It's good to see you again," I said, once we were alone. "These past weeks have proven very sad. All that planning Lancelot and Reginald did so they could find their own happy endings. And then murdered because they refused to fit in."

Tears threatened an arrival but I swallowed them back.

"We must live and love for them," she replied, "in defiance of everything."

"I worry for us as well. Stovell has proof we frequent the Styx."

"You can say you were following a lead," she said. "You knew Lancelot had visited the club."

"What will you say? Stovell's the type to hold a grudge."

"Oh darling, I'll persist," she replied. "My people have known your people's hate for centuries, and here we still are."

I sensed the unspoken histories, vast as a cavern between

us. I struggled to think of the right thing to say, so in the end, I opted for the truth and hoped it was enough.

"I wish the world didn't think our passion morbid."

"Let's not think on pathologies and definitions," suggested Lady Splendid quietly. "There's nothing morbid about my finding you desirable."

Oh, to be complimented!

"Really?"

By way of an answer, she placed her warm fingers on my cheek and lowered them to trace the curvature of my neck. My pulse quickened at my throat.

"Tonight", she said, "let us discover how blissful our passions can be."

ACKNOWLEDGEMENTS

Many brilliant books have informed this one. They include *The Invention of Heterosexuality* by Jonathan Ned Katz; *Straight: The Surprisingly Short History of Heterosexuality* by Hanne Blank and *Can the Monster Speak?* by Paul B. Preciado. Thank you to Matt Houlbrook, author of *Queer London* and *Songs of Seven Dials*, for answering my questions about the 1930s, and to the wonderful tours team and archivists at the Royal Albert Hall.

I would like to thank my agent, Antony Harwood, and everyone at Titan Books including my editors Fenton Coulthurst and Rufus Purdy; Bahar Kutluk, Katharine Carroll and all the publicity team; and Julia Lloyd for another beautiful cover.

Many friends and fellow writers have read my novel and helped make it better – I am deeply grateful to Sally May, Jo Cunningham, Sean Lusk and Elizabeth Holtom – my mum! Thanks to David Kenworthy for his knowledge on policing and to Aerica Shimizu Banks of Shiso Consulting for her invaluable sensitivity read. Finally, I would like to thank Duckie for hosting Lady Malcolm's Servants' Ball at the Bishopsgate Institute back in the summer of 2016 – I had a ball.

ABOUT THE AUTHOR

ROBERT HOLTOM is a novelist, award-winning playwright and storytelling coach, based in London. Their debut novel *A Queer Case* has been shortlisted for the 2026 LGBTQ+ Mystery Lammy Award. Their play *Dumbledore Is So Gay* won a VAULT Festival Origins Award for new work and an Offies Commendation. It has since played at the Pleasance and the Southwark Playhouse, receiving five stars from the *Daily Express*, *Broadway World* and *Theatre Weekly*. Robert also runs workshops in writing and communication skills. You can find Robert on Instagram at @robertholtomwriter; Twitter/X at @Robert_Holtom; and at their website robertholtom.co.uk.